Praise for the
Dark Ink Chronicles

Eventide

"I had high hopes for the third book in the Dark Ink Chronicles and I was not disappointed. . . . *Eventide* is an action-packed trip into the heart of Riley's journey and I can't wait to see where she and Eli go from here."   —Night Owl Romance (top pick)

"[*Eventide*] will elate fans. . . . The lead couple is at their best, but this is Riley's show."

—Genre Go Round Reviews

"The author's use of vivid descriptions to build her world of vampires and hunters is outshone only by her creation of multifaceted characters." —*Romantic Times*

"Riley is funky, is comfortable in her own skin, and loves and protects those close to her. . . . Some new characters are thrown into the mix and I feel that a lot of great things will come of their arrival in future books."   —Urban Fantasy Investigations

Everdark

"One of the things I love so much about this series—besides the smoking-hot scenes with Riley and Eli—is that Elle Jasper writes so descriptively that I feel like I'm in the story. . . . When it comes to waiting for new books in a series . . . Elle Jasper will make it worth the wait."   —The Romance Dish

n."

—Dark Faerie Tales

continued . . .

"Ms. Jasper has a great voice that draws the reader in and writes a solid paranormal series that adds a fresh perspective on vampires, magic, and the South. I can't wait to see what she comes up with next."

—Night Owl Romance

"The characters are personable and vibrant."
—Smexy Books Romance Reviews

"Add in voodoo, the Gullah culture, and the town of Savannah and you have the makings for a great paranormal series. . . . This is a must read for all major paranormal fans."   —The Romance Readers Connection

"Serious action sequences—we're talking training, free running, vampire fight club, throwin' knives, etc.—but at the heart of [the story] is the bond between [Riley and Eli]. . . . You will love *Everdark*."

—Vampire Book Club

Afterlight

"Sultry, sexy, spooky Savannah—the perfect setting for hot vampires. . . . Beware of reading *Afterlight* after dark!"

—*New York Times* bestselling author Kerrelyn Sparks

"*Afterlight* is a book every paranormal lover is going to fall in love with. . . . Ms. Jasper penned a winner. . . . This is a must-read paranormal book and it comes highly recommended."—Night Owl Romance (5 stars)

"Darkly atmospheric and steamy."   —*Booklist*

"There's a certain thrill that goes with realizing you might have discovered the best book you've read in a long, long time. . . . *Afterlight* is beautifully written with mind-numbing possession over the reader. It's edgy and modern, with just the right amount of good versus evil. . . . The most absorbing, enticing, and unique paranormal world I've read in years."

—Romance Junkies (5 blue ribbons)

The Dark Ink Chronicles
by Elle Jasper

Afterlight
Everdark
Eventide

Black Fallen

THE DARK INK CHRONICLES

ELLE JASPER

A SIGNET ECLIPSE BOOK

SIGNET ECLIPSE
Published by New American Library, a division of
Penguin Group (USA) Inc., 375 Hudson Street,
New York, New York 10014, USA
Penguin Group (Canada), 90 Eglinton Avenue East, Suite 700, Toronto,
Ontario M4P 2Y3, Canada (a division of Pearson Penguin Canada Inc.)
Penguin Books Ltd., 80 Strand, London WC2R 0RL, England
Penguin Ireland, 25 St. Stephen's Green, Dublin 2,
Ireland (a division of Penguin Books Ltd)
Penguin Group (Australia), 707 Collins Street, Melbourne, Victoria 3008,
Australia (a division of Pearson Australia Group Pty. Ltd.)
Penguin Books India Pvt. Ltd., 11 Community Centre, Panchsheel Park,
New Delhi - 110 017, India
Penguin Group (NZ), 67 Apollo Drive, Rosedale, Auckland 0632,
New Zealand (a division of Pearson New Zealand Ltd.)
Penguin Books, Rosebank Office Park, 181 Jan Smuts Avenue,
Parktown North 2193, South Africa
Penguin China, B7 Jiaming Center, 27 East Third Ring Road North,
Chaoyang District, Beijing 100020, China

Penguin Books Ltd., Registered Offices:
80 Strand, London WC2R 0RL, England

First published by Signet Eclipse, an imprint of New American Library,
a division of Penguin Group (USA) Inc.

First Printing, January 2013
10 9 8 7 6 5 4 3 2 1

ALWAYS LEARNING   **PEARSON**

Black Fallen

Part One

THE CRESCENT

I saw the angel in the marble and carved until I set him free.

—Michelangelo

A feeling of complete and utter disaster has settled just below the surface of my conscience. I hope these new team members can help make a difference. Something has to.

—Gabriel

Edinburgh, Scotland
Old Town
Late October

Blood. Holy Christ, there's so much of it. Everywhere. Bodies. Human bodies. Crumpled, laying in distorted ways, jagged bones jutting through ripped clothes as they lay lifeless on the cobbled stones. Against the buildings. So many. My stomach rolls, and I look away. I breathe, carefully picking my way through. It's cold. Windy. Now the streets are barren. Where did the blood, the bodies go? I'm not here alone. I feel a presence.

It's behind me. Hugging the shadows. So fast, I can't tell if it's running, flying, or scaling the walls.

Doesn't really matter. Either way, I'm being stalked.

And it's one of the Black Fallen.

Hurrying along the sidewalk, I slip into a narrow

alley and press my back against the aged stones. A dim streetlamp overhangs the eve above, and the shadows reach long and jagged toward me. I listen closely. The air suddenly shifts, and in the next second I leap over the alley to the opposite wall. I climb, and in seconds I'm on the roof. I crouch, my fingers curled around the ledge, peering into the pitch darkness below. Waiting.

I know he's coming for me.

I want him to.

Leaning back on my heels, I find the hilt of my silver blade that's tucked into the back of my jeans, and palm it tightly. My eyes search the alley, the street and shadows below. Then I lift my gaze to study the jagged rooftops. It's here. Hiding. Lurking. Adrenaline rushes through me, and I draw a deep breath—

I'm on my back, rolling away, then I lurch up and crouch several feet from the ledge.

No one is there. My blade is drawn, my body rigid. Ready.

"You're fast," a voice whispers behind me.

I whip around, and slash my blade.

A figure jerks back, then laughs darkly. "Almost too fast. But not quite."

Suddenly, he's in front of me, and strong fingers grasp my throat. I'm lifted off my feet as he walks toward the ledge. I try to slash at him with the blade, kick, throw my legs around him, but I'm paralyzed. I can't even scream. The shadows fall onto his face, blurring his features together. I can do nothing more than stare.

"You're powerless, my young mixed-blood," he says. His voice is deep, his accent . . . old. "You can do nothing to stop me." He swings me out and shakes me over the ledge. Nothing but air separates me from the stone cobbles thirty feet below. He's using some kind of mind-power shit on me and it's pissing me off. My gaze never leaves the vicinity of his.

"Oh. Strong-willed, are you?" he says. I can hear laughter in his voice, shaking me again. He's only toying with me, amused. "Strength will get you no-where with me," he warns, and gives me another shake. "See how you're nothing but a weak mortal now? All those powers you've acquired? Gone. You'd be better off to join us." He cocks his head. "Would you?"

I try to answer, but my throat is squeezed shut.

He laughs. "Oh. Forgive me," he says, and loos-ens his grip on me. "Now, what was that?"

"Go fuck yourself," I say in a hoarse whisper.

Instantly, my throat is released, and I'm falling fast, the cobbles reaching up to me, and his laughter resonating off the stone walls, and the broken bodies along the cobbles begin screaming my name—

"Riley?"

"What?" I jerk up, my eyes fluttering open.

"You were sleeping," a raspy, familiar voice says. "Are you all right?"

I turn my head and look. It's Eli. Relief washes over me. "Yeah, I'm okay."

Eli's blue eyes narrow. Nail me to my seat. "Liar."

I smile. "Just a dream, big guy. No big deal. Honest."

Eli's mouth tips at the corner. "You don't have normal dreams, Ri."

He's right. I sure as hell don't. "I just dreamed a Black Fallen kicked my ass."

Eli sighs and closes his eyes. Frustration rolls off him in waves. "Riley," he begins, and looks at me.

"I know, I know," I finish. "Cross my heart, I will let you know if anything weird happens."

His cerulean stare is disbelieving. I really don't blame him, either.

"We're almost there. Fifteen minutes, tops."

I lean forward a little and glance past Eli at Jake Andorra. My new boss.

He grins. "I promise."

The Rover pitches forward and my hand involuntarily tightens around the leather strap suspended above the door that I've had a death grip on ever since the vehicle left the parking lot at the airport. Our driver, Peter, is an old guy with a shock of gray hair covered by a tweed cap. Peter is clearly insane and lacks an updated driver's license. Maybe he's never even had one. Peter hits the gas and passes a slower driver. We all lunge forward. My stomach turns.

"Och. Sorry 'bout that," says Peter nonchalantly in heavy Scottish brogue.

Jake chuckles.

"Ignore him," Eli says, and leans close. His lips graze my ear, and I'm not at all surprised at the shiver it causes within me. "He likes to get you riled up."

I glare at Jake, who shrugs. "It's true," he admits.

I turn away and ignore him. Eli's right. Jake is one cocky ass. Hot as mess, but an ass all the same.

"Thank you," Jake says.

I shoot him another glare. Mind readers suck. And I'm surrounded by them—including my immortal druid boss and the gorgeous vampire sitting next to me.

Staring out of the window, I can see my ghostly reflection in the glass. I finger my long bangs. Gone are the magenta highlights I've worn in my hair forever. My varying layers now hang straight in solid sheets of jet-black. Jake had advised me to draw less attention to myself. That almost makes me laugh out loud, even now. As if the inky angel wings tattooed at the corner of my left eye and the massive dragon etched into my back and down both of my arms aren't enough of an attention grabber. I had agreed, though, to axe the highlights for now. Besides, they were work to keep up with. And they seemed to fit my lifestyle back in Savannah as master tattoo artist and proprietor of Inksomnia. Back when life was easy and uncomplicated. Greasy Krystal hamburgers and hot, melting Krispy Kreme doughnuts. Chick-O-Sticks and RC Cola. Boiled peanuts. Crabs and oysters.

Nothing will ever be that easy again.

Jake Andorra recruited me to join an elite task force known as WUP, or Worldwide Unexplained

Phenomenon, a few months ago. Up until then I'd been a slayer of all things otherworldly and dangerous—until I became both of those things myself. Now everything has changed.

I study the Edinburgh skyline as it emerges through a hazy gray mist. The heavy, salty scent of the ocean—a smell that I'm very familiar with—seeps in through the cracks of the car and infiltrates my nostrils as it rolls in from the North Sea. A small slice of familiarity to keep me from missing home, from missing my little brother, Seth, or my surrogate grandparents, Estelle and Preacher. Or my best friend, Nyx. But this is my first task for WUP, and I have to give it my very best.

We're in a steady stream of traffic as our convoy of four vehicles moves along the M8 toward Edinburgh. We'd landed in Glasgow and met up with a man named Darius, who now trails behind our Rover of Death, piloted by Peter the Insane, in another vehicle. Although Darius helped save my life once before, I don't know him well. He's an ancient immortal Pict warrior, and I mean ancient as in from the days of Merlin kind of ancient. From what Jake tells me, Darius is a powerhouse of strength. Mind and body. But that's all I know. Behind Darius are two other elite WUP crew members: Ginger Slater and Lucian MacLeod. The only werewolves I've ever met. Like Darius, I still have more to learn about them.

In the final car are two people—or vampires, if you want to be exact—from home who were also recruited to the Scotland task force. One, Noah Miles.

Eli's best friend and head guardian of Charleston, South Carolina. A total bad-boy vamp who pushes every single limit thrown his way. Easygoing and full of southern charm, it's almost like watching a magic show when he morphs into full-fledged fighting vampire. It's a thing of beauty. To me, anyway. And he's saved my ass more times than I can count.

And then there's Victorian Arcos. Our history is so complicated it could fill a book. Even as I think about the strigoi vampire who bit me—whose DNA flows through my veins—I have to look away from Eli. A scrutinizing look from him, and I can tell he knows where my thoughts are.

I blow against the window and the glass fogs from my surprisingly still-warm breath. Outside, the air is chilly, everything a stony gray. Because I have the ability to hear things acutely miles and miles away, I have to work extra hard to tune everything out and concentrate on just my thoughts. Of who and what I am. Of what's become of me.

I was bitten by not one vampire, but four in total. Three of those bites came from deadly, powerful strigoi vampires. One came from Eli, simply because he wanted some *normal* vampire venom flowing through my body. Three were courtesy of the Arcoses, including the one who now rides with us through the streets of Edinburgh. It makes things tense between all of us, and it makes me . . . special. I carry a little of each of their extraordinary traits. I'm not quite strigoi, yet there's very little of the human left in me now. But after that dream I just had, who the hell knows how much help I can be here. What if the Fallen have the power to strip me of all my strigoi abilities? I can't even think that way now. I have to concentrate. Fight. Stay alive.

Eli's fingers lace through mine and he squeezes my hand. He knows me so well; he's trying to distract me from thoughts that he knows disturb me.

Eligius Dupré. Deadly predator. Violent vampire. Fiercely loyal. And now he's my fiancé. My sensitive, hot, kick-ass vampire fiancé. We've been through a lot together. He saved not only my life, but my brother's as well. I owe him everything, and there's nothing I wouldn't do for him. I'm almost a completely respectable woman now. Who would've ever thought that I, Riley Poe, ex-gang member, troublemaking punk kid could have a degree in art, own her own ink shop, and be engaged? How's that for crazy? We haven't set a date yet, but I'm pretty sure we won't even have time to think about that until matters are finished here in Scotland.

I glance outside to check on our progress, and we are much closer to the city. Tall dark spires and ancient stone architecture poke through the mist, and the formidable Edinburgh Castle looms above Old Town in its gloomy, ominous splendor. I'd Googled the city to familiarize myself with it, and I admit: it's pretty freaking cool. Even knowing evil resides here and what we face in taking that evil down doesn't deter me from wanting to check it all out for myself. Scottish history seems interesting and this place is loaded with it. So says Jake.

Peter exits the M8, and in minutes we're weaving through the narrow streets of Edinburgh. I stare at the old architecture, the people. It all looks so normal, like any medieval-born European city that I've seen in books. Everything's made of dark, aged stone, and it's easy to imagine horses, carts, and people from times past wandering the streets and throwing buckets of pee out of the windows. If I didn't know evil lurked in the shadows, I'd never guess it was here.

But it is here. Dormant for now, but just below the surface. And they're waiting for us. The Black Fallen. And after that short dream, I feel they know me. I'd better watch my ass good.

Peter takes a turn that I'm pretty sure sets the Rover on two wheels, and my hand tightens against the strap once more. From the front seat Jake chuckles. My eyes follow the cars coming toward us as we drive on the opposite side of the road, the city's notorious black cabs littering the cobbled streets and zooming past us. My brain won't accept it yet. It's just weird to be on the other side of the road. Yet I have this insane desire to give it a try and take a drive myself. Maybe later. After we've taken care of business.

Merchant storefronts line the street, most with their own quirky, painted signs hanging above the entranceways. A bakery. *Yes!* My stomach growls at the thought of what lies in the display cases. And there's a chip shop—battered, fried fish and fried potato deliciousness. A corner market swings into view.

As we pass by storefront after storefront, I wonder if any of them are the place Jake mentioned: a restaurant with take-out ice cream. Vittoria's. It's on my list of places to find first.

Jake has informed us that Gabriel, another WUP member and an immortal Pict like Darius, will meet us and introduce us to Old and New Town Edinburgh. Gabriel is WUP's Edinburgh contact and has been here since before the organization was even formed. He knows the streets, backward and forward. I hope I don't get lost. Savannah is easy. It's not a big city at all and is easily navigable via the town squares. I'm thinking this will be a little tougher. I'm ready, though. I like a challenge.

Peter turns onto a one-way cobbled drive and squeezes the Rover under a stone arch with an aged plate sign that says OLD TOLBOOTH WYND. I want to close my eyes, the Rover is so close to the sides of the archway. Instead, I glance behind us at the other WUP vehicles.

"Tight fit, aye?" Old Peter says with a cackling laugh.

I meet his twinkling gaze in the rearview mirror. "You barely squeaked by," I answer.

Peter and Jake both chuckle. Eli shakes his head and grins at me.

Once through the arch, the cobbled path opens up to a small, ancient, bricked courtyard flanked by a weathered wrought-iron double gate, which stands open. Through the gates the path winds around a stone fountain. I check out my immediate surroundings. Behind the fountain is an old, narrow, crescent-shaped stone building, three stories high and flagged with windows. Several steps rise to the red double doors.

"This used to be a school," Jake says, turning halfway in his seat to face me. His accent is odd. Not thick and modern, like Peter's, but older. "Gabriel has owned it for a verra long while. Since it closed, anyway." He turns back in his seat. "Now 'tis WUP's active Scotland headquarters."

Peter stops the Rover and puts it in park, and I release the door and get out. A light mist falls, and the wind cuts through the courtyard, sharp and brisk, and stings my cheeks. I don't get cold much anymore, but this weather sinks straight to the bone. Shoving my hands deep into the pockets of my ankle-length black trench, which does at least keep my clothes dry, I study the fountain as I pass. It strikes me. I can't help but stop and stare. In the center is a derelict angel, wings hanging limply behind him, his hands raised and cupped over his mouth as if shouting something at the top of his lungs. Water spurts from his hands and washes over him into the fountain's pond. For some reason the statue chills me. Overhead, ravens screech, and as I glance up a swarm of black moves from one side of the crescent to the other as the birds fly in a flock. I notice the only sound I hear besides the water falling over the angel are the ravens' wings beating against the wind. They sound like harsh whispers. Freaky weird.

Then I sense it. My eyes dart all around me. Searching. Seeking.

"You can feel it, aye?" Jake asks close to me.

I meet his alarming green eyes. "Evil," I say. It's so heavy. It feels like a wet, hot blanket draped over my body. While the city doesn't look it, there's definitely a feeling of it in the air.

"Pure evil, through and through," he says.

Our gazes lock, and there's an immediate understanding between us.

"Lucky for us, though," he says, "we're in the window."

The sound of car doors slamming silences my next question (What window?) and draws my attention back to my immediate surroundings. I turn to watch the other WUP members climb out of their vehicles. Darius is closest, and he walks toward me with long, purposeful strides. He's tall and muscular, with dark auburn hair pulled back at the nape of his neck. Beneath the dark shades lies a pair of disturbing, ancient amber eyes. He stops a foot away. "Riley," he says, giving me a slight nod. "Ready to begin?"

There's an air surrounding Darius that reeks of, I don't know. . . . mystical madness. "I hope I can help."

A smile splits his face, revealing a dimple in his right cheek and straight white teeth. An amazing transformation, that smile. Truly handsome. Breathtakingly so. "You will."

Eli is suddenly beside me. I'm pretty tall for a woman, but Eli towers over me. He's just a big guy. He doesn't touch me. He simply stands. Protectively. Something we're still working on, I can assure you.

Eli has been a little overprotective in the past, and
for some of it, I'm eternally grateful. But he knows I
like to handle myself. "Darius," Eli acknowledges. I
resist jabbing my elbow into his gut.

Darius nods. "Dupré."

Just then the double-hung, red-painted doors in
the center of the Crescent swing open, and out steps
Gabriel, along with Sydney Maspeth. Sydney starts
down the steps first, making her way toward me.
"Riley. Eli," she says, smiling, and grabs my hands.
"So glad you came. I was worried you'd change
your mind."

"Not a chance," I answer. Sydney is shorter than
me, petite, blond, and tough as nails. Yet she moves
with a particular grace that gives away her once-
genteel lifestyle. In another life, she was a grade
school teacher from the Carolinas. Then Sydney
shed her Steel Magnolias persona and now she fights
monsters. Other than her sick ability to read a dead
language, she has no outstanding gifts of strength.
But she's been trained by Gabriel and can fight like
a banshee. She's still graceful as ever. And she's immortal. I guess that has pluses and minuses. Even
dressed in black cargo pants, boots, and a heavy
black turtleneck sweater, with her hair pulled into a
ready-for-ass-kicking ponytail, Sydney moves as
though she's floating, feet barely touching the
ground. Even her hand motions are elegant. She
might as well have on a tutu.

"I see you survived Peter's driving," Sydney re-
marks.

"Barely," I answer. "He's worse than, well, me."

Sydney laughs, and Gabriel is there beside her. "Ms. Poe," he nods, then meets Eli's gaze. "Dupré." He extends a hand.

Eli takes it firmly and shakes. "Gabriel."

Gabriel, like Darius, has no family name. He is Eli's height and just as solid. He has long, straight black hair that he keeps pulled behind his neck in a silver clip. His eyes are a weird mercury color that can stop you in your tracks. I'm not kidding—literally freeze you where you stand. His face is cut and strong. Basically, he's pretty damn sexy.

His stare is almost as profound as Eli's.

I'm punched in the arm. Without even turning around I know it's Noah.

He leans down to me. "Can you feel it?" he asks. Noah has sunkissed brown dreads, and pulls them back in a thick, untamed tail. Crazy silver eyes—much like Gabriel's—stare down at me.

"Hell, yeah, I can feel it," I answer, and I know he's referring to the same ominous evil blanketing the city that I had detected earlier.

"Let's all go inside," Jake says, nodding toward the red doors. "We can get better acquainted with each other," he says, his eyes aimed directly on me, "and with what's out there." With a quick glance to the sky, he jogs up the steps. I wonder what he's thinking. With Jake, you never know.

We all give one another an inquisitive look, then grab our bags from the trunks and move toward the

Crescent building that will, for now, be our new home base. WUP headquarters.

The silver blades in my duffel bag, along with the very special potions concocted by Preacher and Estelle, my surrogate root doctor grandparents, rest as heavily on my shoulder as the solid weight of death I feel hanging in the air around me.

Inside the Crescent it's old, dark, and chilly despite the fire snapping in the fireplace. The air smells of charred wood and musty earth. Dim yellow light spills from several tarnished sconces embedded in the stone walls. They cast a hazy luminescence onto the wood-plank floors, and I notice my shadow stretches peculiarly when I move. Like my arms and legs are twice as long and my head distorted. Weird.

The foyer is empty. A row of old iron hooks, no higher than hip level, lines one wall of the entryway. Coat hooks, probably for the children who once went to school here. I don't know. Something kinda creepy about that.

"You may settle your belongings wherever you wish on the second floor," Gabriel says, his eyes sweeping over all of us. "There are several chambers to choose from. The third floor is primarily for training. We'll meet in the library for briefing in fifteen minutes," he says, then nods at Jake. "Andorra?"

They both exit the room.

Sydney steps forward. Her long blond ponytail brushes the middle of her back, and her dark clothes nearly merge with the shadows. "All right, guys. This way," she says, taking the lead up the wide wooden steps.

Eli's hand rests on my lower back as we follow Sydney. His big body, although not warm, is comforting against mine. Noah, Darius, Victorian, Ginger, and Lucian follow behind us. The wood creaks and groans beneath our feet as we climb to the second floor. Sydney stops just a few feet past the landing. "These apartments were for the teachers of the Crescent School for Unruly Children," she says, wiggling her arched blond brows. "Two shared bathrooms: one for boys; one for girls," she says, pointing to the middle of the long corridor. "And a large linen closet at the end." She points in that direction, too. "Okay, I'll leave you to it. Meet you in the library in fifteen." Sydney disappears down the steps and recedes into the darkness.

"You two," Noah says, looking at me and Eli. "For the sake of all of us, take the room at the very end."

I grin and shoulder my way past him. "No arguments there." Noah shakes his head as I pass.

With Eli's hand still at my back, we walk the long hallway to the last apartment. The corridor is dark, like the rest of the Crescent, and a long strip of faded green carpet stretches straight down the middle. The walls are of stained wood, so dark they appear black. Several old photographs in oval frames grace the wall in a straight line. Stone-faced women, their hair pulled back severely in tight buns, and men just as stony stare back. No smiles.

All business. I swear, it looks like they're straight out of a horror movie.

Ginger and Lucian take the first apartment at the opposite end of the corridor from us. Vic is across the hall from them, Noah is one door down. Darius is next to us.

I drop my duffel on the floor and take quick stock of our room. It's—surprise, surprise—dark. I move through the low light filtering in through the window to flip on a lamp perched on an old desk in the corner. The room is cast in a muted blond haze and illuminates a fireplace; a queen-sized bed, complete with heavy green curtains; a nightstand on either side of the bed, each with a lamp; and a tall armoire in the corner. A wooden chest is situated at the foot of the bed. I walk to the window and look out. It's gray and bleak, and my attention is drawn to the distraught angel in the center of the fountain. I stare at his face, chiseled in stone and chipped with age. His eyes are squeezed tightly shut as he cups his hands to his mouth.

Suddenly his features blur, becoming distorted, and I blink. When my eyes focus on his face, he's staring directly at me. A shot of adrenaline ripples through me.

"Ready?" Eli says, his lips brushing my neck.

I blink again, and the angel's face returns to its original stony state.

What the hell?

"Ri?" Eli says, then turns me around and stares down at me. "What's wrong?" Instant concern flares in his cerulean eyes. The muscles in his jaw flinch. Like I said, he can be overprotective.

I smile. "Nothing. Just getting used to this creepy place I guess." Not a lie. "Let's go before Jake gets his knickers in a wad."

Eli stares a few seconds more, weighing what I say and determining if he believes me or not. He probably doesn't, and with good reason. I'm not sure I believe myself at this point. "All right, Poe. Let's go."

A familiar feeling fills my insides as we leave the room and step back into the shadows of the corridor. It's a feeling that's becoming too much a part of my everyday life. I guess I have to just get used to it.

Dread.

Part Two

THE TEAM

I believe a man lost in the mazes of his own mind may imagine that he's anything.

—*Dr. Lloyd*, The Wolf Man, 1941

Already, this place is eating at me. The moment I stepped out into the air, evil seeped through the seemingly innocent stone and mist of Edinburgh. I don't know exactly what we face, but I know it's going to make killing vampires in Savannah look like playing with Barbie dolls. The Black Fallen? They're bad. Really, really bad.

—Riley Poe

Unlike the bleak entryway and second-floor apartments, Gabriel's library is nothing short of stylish. A massive room with wall-to-wall mahogany shelves lined with volumes and volumes of books. A colossal fireplace that takes up nearly a whole wall. And in front of the crackling fire, a long, dark leather sofa, love seat, and several chairs. A chandelier made of intertwined stag antlers dangles overhead. Several table and floor lamps with Victorian-era shades of claret, green, and cream add to the soft glow from the fireplace. As we all file in, I notice Jake and Gabriel near the hearth, their dark heads together, deep in conversation. Simultaneously they both glance up and step forward.

"Sit," Jake says, nodding to the seating before the fireplace.

We all do. Noah plops down on the sofa beside me, and on my other side, Eli. Darius takes a chair; Victorian takes another. Ginger and Lucian take the love seat. Sydney is already positioned in the over-stuffed leather chair closest to the hearth. I take notice of my companions. It still floors me to know what really, truly exists in our world. I call them otherbeings, for lack of a better term. And they are beings, with feelings. Tempers. Attitudes. But they're also vampires. Werewolves. Immortals. And then there's me—whatever the hell I am. I guess I fall into a weird, in-between category. Not sure yet if I like that or not, but there's no changing it. It is what it is.

"As you all know, we're here to deal with the Black Fallen," Jake says. My eyes cut to Eli. We're both thinking the same thing: this guy doesn't waste time. Jake crosses his arms over his chest and his eyes sweep over us with a hard gaze. "The Black Fallen are angels engulfed in the darkest of magic. They're obsessed, powerful, and completely unde-tectable. They've zero conscience. They move among humans as one of them, and only another fallen one can recognize them straight away. They're from an ancient realm of holy and unholy, if you believe in that sort of thing. And they'll not stop until they have what they desire."

"Swell," Noah says, rubbing his hands together. "I love a challenge."

I turn my head to look at him. He returns my stare. "What?" he says. "I do."

"Well, you may change your mind soon enough, Miles," continues Jake. "No matter how powerful you are, there's always something out there more powerful than you." He looks directly at Eli. "For a vampire, it's the Black Fallen."

"Why are they here?" Ginger asks.

"And what do they want?" Lucian adds.

"Darius will brief you on their history," Jake asks. "He's more knowledgeable about the matter."

Darius takes up the story. "Centuries ago, my brethren and I were forced to destroy another sect of druids called the Celtae. They'd stolen an ancient tome of magic called the Seiagh, filled with the most potent and powerful of evil spells. Dangerous not only to themselves, but to mankind. It poisoned their minds, and they had begun using it for their own personal gain. For money. Riches. Sex. Power. Only later did we realize they had stolen it from the Black Fallen. The Seiagh's power was legend. It needed to be destroyed." He takes a breath in. "Little did we know that the Celtae had hidden it so elaborately that even we wouldn't be able to find it. The bloody thing is masked with magic. 'Tis been nearly an impossible task to find it. Until now."

"So why here and why now?" I ask. "Why have the Fallen suddenly shown up seeking it in Edinburgh?"

Darius meets my questioning gaze with intense amber eyes. "A perfect example of Jake's earlier words," he says solemnly. "There are always others more powerful than you. The Celtae, whilst not exactly more powerful, were cunning. And determined." He rubs his jaw with his hand. "They used magic from the Seiagh to conceal it from the Fallen, yet were so convinced they could overcome their deaths and reclaim the book, they created an intricate path, filled with riddles and clues, to the Seiagh's location. My brethren and I knew then that the Seiagh would need protecting, to keep others from finding it. We appointed our own bloodline as these protectors. Sacrificed peaceful eternity in order to guard the book and make sure it never, ever reached the hands of others." He sighs, and glances at Sydney Maspeth. "We then appointed an Archivist—one who, centuries after the book had been gone, would be the only one left who could read the ancient language. That would be Sydney, and she's the only Archivist in existence. Once the Seiagh is located, her job is to read the one ancient spell that will destroy the book itself."

I gaze at Sydney, who merely stares back at me. So her destiny had been decided centuries before she was even born. Damn. Maybe all of ours were.

"And the Black Fallen?" Eli asks beside me.

"Call it . . . prophecy. They are in the position to know things of a higher power. They created the Seiagh. The spells within gave them their power on Earth. It was stolen from them. They know its capabilities. But they could not undo the spells keeping the book masked." He again glances at Sydney. "But they were very much aware of when the Seiagh would reappear: with the appearance of the Archivist."

"So now they're just . . . waiting?" asks Victorian.

Darius shakes his head. "Not exactly. For as powerful as they are, they do have a weakness. In order to maintain their human form, they must find souls to replenish their unholy forms." He looks at me. "Without them, the Fallen will disintegrate in a matter of time. They are not meant to exist on this plane."

My head is spinning. So much to take in and remember. So much stuff to learn about otherbeings. So many rules. Who makes up all these rules anyway?

"Depends on what you believe in," Jake answers my thoughts. "Where matters of Heaven and Hell are concerned, well, I'm sure you know who makes those rules up."

"And how do the Fallen manage to get willing participants to just give up their souls?" asks Noah. He leans forward, muscular forearms resting on his knees. "Do they have mind control?"

Darius answers. "Yes. But they have to use a medium to lure their victims."

"And what is that?" asks Lucian.

"The Jodís," replies Darius. His amber gaze scans the team. "Jodís are demonlike beings created by the Fallen. A concocted being pulled straight from the pages of the Seiagh itself. They're made to appear human, but they're anything but. They are . . ."

"Hideous," I answer.

All eyes turn to me.

Eli's hand slides over my lap and his fingers lace through mine. He squeezes. "Riley experienced a vision through Sydney's eyes once before," he clarifies.

"It can be overwhelming," Jake says, as if reading my mind. Then he looks pointedly at me. "But I wouldna have chosen you, or the others, had you not been capable of comprehending. As for the souls . . . the Jodís take the victim's heart. Literally. Take it straight to the Fallen."

"Damn," I say, and I say it again to myself. *Damn.* "That's brutal."

"Aye. It is."

I meet Jake's gaze. "I can handle it."

His eyes smile. "I know that."

"The only way to kill a Jodís or a Black Fallen is by beheading them," Gabriel announces.

I groan out loud.

Several chuckles fill the room.

"Not to worry," Gabriel adds. "Part of your training will be on the handling of a broadsword."

"What's the other part of training?" Noah asks, all too excitedly.

"How to keep it concealed," Sydney finishes. "Not as easy as you might think."

"Back to the tome," Darius continues. "In order to find the Seiagh and vanquish it forever, there are three ancient relics that must be found. Before the Celtae were killed we . . . extracted some information from them. Not everything, but enough."

I shudder to think of what that extraction consisted of. Torture. The Celtae must've been some hard asses.

Darius gives me a slight nod, proving my assumption. "Each is encrypted with a verse that, when all three are combined, will lead to the physical location of the dark tome. Once the tome is found, only Sydney—and the Black Fallen—can read the incantations. There is only one that will disintegrate the Seiagh."

"So, basically, it's a race to get the book first," Victorian says. "Why don't we simply kill the Fallen?"

"As long as the Seiagh exists, mankind is in danger. It has to be destroyed, as well as the Fallen," Gabriel says. "Unfortunately, we will have to lure them. And they want Ms. Maspeth almost as badly as they want the Seiagh."

Jake crosses his arms over his chest. "We've become more than just slayers of otherworldly beings." He sweeps us all with a stealthy glance. "We have to keep as many innocents alive as possible. And Ms. Poe has certain . . . gifts no one else possesses."

"Yeah," Noah says. "Like she can fight like unholy Hell? And she's mean as shit?"

I grab a piece of thigh muscle through Noah's jeans and pinch. Hard.

His face actually turns red.

"She does have dominant mind control now," Eli says. His voice is low, tinged with unease. "Let me guess. She's going to be used as bait." He glances down at me. "She'll be more than up for it, unfortunately."

Jake rubs his jaw. "Her skills, aye, they'll certainly come in handy. Her mind control is indeed a major factor, as well. We do have one small advantage," he continues. "Whatever spell they use to create the Jodís exhausts them. It takes three to four consecutive days for the Fallen to regenerate. We know this to be accurate, as the last two batches of Jodís Gabriel and Sydney have vanquished did not regenerate until the appropriate amount of time had passed."

Sydney nods. "The spell drains the Black Fallen, so it must be a pretty potent one."

"Indeed," Jake continues. "The Fallen have names." He looks at me. "Canthor. Danu. And the youngest, Athios. Two have been condemned for some time. But we know very little about the youngest one, Athios."

I have to wonder which of the three appeared in my dream earlier.

"So, how are we to find them?" Ginger asks. "They're undetectable, right?"

Jake, Gabriel, and Darius share a look, then turn their stares to me. "That's where Ms. Poe comes in," Gabriel says.

"We have to infiltrate their circle," Jake continues. "They might be undetectable to look upon and pick out of a crowd," he says. "At first. But then, so are we."

"Their desires and mannerisms are predictable," Darius states. "They are not unlike other fallen angels. They crave power. Sex. They're posh. And they like . . . flashy things. Plus there's a chance Riley may be able to actually hear them, if she concentrates, as she has remarkable hearing and a sense of smell that far exceeds even her vampire benefactors."

I glance at Noah. "It's true. I do."

Noah grins.

"And they don't like to get their hands dirty," Jake clarifies. "It's one reason why they've created the Jodís." He looks at me. "To bring the souls to them."

I draw a deep breath, push it out slowly between my teeth. "Are the Jodís detectable?"

Darius nods. "Aye. Their pupils aren't normal. They're vertical."

I stare back. "So we have to be close enough to see their pupils before taking them out?"

"No," Sydney says. "They cannot tolerate the daylight. And they have a certain scent only another otherbeing can detect. They stink to high Heaven."

My brain twists at all that's been said. So much to know, so much to understand.

"Taking out newlings is much easier," I say under my breath. Just months ago the extent of my dealings with the paranormal extended to slaying newly created vampires. I could tell this would be a lot more challenging.

"That's why we'll begin training right away," Jake says. "You'll break into groups. Darius, Gabriel, and

I will enlighten you on the use of a broadsword. We've a couple of specialists paying us a visit later on. Quite proficient in the use of a sword, these two. You'll appreciate their expertise."

Beside me, Noah rubs his hands together in anticipation. "I love swords."

"Well," I say, standing. My insides are already taut with anticipation. "Let's get at it, then."

"Let me emphasize one thing. For all we know, the Fallen have found a way to overcome their regeneration time. I don't trust their window, or them," Jake adds. "It's safer to assume they're strengthened now, creating more Jodís."

"Which means more innocent kills," I say.

"Unfortunately, yes. Sydney and Gabriel just disposed of the last of them two days ago. But they're fast and difficult to spot, especially after they've been newly created. Perhaps with more of us we can eliminate the number of innocent victims. We'll spend what free time we have now to familiarize you with Edinburgh and her fishbone streets, closes and wynds, as well as honing your skills. We'll break to eat first," Jake says, then scans the group. "For those who eat food, the kitchen is fully stocked, or there's a chippy just out the gates of the Crescent on Canongate, across the street. Bene's Fish and Chips. Great takeaway. Plus numerous other establishments along the Mile. For those who prefer to drink," he says with a grin, "yours will be in the red refrigerator. Courtesy of Preacher. There is a month's supply. Let's meet upstairs in thirty minutes. And if you go out, watch your backs."

As I fix my gaze on Darius, Jake, and Gabriel, I have a feeling training with three ancient Celtic immortals will be slightly different than hand-to-hand fighting with the Dupré family.

Part Three

·—+‡+—·—·—+‡+—·

SKILLS DAY

In London there is a man who screams when the church bells ring.

—*H. P. Lovecraft, "The Descendant"*

I already can see a sisterhood forming with Riley, and I'm glad. Grateful. I've been feeling so alone in all this, like the only female thrown into a world of evil chaotic males. Well, Darius and Gabriel are far from evil, but you get my drift. It's nice to have another female in the mix. Ginger, too, although she's relatively new to the team. I'm not sure they're entirely aware of what's coming, the black storm of evil that's descending upon Edinburgh. But they will. And I can tell we are all better off having Riley on our team.

—Sydney Maspeth

Bene's proves to be a potential favorite place to eat in Edinburgh. Just enough room in the small take-out spot to step inside, drool over the selection of foods (excluding haggis—um, no, thank you), give your order, and either step back outside or hug the wall and wait. The guys behind the counter were superfriendly and fast. Both only briefly glimpsed at my inked wings and then continued on with their cheerful, brogue-tinged conversation. I like that, and it makes me think Edinburgh is as diverse as any other city; even the folks at Bene's aren't surprised by a girl with tattooed black wings on her face. I haven't explored other eateries yet, but, man—Bene's big batter-fried slabs of haddock, and mountain of chips dowsed in malt vinegar and some weird-looking but delicious brown sauce? Let's just say the voracious appetite that is now part of my Frankenstein-like genetic makeup overdid itself. I ate like a freaking hog. And I'm feeling it. I almost want to let out the top two buttons on my jeans.

It was *so* good.

We're getting ready to start training with the swords, and I don't want to be impaled because I can't breathe from too much Bene's. I leave Eli, who is talking to Jake about the layout of Edinburgh, in the kitchen and hurry through the front sitting room, where Lucian and Ginger are talking to Victorian, and bound up the steps to the second floor. Jogging to the end of the corridor, I slip into my and Eli's room, cross over to my duffel on the floor where I dropped it earlier, throw it onto the bed, and start rifling through it. I find a tie for my hair and pull it back into a ponytail. Next, a pair of black Lycra pants. I toe off my boots, unbutton my jeans, and slide them over my hips. Kicking them into a pile, I pull on the Lycra and fish in my duffel for a shirt. Finding a black tank top, I grab the hem of my sweater and pull it over my head.

"How long did it take to ink that dragon onto your back?"

I don't jump in surprise, nor do I snap around and cover myself. My modesty went out the window years ago. "I heard you cracking your knuckles as you left your room, Noah Miles," I say. I pull the tank over my head and turn around. "You don't think you can possibly sneak up on me. Do you, bro?"

"Maybe. But I don't see how you can sneak up on anyone, woman. I can hear the fish and chips sloshing around in your gut," Noah says. He's leaning against the doorframe of my room, arms crossed over his chest, grinning. Clad in a pair of black running pants and a plain white T-shirt, he looks about as average as any guy in a gym. Well, except for his extraordinary good looks. Painfully good, even.

He grins. "So. How long?"

I ignore the fact that he randomly reads my thoughts any time he wants. "It took several sittings, maybe four to five hours each," I answer. "You outline first, then once it heals, maybe in three to four weeks, the color is added."

"You miss it?" Noah adds. He walks over, lifts one of my bare arms, and studies the intricate dragon's tail winding from shoulder to fingertip.

"Yeah," I say. "Why—you want one?" I grin at him.

Noah's head is bent over my forearm. "Maybe," he says, lowers my arm, and looks at me. "You're going to have to keep covered while we're here," he says. "You know that, right?"

Grabbing my black Nikes from my bag, I pull them on. "What do you mean?"

"Like Andorra says, you need to draw as little attention to yourself as possible," Noah says. "This isn't Savannah, babe. Your ink sticks out. Draws unwanted attention you don't want to have to deal with. Locals." With a knuckle, he grazes the wings at my eye. "And, yeah, I know you can handle yourself."

He does, too. I like that about Noah. He has my back if I need it, but I seriously have to need it before he jumps in to cover me. He respects my abilities. Gotta love that about a three-hundred-year-old vampire. With dreads. And, maybe he's right. Although the guys at Bene's accept my body art, I definitely don't want to stick out.

"And my alluring silver eyes, don't forget," he adds, batting his long lashes. Infiltrating my thoughts. Again.

"You're ridiculous, Noah," I say, and I can't help but smiling at him. He's such a freaking kid. Yet . . . to see him change, to see his fangs drop, and to see him fight? Breathtakingly beautiful. I know that makes me sound a little sick, and I guess I am. I punch his arm. "Let's go."

Noah and I walk out of the room together and head down the corridor.

"This place is a little creepy. Don't you think?" he says as we near the steps. "There's something, I don't know, weird about the idea of little unruly schoolkids that freaks me out."

I shake my head as we jog up the steps to the third-floor training area. "Yeah, I agree. Little pale-skinned Victorian-era kids, wearing black dresses and stockings and button-up boots, is definitely creepy," I say.

"Slipping around corners, talking in hushed whispers, and just being . . . weird," Noah adds. "Kids," he says with a shudder.

We both chuckle as we hit the third-floor landing. Halfway down the corridor is an open set of dark double doors. We step through, and Jake, who is standing close by, gives me a grin.

"You've reason to suspect the children once housed here were creepy," he says. "They were"—he strokes his chin—"extraordinary, one might say."

"Extraordinary?" I ask. The others in the room— Ginger, Lucian, Victorian, Noah, and Eli—all turn to listen.

"Aye," he continues. "All had exceptional gifts. Levitation. Mind reading. Transversing space. Just to name a few. Unfortunately, though, their families and the general public of Edinburgh thought they were mad," he says, and looks at me. "Insane."

"We're staying in an old Victorian-era children's insane asylum?" Noah asks. He looks at me. "I knew it."

"The chamber you're residing in, Noah, once belonged to one Professor Gallagher," Jake says.

Noah nods. "And?"

"He was found dead, huddled against the wall near your bed," Jake adds. "An expression of terror frozen onto his weathered face and one hand held up in defense."

"The other hand?" Noah prods, clearly enjoying Jake's tale.

Jake's gaze narrows. "Clutching his rosary."

Noah nods. "I've caused a similar response in

folks myself a time or two, Andorra." He eyes me and winks. "Before I became a guardian, darlin'."

I just look at him sideways. "Hmm."

"The professor was literally frightened to death," Jake continues. "By one of his pupils." He smiles. "Little Lily Johnson."

"Och, Lily," Gabriel says as he enters the dojo. He's wearing black martial arts pants and tunic tied with a black belt. The man is huge—nearly larger than Eli. And all that long, straight black hair clasped at the nape and hanging down his back. Impressive, to say the very least.

"What about Lily?" Noah asks.

Gabriel almost smiles. "Let's just say if you encounter her, dunna look her in the eye."

I stare at Gabriel, and he lifts one brow. I can't tell if he's joking or not. At this point I'll believe anything. Freaky little Victorian Lily equals no eye contact. Besides. Anyone who bears the name Little Lily Johnson? Shudder.

Now we're all gathered in the dojo. A large, spread-out room the size of at least four bedchambers with windows lining the wall and facing the courtyard. Outside it's gray, dreary, and bleak. It *looks* cold. Fortunately, I don't feel temperature the way I used to, so I'm rarely either hot or cold. The floor is covered with a dark gray padded mat, pretty much like the one in the Duprés dojo. Along one wall there's a wooden stand containing a myriad of swords. Big ones. Sharp ones.

Silver ones.

"We're going to break off into groups," Jake says. He looks at Gabriel, then at Darius, who's just entered the dojo. "But before we start with the blades," he scans us all with an inspective gaze, "we're going to see what other skills we all have combined."

"You want us to show off our tricks?" Victorian asks sarcastically.

"We're all going to show off our tricks," Jake replies. "Two at a time. Let's start with . . ." He studies each of us. "The wolves."

Without a word, all of us except Gabriel back against the wall as Lucian and Ginger take the center of the room. Lucian looks at Gabriel. "Human or lupine?" he asks.

I find that very interesting.

"One at a time," Gabriel instructs, his face expressionless. In his hands is a pair of long, wooden training sticks, probably four feet in length. He tosses one to Ginger and she catches it. "Ms. Slater first. Human."

Ginger, wearing a pair of navy blue training pants with double white stripes up the sides and a gray V-neck T-shirt tightens her grip on the stick and moves toward Gabriel. Her face is drawn, intense, and she is concentrating heavily. Her focus is solely on Gabriel. Eyes frozen to his. Without hesitation, she moves in.

Ginger Slater is all of five feet, three inches. Maybe 115 pounds soaking wet, with all of her clothes on. She looks like a porcelain doll; her features are so sweet, skin blemish free. Even her voice is soft. Confident, yet soft. She reminds me of the sweet-spoken female cop in that old comedy *Police Academy*. Seemingly so . . . innocent. Possibly even a pushover. Easy to overtake, especially by a big man—or a big other-being, without a doubt. Gabriel is both and he towers over her, by more than a foot, and outweighs her by God knows what.

She moves like lightning.

It proves to be one of many advantages.

Showing no fear and a face lined with determination, Ginger strikes Gabriel first. Their training sticks collide with repetitive, echoing clacking as they pose offense and defense. I study Gabriel's movements hard, watching everything closely. I'm having a difficult time deciding whether he's working to keep Ginger's stick from knocking him in the head or if he's simply toying with her. As usual, his features are stoic and stony.

Ginger's expression is . . . mean. I can't think of another adjective for it. She looks mean as Hell. But even mean can't fend off a six-foot-three-inch, two-hundred-plus-pound immortal from charging you and throwing you against the wall. I continue to watch her. Ginger's hands grip the stick tightly, and the little muscles in her biceps tighten with each strike she makes on Gabriel. She reflects each of his strikes, too. I glance at Lucian, and a satisfied smile pulls at his lips. He looks at me and nods proudly.

"Lupine," Gabriel simply says.

My eyes are glued to Ginger, because even with all the extraordinary things I've seen in the past several months with vampires, I'm anxious to see another otherbeing. My mind now logically accepts things like vampires, werewolves, immortals, humans with tendencies. I know them to exist. Yet there's a morbid part of me that has to see it in action first. Wants to see it. My insides tighten with anticipation.

The fighting stick drops from Ginger's hands. Before it even hits the mat, it's happened. Her human form blurs, movement shifts like a breeze wisping through a gauze curtain, and she drops to all fours. When my vision focuses, she is a reddish-colored wolf. She launches at Gabriel, paws to chest, jaws wide open and angled over his throat, and has him pinned to the mat in mere seconds.

"Damn," Noah says, admiration clearly in his voice. "That is sick, my friends."

"*Oui*," agrees Eli. Whenever he slips into French, I know he's in deep with whatever he's concentrating on. Our gazes meet, and he grins at me. I return it. Ginger will be a total asset to the team.

Gabriel's expression remains remarkably unreadable. "Well done," he says, looking Ginger the wolf directly in the eye. She sort of bows her scruffy head and backs off of him. Turning her head toward Lucian, he smiles and nods toward the doorway. Ginger takes off at a trot.

"Where's she going?" Noah asks.

Lucian glances over at Noah. "Do you see that pile of clothes on the mat?"

We all glance down. Damn. Even I hadn't noticed. Sure enough, there lay the Nikes, navy blue training pants, and Ginger's T-shirt. Along with a bra and undies.

Lucian smiles. "She's modest." He walks over and scoops them up. "Be right back." He jogs out of the dojo.

Gabriel is up now and scanning the room. "Quite an advantage, those two," he says, his gaze landing on Jake's. "She could have snapped my head off with those jaws."

Jake looks at Gabriel and grins. "I know."

In my head, I'm wondering why, if they have so much vampire power and wolf power, WUP needs my help. The vampires can read minds, and so can the immortals. They can all fight like insane ultimate fighters, and the wolves can bite off heads. Why do they need me?

"Because," Darius says, reading my mind and pinning me with a pointed look. "You are more than just a fighting human, Riley. Your mind control alone is a challenge any otherbeing will have difficulty warding off."

"Victorian has it," I say, glancing at Vic.

"Not to your extent," Eli adds. "We all saw what you did to his brother, Valerian. Don't forget that."

I glance at Jake. His chiseled jaw tightens as he returns my stare. "We did," he answers. "Invaluable."

Oh, great. My mind powers of coercion make me a high commodity in the otherbeing world. Fantastic. Always knew I'd be good for something.

At least five chuckles fill the dojo. Freaking mind readers.

Don't be silly. You're good for many, many things to me, soon-to-be Mrs. Dupré.

I shoot a glance at Eli, who is merely staring at me. One dark brow rises.

I fight a smile and shake my head.

Just then, Ginger and Lucian step back into the dojo, and the sparring continues.

I soon see that Gabriel was, in fact, holding back a little with Ginger. I knew it. Although I do think she could've probably rendered him headless if they weren't on the same team. But when Gabriel and Lucian spar, it's a little more intense. They spar in human form for only a few moments—long enough for us all to see Lucian not only can handle his own, but also watch our backs. Then he morphs into his wolf form and, man, it's . . . breathtaking to watch. Midnight black, he lunges straight at Gabriel, and Gabriel hurls him across the dojo. All the way across it. My mouth drops open. Literally. I feel a finger at my jaw as Eli gently forces my mouth shut.

Noah and Darius spar. Darius, shirtless and a six-pack you could thump a penny off of, amazes me almost as much as Noah does. Both fight in martial arts form, both equally strong. Only Noah can jump. Abnormally high. Moves fast as lightning. Something extremely sexy about a man who can kick so high, his legs are nearly split in half, like scissors.

Noah throws me a grin. Darius takes him out. Flat-out. On-his-back, on-the-mat out.

Next, Victorian and Jake go at it. Both are vampires, and both are exquisite fighters. Jake is a lot older than Vic, though, and his experience shows. Each throws the other across the dojo, and each leaps high into the rafters above. And despite Victorian's looks—he is almost painfully beautiful, in a polished, aristocratic way—he can morph into one freaky-ass, scary vamp. And there's not a single bone in his bloodless body that is scared of anything or anyone. Neither morph, though, but rather keep to hand-to-hand combat. Both are pretty intriguing, to say the least.

Sydney and Gabriel take the center floor next, and Gabriel shows Syd no mercy. I mean zero. He charges her relentlessly, and without flinching or shying away—not even once—Sydney charges back. She, like Ginger, is petite and blond, and while not as innocent-looking as Ginger, she does move with a certain grace that is pretty interesting to watch. She lacks the sweetness Ginger still has, too. Like me. Syd is rough around the edges, yet cultured. Classy.

And she can kick some immortal ass, if I ever saw it.

Gabriel grabs Sydney, her back to his front, and has a choke hold around her neck. I swear, I blink, and when I focus, big-ass Gabriel is flying over Sydney's narrow little shoulders. Gabriel lands on the mat with such force, I feel the floor shudder beneath my feet.

The look on Sydney's face as she looks down at her mentor is one of smugness. Pride. Serious accomplishment.

Totally priceless.

Next up, Eli and Darius. Now, I'm completely biased when I say Eligius Dupré is a vision of beauty when he is in the heat of battle. Well, maybe not. He's the sexiest otherbeing alive, and of that I'm 100 percent positive. But he's a machine when he fights. And he's totally terrifying when he morphs. He and Darius are apt opponents, and they spar for several moments before either is struck. With my eyes I follow Eli's movements, watch his muscles tighten when he moves, and once I focus on his face, I'm lost. Such fierce intensity, vigorous determination. He makes sort of a . . . I don't know, a growling face. Teeth bared, brows drawn. He looks vicious.

"Riley," Jake says, calling a halt to Eli and Darius. The WUP leader smiles at me, and it's not a pleasant, welcoming, friendly smile. Rather, it's one of . . . anticipation. "You're with me, girl."

Eli walks by me, leans down, and kisses my cheek, and at the same time slaps me on the ass. "Go get 'em, Neo," he whispers.

I grin. "Flattery will get you everywhere," I answer. He's referring to my *Matrix*-like fighting skills, no doubt. I have to admit, my new powers are freeing. It's hilarious to think I've traded my thigh-high leather spiked boots, fishnet hose, and plaid miniskirt for Lycra and Nikes. But I have.

Eli grins, and I continue on to the center of the mat. Jake is waiting. He wears a T-shirt and black training pants and is barefoot. His long black hair is pulled back. With his green-eyed gaze, he studies me as I move. Follows my every step. I take in everything about him; weigh him as an opponent in as little time as necessary. I profile him, so to speak. I focus solely on Jake. I block out everything, everyone in the room, and channel all of my thoughts, my senses on just him. The room blurs. Only Jake is crystal-clear in my vision. Everything he does, voluntarily, involuntarily, is magnified. He blinks once, and I hear his lashes brush his cheek. Jake's body relaxes. His muscles flex at his jaw. His nostrils flare as I draw closer to him. Head slightly lowers. Fingers flex. Then his body leans ever so slightly toward me and goes rigid.

Just as he lunges, I leap upward and over him, landing soundly and in a crouching position behind him. Jake whips around and meets my gaze.

"Nice," he says, his voice low, even. "Verra nice—"

I dive toward him and have my legs wrapped around his neck, and we're falling to the mat before he finishes his sentence. We both hit with a thud. Jake's trapped in my leg lock.

Eli lets out a whistle. I know it's Eli because, well, I know his whistle. I don't spare him a glance, though, because despite my little victory over Jake, I don't trust him for a second.

I'm on my back in less than a second. Jake is strad-dling me, my arms pinned above my head. Just that fast, it happens. The room tilts; my vision blurs even as I stare up into his face. A smile touches Jake's lips, and I know he knows exactly what he's doing. My new gift. The one I can't quite control yet.

I am Jake . . .

The night is verra dark, and cast in an insipid flush by a thumbnail moon. Shadows extend in awkward lengths along the barren road. It's damn cold outside, and the stark moors are no barrier for the harsh Highland winds. His horse stamps against the gales, mayhap anxious to reach a nice barn filled with hay. Even through the thick, coarse wool of breeches and a heavy coat, the chill seeps deep, through each bloody layer, far into his bones. He canna recall the last time he was warm. Verra likely 'tis when he last lay next to his wife. Elizabeth's image comes to mind, her long midnight hair trailin' over skin so pure and white it nearly glows. Her eyes, large and green, are filled wi' love for him and their three bairns. 'Tis the image that keeps him goin'. Keeps him warm enough.

He's no' far from home—mayhap a league, just over the next hillock. Jake nudges his mount onward, and they pick up speed. At once he sees a red-orange hue plumin' in a flickering cloud. Far in the distance, in the direction of his home. On the next gust of wind, the acrid scent of smoke reaches his nostrils. His insides freeze and his heart leaps. They've no neighbors. Jesus Christ. It has tae be their home.

Jake sinks his knees into his horse's sides and tears across the moors. Fear clasps his insides. Closer, closer, they grow, and 'tis only when they're no more than a score of minutes away that he's swept off his horse.

Only then does he hear them.

They're all around. They're above.

Stunned only for a moment, Jake pushes hard to his feet. His heart pounds against his ribs, and it's then the screams reach his ears. These . . . men—there are five in all—they stand round him, circling. He breaks hard and tries tae run past them, toward his family, his burning house. One grabs his shoulder and flings him harshly tae the ground. The air whooshes from his lungs. He's lying on his back when the one who flung him walks toward him, placing a booted foot upon his chest. Young, smaller than Jake, and with the palest of skin, his gaze holds and locks.

"They're already dead," he says bluntly.

"Nay!" Jake forces the words out of his mouth. He tries to shove the foot off his chest, but he can't budge it.

The man laughs. "No need to try heroics. It won't work for you"—he glances off toward Jake's home—"or for them."

Jake growls. "You killed them!" he shouts at the top of his lungs. Still, he can't move. Grief and anger choke his words. "Why?" He thrashes about, trying tae remove the man's foot. "I've got tae get them!" Jake yells.

"Oh yes," another, in the shadow, says. "He'll be quite an addition."

"Aye," yet another agrees. "His size alone makes him worthy."

All at once, the men disappear, save the one pinning him to the ground, and a cacophony of beating wings fills the night air. Jake canna tell if 'tis the wind or if they're flyin'. They canna be flyin'. They're just men. . . .

"Ah, good man, we're much, much more than mere men," the one holding him captive says. "As are you."

Frozen in place by the man's single foot, Jake stares with hatred into his emotionless dark eyes. There is no *way he can possibly know what Jake is. No one does. Not even his beloved wife. Centuries ago Jake was sworn to secrecy. The rest were slain. He's the only one left. "I am going to kill you," Jake says, his voice eerily calm.*

With one slender hand, the young man leans down, grasps Jake by the throat, and removes his foot and lifts him straight off the ground. "I know what you are," he says, his voice even. "Because 'twas I who slaughtered your brethren. You're immortal." A slow smile stretches across his face. "And now you'll become one of us."

In less time than it takes Jake tae blink, the man transforms. No longer a man. Sharp teeth drop from his gums into long, pointed shards; his lips pull back into an exaggerated grimace. His jaw extends. And his eyes are now merlot red. Jake knows what he is. His brethren hunted them long ago.

Vampires.

Tightening his grip around Jake's neck, Jake gasps for air. His limbs are paralyzed and he canna even strike out to defend himself. And in his next breath this monster has ripped open Jake's shirt and exposed his chest. He sinks those sharp fangs straight into Jake's heart. Intense pain rips through his body, and blackness begins to suffocate him. Jake allows it.

The last things Jake hears are their voices. Their laughter. But he doesna understand what they're saying. In his recent memory he retrieves the sound of his children, his wife, screaming. They're dead. He knows he'll never see them again. A pain much worse than the physical one his body is experiencing takes over. Fills his mouth, his eyes, his soul, with an acrid blackness. And then he remembers no more. . . .

"Riley?"

My blurry vision clears and I stare up into the modern-day face of Jake Andorra. I understand him a little better now. My arms are above my head, pinned by his extraordinary strength. He is smiling, proud that he's pinned me so efficiently. Rendered me helpless.

So he thinks.

I'll go easy on him. Sort of. I mean, he says he knows what I'm capable of, yet he shows no fear. Mocks me, even, with that silly grin. Dares me with that eye twinkle.

My stare fixes on Jake, and I concentrate on what I want his body to do. I tell Jake what to do. With my mind. Like before, everything around us goes silent. Turns hazy. Only Jake is in focus. I stare, concentrate, targeting his mind. It's like being in a dark, winding tunnel. He's at one end. I'm at the other.

Balls, seize like you're being squeezed between a pair of vise grips. Breath, catch in throat. Eyes, widen. Pain, take over until I say stop.

Jake releases me, grabs his crotch. His breath catches and a little squeak emerges. His eyes widen, and he rolls right off of me. Groaning in pain. Clutching his 'nads.

I bask in the glory for only a second or two.

Pain, stop.

Immediate relief eases the lines of pain on Jake's

face. His body relaxes. A stare of intense curiosity and admiration fills his eyes. "That," he says, pushing up and standing to face me, "was impressive. Dirty, but impressive."

Drop to your knees and freeze. This is directed at Noah, who has eased up behind me, ready to grab me. He never makes it. Noah instantaneously drops to his knees behind me. Frozen in place.

Tell me I'm a goddess.

"You are a goddess," Noah says involuntarily.

Chuckles fill the room.

And say, "I'm such a ding-dong."

"I'm such a ding-dong," he says.

Now it's all-out laughter filling the dojo. I cover my mouth, trying be serious. Kinda hard when a centuries-old vampire is on his knees, calling himself a ding-dong.

Get up.

Noah shakes his head and stands. Only then I notice everyone else staring at me, wide-eyed. Noah drapes his arm around my shoulders.

"Pretty sick trick, babe," he says with a grin. He gently cuffs my jaw with his fist. "Glad you're on our side."

I can't help but smile. It *is* a sick trick. *Thanks, Julian Arcos. Word.*

I notice Gabriel has his cell phone to his ear. He speaks in a low voice, then puts the phone in his pocket. "De Barre and Conwyk are close," he says to Jake. "We're ready for the swords?"

"Aye," Jake answers, and as the others talk in groups, Jake inclines his head toward the far wall. "A word?" he asks.

I feel Eli's gaze on mine, and I look at him. He's standing next to Noah. I smile and walk to meet Jake. I already know what he wants.

Jake looks uncomfortable. With his arms folded over his chest, he bends his head close to mine. Green eyes—eyes I now know have seen more than their fair share of pain and heartache—study me. Hard.

"What did you see?" he asks. Jake leans close and he all but crowds me, he's so big.

Without hesitation, I meet his gaze. "The night you were taken," I answer. "You were jumped by several vampires. You didn't know what they were at first because they attacked you from above." His face flashes with pain as memories race through his head. "They killed your family," I say quietly, and rest my hand against his forearm. "They turned you that night. I'm sorry, Jake. I know what it's like to lose someone you love. I can't imagine losing three at once."

A waver of vulnerability flares in his fathomless eyes. A glimpse of his past rests there, and I can see it. I can feel his pain all over again, feel the love he still has for his wife and children. So many years ago, yet in those flash of seconds, he relives it as though it has just happened. His eyes soften as they stare at me. *Not a day goes by that I don't think of them. Time has eased the pain, though.*

I narrow my eyes. *Liar.*

A smile touches Jake's mouth. *Somewhat.*

"They're here," Gabriel says, interrupting.

Jake gives Gabriel a nod.

"Who is here?" I ask, looking between the two.

Jake meets my questioning gaze. "Two of the fiercest, most lethal swordsmen," he says with a grin, "of the twelfth and thirteenth centuries." He slaps my back, and I buck forward. "Your new mentors."

A grumbling voice catches my attention from outside, and I tune my acute hearing to pick it up. The accent is . . . odd. English with a little French, and old. Ancient.

"Andorra! Where the bloody hell are you, man? Damn me, this manor reeks of something chilling and evil. Don't you think so, Conwyk? Conwyk, where are you? Damn."

I glance at Jake, whose slow smile leaves me wondering if I'm in a lot more trouble than I initially think.

Oh, you most certainly are.

I resist the urge to smack Jake on the back of the head, and I anxiously await the booming, strange voice to enter the dojo.

Part Four

✦━◆━✦

OTHERBEINGS

There was something awesome in the thought of the solitary mortal standing by the open window and summoning in from the gloom outside the spirits of the nether world.

—Sir Arthur Conan Doyle, "Selecting a Ghost"

It gives me some relief to know the extent—or at least most of the extent—of Riley's powers will more likely than not keep her safe. I knew I'd made the right choice by inviting her to join the team. She's invaluable. The Fallen will not be easy foes to manipulate, so hopefully she'll have the power of suggestion as a complete surprise to the bastards. Otherwise, we'll all be holdin' our crotches.

—Jake Andorra

The very second I think to myself that the dojo can't become any more crowded with enormous, ancient, testosterone-filled otherbeings, I'm proven wrong. A man ducks into the dojo.

Swaggering. As if he owns the place.

His massive body alone nearly fills up the entrance.

"Andorra!" the man yells.

Jake laughs and walks toward him. "De Barre, you fool, I'm right here." He walks over and grabs the big man by the shoulders and shakes. "Glad to see you, man."

"Aye, aye, the same here," De Barre answers, grasping Jake's shoulders in return.

What kind of name is that—De Barre? I'm sure I'll find out soon enough.

"Where's Conwyk?" Jake asks.

"No doubt took a bloody wrong turn," De Barre answers. He looks around. "This place. It gives me nightmares just standing here. There's something unsettling about it."

We have one thing in common so far.

Jake laughs. "The Crescent has its own particular . . . charm. And that's funny, coming from you, my old friend." He turns and eyes me. "Come on, man, and meet your new pupils."

I watch the two big men cross the dojo, hugging the wall and making their way toward me. Even I, surrounded by unusually gorgeous otherbeings, have to admit that besides being massive, he's one handsome guy.

And apparently old as dirt. Jake had mentioned twelfth and thirteenth centuries. I can see that, looking at this guy. He's all of six feet, six inches. At least. He is taller than Jake, Gabriel, and Eli. Heavily muscled. Broad shoulders. Dark wavy hair to his shoulders, partially pulled back at the nape. Piercing eyes lock onto mine as he walks. Struts, rather. He definitely has swag. Definitely swagalicious.

Across the dojo, Eli all but growls. I try not to laugh. I shoot him a mock stern look and turn to meet my mentor.

"Tristan de Barre, this is our newest and most human WUP member, Ms. Riley Poe," Jake introduces, and looks at me. He lifts a dark brow.

Before I can acknowledge the intro, Tristan de Barre grasps my hand and lowers his head over it.

His eyes, a striking shade of sapphire, fix on mine. "My pleasure, lady," he says, then brushes his lips over the top of my hand.

It happens too fast.

I really need to learn how to control this gift.

The room spins, tilts, and I feel myself losing gravity as a suffocating blackness swallows me. I know what's happening the second it begins.

I'm him. Tristan. I concentrate hard, and this time, I'm able to watch, as if peering through a window. It's a long-ago century, that much is for sure. A musky, dank dungeon. It's cold, and Tristan is shackled to the wall.

Then, everything happens in fast-forward. A man, trusted by Tristan. Murder. A curse that lasts centuries. Tristan and his knights are spirits . . .

"Lady? Is there aught amiss?"

My body is shaken by strong hands. None too gently. I feel it, but I'm still watching . . .

"Lady?"

I blink and focus on Tristan's face no more than a few inches from my own. He is holding me in his arms. He blinks.

"Why are you unwell?" he asks. Sapphire eyes narrow. "Is Andorra tasking you overmuch?"

Tristan speaks in the weirdest of ways, yet I seem to get most of what he's saying. I slip a fast glance at Jake Andorra, who is standing close by, then look back at Tristan. "Yes. He is."

A slow, sexy smile spreads over Tristan's face. "You remind me of my lovely wife, Ms. Poe. Quite feisty, you Colonists." He fingered the wings inked

into my cheek. "Although you've a few more un-
natural attributes." He sets me straight on my feet
and looks down at me. "She's got speckles," he drags
his finger over the bridge of his nose. "Just here.
Now, then. What did you see when I touched you?"

The others are standing close behind me now, all
awaiting my answer. "You're called Dragonhawk,"
I answer, meeting full-on his inquisitive gaze. I tell
him everything I'd just witnessed. "Your foster father murdered you and your knights. Not sure
which century but I know it was a helluva long
time ago." I cock my head. "So . . . how are you
here now?" I poke his chest. "You seem solid
enough, but you were all ghosts for centuries. Are
you immortal, too? I don't know what year it was,
but"—I glance down at his thick thighs clothed in
black martial arts gear—"you looked like you were
wearing pantyhose under all those steel chains."

Tristan's compelling blue gaze fixes on mine. He
studies me for a moment before throwing his head
back and laughing.

I stare at Jake.

"Damn me, but you're a witty wench," Tristan
says. "Aye. My men and I were murdered by my foster father. 'Twas in the fourteenth century. We
walked the earth as spirits after that. Ghosts cursed,
for nearly seven hundred years. 'Twas not that long
ago that my bride swept into my life and saved me."
His blue eyes shine. "Saved us all."

Wench?

"I guess we all have a lot of catching up to do," I

say. "Where does that accent come from? Besides the fourteenth century?" I smile.

"Ah," Tristan says, nodding. "'Tis my English-French Norman accent you fancy. As does my bride, Andrea."

I nod my approval.

"When we sup I shall tell you all about it," Tristan promises. He glances around. "There are beings in this chamber who still consume food, aye? Mortal food?"

"Riley definitely does," Noah says. He walks up and sticks his hand out to Tristan, and the two shake. "Noah Miles. I've heard quite a lot about you from Andorra."

"And I, you," Tristan answers. "I hear you have a fine 'sixty-nine Camaro you've restored single-handedly."

Noah's eyes take on a shine that I've seen in other-beings and human males alike. It's that . . . car-shine. A deep, weird love of iron and steel and whatever else with four tires. "I did," Noah says. "Smooth and fine."

See?

As Jake introduces Tristan around the room, I lean my back against the wall, cross my feet at the ankles, and watch. It's sort of a surreal scene. I'm in an old manor, once a school for weird, freaky little kids with unexplained powers, and I'm training under a medieval knight who was murdered centuries ago but gained another chance at mortality. I'm part of an extermination team comprised of vampires, immortal druids, and werewolves. We're in old Edinburgh, where three nasty fallen angels can create human-looking monstrosities to apprehend innocent souls for their own selfish needs.

And then there's me. Probably the most . . . normal of the bunch.

With the exception of Peter. The old, crazy driver.

Seriously, even growing up with my surrogate Gullah grandparents and their hoodoo and root-doctor beliefs, I never suspected such otherbeings existed on the same plane as mortals. To look at them all now—Tristan, Jake, Darius, Gabriel, Eli, Noah, Victorian, Lucian, Ginger, and Sydney—they seem to be ordinary, although beautiful, regular-Joe human beings. Skin. Flesh. Muscle. Bone. Blood.

Well, some without blood.

It's all seriously mind-blowing.

Despite the long windows lining the dojo wall, the already-bleak grayness from outside now grows darker, shadows begin to extend, and the chamber takes on a distinctly creepy, eerie feel. It's almost as if I'm looking at an old black-and-white roll of film or one of the silent pictures from the 1920s. Surreal. That's about the only word that fits it. I almost feel displaced, as if I'm not really here, but rather looking down through a hole and seeing all of this going on. Weird.

"Grimm. How nice of you to find your way up here and join us," Tristan says, causing me to glance at the doorway.

And things only get weirder.

Now there's the guy standing in the entranceway. I immediately sense something different about him, other than being from a long-ago century. Something unearthly. Not so much . . . otherbeing, but, no . . . yeah. Otherbeing. Holy? Definitely ethereal. With dark, wavy auburn hair worn loose around his shoulders, he isn't as big and bulky as Tristan. Lean. Strong. Broad. He also wears black martial arts gear and a black jacket. His name is Grimm? Seriously?

"Aye, well, I was detained by Peter," he replies. He moves his gaze to Gabriel. "Gabriel, quite a . . . unique place, this."

Gabriel gives a slight nod. He even almost smiles. "It is."

I study Grimm. A unique sort of accent he has, too. Old. Medieval, like Tristan's, but different somehow. I'm already anxious to hear his story.

Or see it.

Jake introduces him to the team. "Gawan of Conwyk, of Castle Grimm, and a longtime best mate of de Barre here," he says. "Conwyk, the team."

Gawan Conwyk, also, apparently, called Grimm, glances over us all, and his eyes rest on me. It's not difficult to follow his eyes as he takes in my inked wings. He gives a slight nod of acknowledgment.

Why do I feel as though I've been the topic of convo between these guys?

Because you have, love, says Jake in my head. *You are somewhat of an anomaly, Ms. Poe. Get used to it.*

A snort escapes me. I can't hold it in. Swear to God, I can't help it. I'm the anomaly here? Seriously?

All eyes turn to me.

Jake smothers a grin.

"All right," he finally says. "Why don't we break into groups?" He points. "Eli, you're with Conwyk. Miles, you're with Gabriel. Lucian, you're with me. Ginger, you and Sydney are with Darius." Jake's gaze latches on to mine. "Riley, you're with de Barre. We'll eventually all rotate partners, to get the feel of each different technique used in sparring. For now"—he throws a probing look over us all—"let's see what you have. Miles, MacLeod, help me with this mat. Aye?"

We all step off the mat and hug the wall, and Jake and the guys roll up the mat and push it to the end of the dojo. Beneath it lays the old wooden floor. I notice every couple of feet are four grooves embedded into the wood. When I glance up, Jake's grinning at me. "Desks. For the children."

God, that freaks me out.

Jake laughs.

"Ms. Poe?"

I turn and look up—way up. Tristan is standing there, waiting. "Ready?" he asks.

"Always," I respond.

Together we cross the dojo. I catch Eli's gaze, he gives me a smile, and he turns to talk to Gawan. I have to say, I extremely need some Eli Time. Soon.

Good to hear, Poe. Now pay attention so you don't get hacked with a blade, oui?

I smile to myself and notice then that Tristan is staring at me as we walk. "That's an interesting bit of artwork on your face, Ms. Poe," he says. "Does it mean something?"

I laugh. "Yeah," I say. "It means I was wasted when I got it," I answer. "I honestly don't even remember getting inked. I was . . . young. Stupid."

Tristan's stare is profound and lasts for several seconds. "Aye, well, we've all been that at one time." His eyes are sincere. "It means something now, aye?"

I consider his words. "Yeah, I guess it does." The big guy seems to be a bit more perceptive than I gave him credit for.

The sound of steel sliding against metal catches my attention, and I glance over to the rack of blades just as Eli is withdrawing a sword. Damn, it's big. Only then do I notice Gawan, who has pulled off his jacket. The black, billowy sleeves of his martial arts tunic come only to just below his elbows. Extending down each arm is a series of pitch-black markings all the way to his fingers. I'm too far away to see them in detail, but they intrigue me.

"Try this one out for size," Tristan says, and I turn my attention to the sword he's holding out to me. "Grasp the hilt like so," he instructs, and I do as he says. "Feel the weight of it in your arms. Make sure it's distributed from hilt to sword tip."

Extending it just in front of me, I measure the weight. It's not too heavy; my muscles tighten as they control it. "It feels okay."

"Just okay, or does it feel more like an extension of your arm?" Tristan asks.

I heft it up and down and then smile. "Okay, yeah, I can feel it from my shoulder to my fingertips."

"Aye, 'tis a good sign, then," he answers. From a large black leather scabbard, he withdraws his own sword. A sapphire stone commands the hilt.

"Nice," I say, looking it over. I glance up at Tristan. "Big."

He hefts it a time or two. "Aye, but at my size 'twould do me no good to use a splinter, like the one you have. Now, would it?" He grins.

"Splinter?" I reply. I tap my blade to his. "Talk is cheap, big guy. Teach me, and I'll show you what I can do with a splinter. Show me what's what."

Tristan nods. "Very well. Put your blade back in the rack."

I blink. "Say what?"

"You've got to see a pair of true sword fighters duel before handling a crash course yourself," Jake says.

Conwyk steps forward. Both men disrobe down to just their pants. My eyes nearly bug out of their sockets.

Across Gawan's chest, down both arms, and from shoulder to shoulder and down his spine are intricately inked markings. Old-looking.

Very old indeed. They're Pictish symbols, Jake offers in my head. *Each stand for a number of men killed in battle.*

Well, damn. I don't even know what else to say about that.

Tristan and Gawan draw their swords, move to

the center of the dojo. I, along with the team, move to the edges to watch. Beside me, Lucian and Eli. Each swordsman takes his position—back straight, legs apart and braced—and taps the other blade with his own.

Then the swinging and hacking begins.

Steel against steel rings out in the dojo, and I almost cover my ears at the sound of it. The muscles in both men's arms tighten, flex, and rip as they swing, clash, and charge one another. They literally look as if they mean to hack off the other's head. It's amazing to watch. Sweat plasters their hair to their heads, rolls off their biceps and down their arms. Each makes a fierce grunt as they swing and lunge and steel collides with steel so fiercely, my insides quiver. In a move so fast I almost don't follow it, Tristan flicks his blade at Gawan's shoulder and nicks him. Gawan, almost as fast, flicks Tristan on the chin. Both draw blood.

In a chamber filled with vampires.

Eeesh.

My gaze immediately shoots over to the one vampire I least trust to control himself around spontaneous bloodletting: Victorian Arcos.

A slow grin lifts his lips. One dark eyebrow rises.

The clamoring of steel drags my attention back to Tristan and Gawan. I study their steps, their movements, and I can't help but notice how graceful such large men can be. I know I'm witnessing an ancient art of combat—actually accomplished in ancient times—at work.

It's beyond breathtaking.

Finally, the two warriors are pressed close, face-to-face, their blades pushed against each other. They're both breathing hard, but not nearly as raggedly as I would expect after all that combat. Then, with his free hand, Tristan punches Gawan in the head.

In. The. Head.

Gawan lets out what can only be a string of weird, unintelligible medieval curses, rears back the hilt of his sword, and cocks Tristan in the jaw.

Godalmightydamn.

"Halt!" Jake yells and steps in probably just before the two get ready to throw down on the floor and wrestle, or just plain beat the crap out of each other. "Enough. Top form as always, Dreadmoor. Grimm, you've still got it. Simply amazing."

Tristan wipes his brow with his forearm. " 'Tisn't as easy as it once was, I fear," he says. "Whilst I have an interesting past, I'm one hundred percent mortal now." He flicked a hank of his hair. "I vow I saw a gray hair yesterday morn."

"You know I can change that for you," Jake says, grinning. "If you wish."

Tristan frowns. "Keep your fangs far from me, Andorra. I've existed longer than you, my boy, and I look forward to growing old with my bride."

I like hearing that come from Tristan.

Over the next few hours, we remain in our original pairs and practice stance, movement, and thrusts. It's a lot more involved than leaping, climbing up a newling's back, and plunging a dirk into its heart. Of course, the sparring probably won't be all that necessary.

We only have to take off their heads. That's it.

We don't have much time for practicing. And we still have to learn our way around old Edinburgh so we can actually hunt them.

"Damn me. Can we sup now?" Tristan bellows over the dojo. "I vow my gullet is empty. Andorra!"

Jake laughs. "Aye. Just for you, Dreadmoor."

Tristan gives a satisfactory nod. "Appreciated."

"Your markings are interesting," a voice says from behind.

I turn and find Gawan standing there, his perceptive brown eyes taking in my exposed, inked arms. I shrug and smile, then incline my head toward him. "Yours are pretty intense, too," I say. I draw a little closer, my eyes peering at the finely detailed black marks. "Jake tells me they represent deaths in battle," I say. "But what are they?"

"At one time, marks of valor," Gawan answers. "Now they're naught but reminders of a time I'd rather scrape from my past."

"That bad, huh?" I say, and stare at a particularly fascinating mark. "No disrespect, Gawan, but these symbols are beautiful." I lightly finger one on his shoulder.

And that's all it takes.

That simple grazed touch of my finger pad to his shoulder.

For the third time since arriving in Scotland, it happens. A wave of nausea washes over me and vertigo sends me spinning, turning head over heel, and shadows fall over me until I'm engulfed in blackness.

I'm now Gawan. It's the time of the Crusades. I sacrifice my life for an enemy's young son. I'm granted an earthbound life as a guardian angel . . . life flashes in frames, faster and faster, up until the present . . . Until Ellie . . .

"Riley?"

Eli's voice pulls me from the dark mist. His hand is there against my back. His body is close. My vision comes into focus on his face, which is looking quizzically back at me. Gawan is next to him, his profound stare boring into mine.

"You were just saying how interesting that particular mark was," Gawan says. " 'Tis strange that you noticed it first. 'Twas my first mark."

I look at Gawan. I glance at Eli. The rest of the team is hanging out, just talking. Everyone is pretty much in the same spot as when I swirled out of control and into Gawan's past.

Had it happened that fast? Mere seconds?

At least I didn't hit the floor this time.

"The symbols are fascinating artwork," I say to Gawan.

" 'Twas fine craftsmanship indeed," he answers. Then, he studies me. "Andorra told Dreadmoor and myself of your abilities. Did you see thusly into my past? Just now?"

I nod. "Yes." I cock my head, remembering everything I'd seen. "The girl. Ellie? Was she dead?"

A slight smile touches Gawan's lips. "She is now my wife, but aye, she was more . . . in betwixt, as we say. Not quite dead. Not quite alive, either." He looks at me. "I'll tell you all about it soon enough."

Now that I know Gawan's past, or at least a small piece of it, I find him to be more than curious. There's something else about him that strikes me. He's more than just an ex-warlord and sword-swinging badass Crusader from the twelfth century. He's more than a warrior once proud of how many men he'd killed. There's something about him that wasn't fully revealed to me in the vision, and is teasing at the edge of my consciousness.

I just can't place my finger on it.

Maybe I should start wearing long gloves? Seems I can't even graze someone's skin without jumping into a portion of their lives. At the very least I need to learn control.

"Let's clean up and meet downstairs in half an hour," Jake says. He starts for the door. "Dreadmoor, Grimm," he calls, "this way."

With a nod, Gawan follows Jake and Tristan out of the dojo. Eli kisses the top of my head. "We should hurry," he says. "I can hear your stomach rumbling from here."

I link my fingers through Eli's and we move toward the doorway. A spark of excitement rushes through me at the thought of learning my way around the streets of old Edinburgh, the catacombs, the narrow alleys.

And bringing down the Fallen as soon as damn possible.

I'd like to go ahead and return to some sort of normal life.

I glance at Eli. One brow is raised.

Maybe that won't happen for some time.

Part Five

❖

CITY OF THE DEAD

'Tis now the very witching time of night,
when churchyards yawn, and hell itself breathes out
Contagion to this world.

—*William Shakespeare,* The Tragedy of Hamlet,
Prince of Denmark

*Aye, this lass is by far the most intriguing of Andor-
ra's pack of misfits. Riley Poe. I vow she'll give the
Fallen a run for their coin. Makes me want to stay and
join the team, although I know my bride, Andrea,
would no doubt clout my ears for doing so.*

—Tristan de Barre, of Dreadmoor Keep

"Oh, hell. Go ahead. I'll catch up with you guys
downstairs," I say to Eli, just as we start to
leave our room. Noah's at the doorway, waiting.
"What's wrong? Forget your purse?"

Idiot knows I don't carry a purse. Not that there's
anything wrong with purses; there's just no room on
my person. Not while I'm lugging a sword.

Our task for tonight: conceal a sword while ma-
neuvering through the fishbone streets of Edinburgh.

"Where's *your* purse?" I throw at Noah. He grins
and shrugs.

Eli kisses my nose. "See you downstairs, then."

I love the way his blue eyes take on a dark shine
when he looks at me.

"I think I'm gonna throw up now," Noah says,
then turns and walks off.

Eli joins him. Funny how normal a pair of vampires can be.

I turn back to our room. Hurrying inside, I cross over to my duffel—I haven't even unpacked it yet—and find the concealed leather sheath containing a silver dirk. I'm wearing a snug black long-sleeved Under Armour shirt that clings to my body. I assemble the thin leather straps of my holster—thinner than a Victoria's Secret bra strap—adjust it over my shoulders and around my waist, and slip my sheathed dirk inside. I grab the black, ankle-length oiled canvas coat, which will completely hide the sheath, dirk, and sword, and turn to leave.

I noticed you the moment you set foot in Edinburgh. And I'm completely and irrevocably intrigued.

Adrenaline surges through me and I snap my head around. I search the room. There's no one around. Of course there's not. The voice just formed in my head.

So who the hell is it?

Aye, in time we shall meet. And I look forward to it, Riley Poe. This changes things, you know. You being here. It changes . . . everything.

"Who are you?" I ask out loud. "Don't be shy. Give up a name."

Ah, if only I could. We'll meet soon enough. Then you'll know more than my name. Until . . .

I know the voice is now gone. I can no longer feel it residing in my mind. I have no idea where it came from, but I know it's not someone on the team. Is it another vampire lurking in the city? Another otherbeing? One of the Fallen? The voice is almost familiar. Almost, but not quite. All I know is that it leaves within me a quiver in its wake.

Just as I jog through the doorway, I jerk to a stop. A sensation of dread fills me. I glance behind me, look into the gloom of my room, and see nothing there but long, stretching shadows and furniture. The moment I turn back around, she's there. She wasn't seconds before. Standing just on the other side of the threshold is a young girl. Black hair. Black dress. Black stockings. Black shoes. Her skin is pasty white, and large dark eyes stare at me.

For a moment or two, I'm paralyzed. I can't even speak. Despite being surrounded by otherbeings on a daily basis, this one feels different.

With mouth wide open and distorted, as if releasing a silent, strangled scream, the strange little girl throws herself straight at me. *Through me.*

My body jerks, and I gasp. I'm filled with icy cold. Not a cool draft on my skin, but freezing cold *inside*. Like it sifts through my skin, freezes my blood, and scrapes my bones. I shiver and spin around.

She's gone. Only the eerie shadows in my room remain. I blink several times.

"What's wrong?" Victorian says behind me.

I turn toward him. I didn't even notice him approaching me. "I think," I say, glancing around. "I swear I think I just saw a ghost," I say. "That, or this place is just getting to me. This creepy old house totally gives me the freaking willies. Let's get the hell out of here." I head out and shut the door behind me.

"What's a willie?" he asks.

With a sideways, mocking glare, I shake my head. "Nothing, Vic."

"I want to know in case I have them myself," he pushes.

I can't help but laugh. We hit the steps and I jog down, Vic right beside me. "You know," I explain. "A creepy-crawly feeling, like under your skin. Your hair stands up on your neck? Goose bumps?" By the blank look on Victorian's face, I can tell he's never experienced the feeling.

"Probably because I'm usually the cause of the feeling," Vic says.

I roll my eyes. He's probably right.

At the bottom of the steps, the others gather. Twelve of us in all, dressed in various shades of black and gray we look like a funeral procession. I turn my attention to Jake.

"We'll break into three groups and take separate directions," Jake says, then explains. "I think a group as large as ours walking together would cause unwanted notice."

"Sir," Peter says as he emerges from the sitting room. "You may wish to see this." He shakes his head. "Horrible."

Jake, Gabriel, and Darius lead the way to the sitting room, and we all follow. I look at Eli, who merely shrugs. A large flat-screen television on mute takes up a good portion of one wall.

"Turn it up, Peter," Jake asks.

Peter unmutes the TV, and immediately a blast of sirens echoes through the room. A scene of an apartment building and a reporter standing on the sidewalk in front of the entrance. Lights from the fire and police vehicles flash across his face. "There appears to be nothing else burned, save the victim," the reporter says, and points to the building behind him. "The victim's name is being withheld until the next of kin is properly notified, but its been reported that, nothing else seems to be charred except the body." He looks at the camera. "Human self-combustion? What else could cause such an atrocity?" The reporter turns away. "This is horrific. I am positive the authorities will have answers soon."

"I recognize the building. It's in the flats close to St. Giles'. Lets go check it out," Jake says.

"Why?" I ask. "What do you think it is?"

"I canna say," Jake answers. "For now, we overlook nothing. Could just be a junkie who lit himself up huffing the wrong can of aerosol."

I get that. Druggies do crazy shit.

"The layout of old Edinburgh is verra simple," Gabriel says, turning to face us. Eyes scan the team. "Think of the Royal Mile as a fishbone. At the head of the spine, the castle. At the tail, the Palace of Holyroodhouse and Scottish Parliament"—he inclines his head—"just down the way. And all the tiny fish ribs are the tightly knit closes and wynds in between. As you might've noticed as you approached the Crescent, we are along one such wynd. We'll get to the flats if we go onto Canongate and turn right. I will lead a group. Jake and Darius will head up the other two groups. We can all come together and check out the accident. Any questions?"

I don't have any, but I think that's the most I've heard Gabriel speak. Ever.

"Right. Let's go," Jake says, heading toward the entryway. Only then do I see the swords and scabbards leaning against the wall. Three are notably smaller than the others. *Chic blades.* "Each of you grab a blade, strap on the scabbard, and practice concealing as you move through the city." Jakes says with a sly grin. "It won't be as easy at you think. And, yes"—he looks at me—"the slighter ones are for the ladies."

Within minutes, we're all geared up. We split into groups, and I'm with Jake, Tristan, and Eli. The moment I step over the threshold, I feel it. The only way I can describe the sensation is like a hot, wet death shroud pulled over my face and suffocating me. I feel it everywhere. My eyes dart to the corners of the shadows, the areas illuminated by the recessed lights of the building, any nook and cranny something could be lurking in, and I see nothing. I don't care if the Black Fallen are possibly, hopefully still recovering. Their presence lingers in the air like a heavy fog. I don't like it. Not one damn bit.

Eli's hand slips inside my coat and around my waist. I glance up at him, and in his eyes I find complete understanding. I lean into him, feel his hard chest close to my cheek, and it comforts me. I know—sounds pretty girly. Love does that to a person, I guess.

Eli squeezes me and kisses the top of my head. *You look endearing with that sword strapped to your side. Turns me on.*

I elbow him in the ribs. *What doesn't turn you on?*

Eli's smile is predatory. I like that.

Outside the Crescent, darkness has fallen. The air is crisp, and the sound of the fountain echoes against the aged stone walls around us. A tall lamp near the edge of the Crescent casts a light over the courtyard, causing the shadows to creep and stretch over the angel in the fountain. Damn, that is one creepy-ass statue. The weathered stone, with its decayed chips and discoloration, leaves me unsettled inside. I'm not sure what the death-shroud feeling was, but I know I'll find out sooner rather than later.

Sounds of traffic aren't far away. I strain to hear the noise of the city, the drone of thousands of people talking at once. I tune in deeper and distinguish conversation on the street, just outside the Crescent. People walking by. Young people heading to Niddry's Pub. I'm going to have to work on deciphering the Scottish accent, because it's pretty heavy. Hard to make out.

"Let's go," Jake says, and we all begin walking toward the gates of the Crescent. Darius takes his group first and heads up Canongate. A minute passes, then Gabriel leaves with his group. They also turn right on Canongate but cross to the opposite side of the street. They all eventually fade into the crowd, which is a little thinner here. Farther up the Royal Mile, there's heavy foot traffic. Lots of activity.

"If we separate, just remember that Royal Mile, High Street, and Canongate are all in one line," Jake says. "And the Crescent is closest to the tail of the fishbone. If anything should happen—anything otherworldly—your best bet is to head straight to St. Giles'. Unless you want to cause a scene on High Street. Your choice."

I give a nod and adjust the weight of the sword strapped to my hip. "How in Hell are we ever supposed to run with this thing?" I ask.

Tristan, his face cast in half shadows, smiles. "Walk first, lady. Get used to steel on your person. In time, it will feel as if it is part of your body."

I look at him. "Women don't think about their *body* the way men do, Dreadmoor," I answer. I shift the blade again, and Tristan's lips twitch. "But I'll try."

Peter emerges from the side of the Crescent, and with a spry walk, approaches. Still wearing that plaid golfer's hat. "Shall I close and lock the gates behind you?" he asks Jake.

"Aye, Peter," Jake says. "And keep your mobile with you at all times," he tells the older man. "Just in case."

In case of *what*?

"Will do, Master Jake," old Peter says.

Now we're on Canongate, walking two by two on the sidewalk. Eli and I follow Jake and Tristan at a leisurely pace. Just out of Tolbooth Wynd is Tolbooth Tavern. I may hit that on the way back. We pass several storefronts—Carson Clark Gallery, an antique

map store with several cool prints framed and dis-
played. A whiskey shop, a few cafés, a kilt maker, a
woolen shop. Part of me seriously wishes I were nothing more than a tourist, browsing stores and cram-
ming delicious food in my mouth. Buying postcards.

Not gonna happen. Not on this trip.

The farther up we ascend the Royal Mile, the
denser the sidewalk becomes with people. I get a
few curious looks at the ink on my cheek, but for the
most part nothing obnoxious. The steel strapped to
my side bounces with each step, and I shove a hand
in my coat pocket to brace the sword against my
thigh. It's already becoming easier to move with it.
Amazing.

I notice everyone around me. I hear them whis-
pering, making idle chatter inside pubs, utensils
clacking against plates as they eat. Laughter. Normal
stuff. We move through the night, and the street-
lights fall over us. Shadows lengthen as we walk.

"Look," Eli says, and points.

Way up on the craggy hill, as if it carved out of
the rock itself, is Edinburgh Castle. It's lit up, and
glows like a beacon over the aged city. "Pretty cool,"
I answer, and truly it is. Different from Julian Arcos's castle in the Carpathians, yet the architecture
is just as breathtaking.

Ahead, several police cars and an ambulance are
parked outside of a row of flats. A news truck sits
outside.

"The combustion," I say to Eli. "I can smell the
charred flesh from here."

"As can I," Eli answers. "Sure you want to go?"

I look at my fiancé and smile. "No, not really. But since I've hacked off several newlings' heads, I am forcing myself not to be squeamish. I need to see it. Helps me understand what we're up against."

"That's the spirit, girl," Tristan says over his shoulder. "A true warrior."

"I'll clear a path," Jake says.

And by that I know he means he'll use his power of suggestion to make all the police and reporters look the other way as we go inside.

Sure enough, the reporter we saw on TV glances once at us, then turns and heads to his truck. The police all do the same. Jake, Tristan, Eli, and I walk straight through the apartment building and to the victim.

The scene is far from pretty. The apartment door is ajar, and the pungent scent of burnt human flesh permeates the hallway. You don't have to have special powers to smell that. Not this close. Jake enters first, followed by Tristan, then Eli, then me.

"By Christ's blood," Tristan mutters. My eyes follow his to a pile of ash and bone, with two curiously unburned legs, heaped in the seat of a lazyboy chair. The TV is on. Smoke smolders from the pile of ash that used to be a human being.

"Why aren't the legs scorched as well?" I ask, studying the horrible scene. On a side table, a photograph of a group of young kids. Probably grandchildren. And from the looks of the remaining legs, it was an older woman. Wearing little black grandma loafers.

So incredibly sad.

"I canna tell what or who is responsible for this," Jake admits. "If it's the Fallen, they've discovered a way around their rejuvenation."

I take one last look at what used to be someone's grandma. "Well, that just pisses me the hell off," I say. I feel dark hatred for the Fallen. Instinct kicks in, somewhere deep inside of me, somewhere within my strigoi powers, and I graze my fingertips across the charred victim's leg. The skin is cold, lifeless, yet immediately my mind hums with the old woman's last moments of life. Flashes of her little apartment blink behind my eyelids. She's sitting in her chair, her feet propped up, watching the television and eating some cookies with her tea. Her face is aged and lined, but kind. A long shadow stretches across the room and across her lap, and when she notices it, she glances around the room. The moment her eyes light on the intruder, shrouded in a black cloak, her heart quickens. The intruder moves closer, and the old woman drops her tea cup to the floor where it spills out. Her eyes are stretched wide in horror. The intruder's face is hidden in the shadows of his hood, and I can't see his face. But as the woman begins to cry, then choke and cough, the shadowy intruder lifts a single hand to her mouth and touches her lips with a long index finger. The old woman tries to cry out, but she's silent. Her heart is erratic now, and pain is etched into her grandmotherly features. Then, she begins to smolder. Smoke streams from her middle. Her gaze lowers to her stomach, pain laces her eyes, and then her heart stops altogether. Smoldering smoke turns to flames. But not before the intruder sinks his hand into her chest and retrieves her heart. I shake my head, and my mind returns to the present. I glance at my companions. I'd seen enough. "Let's go."

As soon as I step from the apartment, my attention is caught. Again.

I hear a man shouting. Angry shouting. I sense a heavy testosterone level in the air. Violence. My eyes scan the street and sidewalk in front of me.

"There," Eli says, inclining left.

Up ahead, the aged spires of St. Giles' Cathedral jut into the night's sky. A young guy is shouting and cursing just outside of the cathedral. He holds his head, turns around, kicks over a metal trash bin. Kicks over the table and chairs to an outdoor café. Two young women, walking toward him, cross the street and hurry toward us. Avoiding the out-of-control guy. They're frightened. So are several other passersby.

Something draws me to him, and I duck behind Eli and cross the street. Three curses sound behind me, and I throw a hasty glance over my shoulder at Tristan, Jake, and Eli. *I got this. Something's not right with this kid. Keep walking.* This I say to Eli and Jake. I turn away before I see if they actually listen to me, and head straight for the guy.

"What the feck are ya lookin' at?" the young guy yells to a small walking tour passing by. They all hurry across the street from him, and he laughs.

I pass through the tour and make my way directly to

him. He's grabbing the sides of his head again, pleading, cursing, and he drops to the ground in a squat. Just as fast, he's up again, pacing. He's maybe twenty years old, if not younger. Hard to tell. Short-clipped brown hair, about five feet, ten inches. Solidly built.

He won't go down without a fight.

When the guy catches sight of me, his eyes widen. "Help me," he says. It's barely more than a whisper.

In less than a split second, his blue eyes darken to nearly black. A slow grin stretches and distorts his attractive features into something gruesome. A face not his own. It's freaky as hell, and I wonder if anyone else can see it but me.

"You think you can save him?" A cracked voice, not his own, emerges.

"I know I can," I answer, and lunge, grabbing both of his hands. My skin contact against his sends tingles up my arm. My head starts to throb. In front of my eyes, a swarm beats wings of inky blackness. But I can't tell what the swarm is. I see long, spindly wings, bones, and ripped flesh. Not birds. Not bats. I blink several times and concentrate. Hard. Through fuzzy vision, I stare into the guy's eyes.

Then, everything spins, and warps. I'm alone, and . . . *freezing rain pelts my eyes and cheeks as I run hard, fast, the muscles in my thighs burning almost as much as my lungs. I grip the leather hilt of my sword tightly, throw a quick glance behind me, see nothing, but I don't slow up. I can hear them everywhere, all around me, a thousand whispers going off at once, and it makes my adrenaline kick into high gear. I run harder. St. Giles'* is the only place I know to go. But is St. Giles' still St. Giles' here? Hell if I know, but I get the feeling its not. It's just a few blocks farther and is the closest sanctuary without taking shortcuts. Shortcuts equal shadows. Here, in this place, in the shadows? Somehow I know they reign, and they're way too powerful and too many of them for me to take on with one blade. I'm too new at this. I'm used to fighting newlings and seasoned bloodsuckers. Not . . . whatever these things are. How did I get here? I glance around, and although I see Edinburgh, I see where I'd just been walking with Eli, Jake, and Tristan, it's . . . different. Am I on an alternative plane? Is hallowed ground still hallowed here? I suppose I'll find out real soon.

Brown, icy slush piles stagnate against curbs, on sidewalks, in potholes and cobbles, and I pound through a big puddle of it as I make my way up the street, toward the ancient minster. Slush? When did it snow? And where in Hell is that kid? Lamppost to lamppost I run, my boots growing heavier with each step as I stay beneath the lights. I somehow know it's always deserted here, and on the cusp of darkness; like negatives from a film camera, it has a sepia tone and there are always shadows. I'm on Fallen terra firma. I arrived the second I touched that crazed kid on the street. I know very little about the Fallen, but I suspect they're in control of my surroundings. Are these winged things demons? Jodis? Has to be something concocted by the Fallen because I doubt it's the angels themselves. Jake said they don't like to get their hands dirty, right?

That guy is in here. Has to be. An innocent soul who relies on me. That's all that matters. And he's here somewhere. I'm gonna find him. . . .

St. Giles' comes into view, which is weird, since I had been standing directly beside it earlier. I run toward it as fast and hard as my legs can carry me. The moment my feet hit the church grounds, the whispers grow in numbers, so much that it begins to sound like a hive of angry bees that someone has just beaten with a stick. They're coming after me. Fuckers. I fly up the walkway, past a stone Celtic cross with a tattered and faded purple cloth draped over it, skid up to the heavy double doors, and grab the knob. Not locked, but the door is jammed. Whispers turn to voices, mocking, almost as though they're toying with me. "Goddamn it!" I curse, grunting, as I repeatedly slam my shoulder against the door. "Come on!" I yell, grunting. When that doesn't work, I kick it—hard, over and over, the flat of my boot striking sharp against the wood. Finally, it gives, and I stumble inside.

The moment my body crosses the holy threshold, the whispers cease. I don't trust it, though, and I move to the first thing I see that can block the door: a broken, decayed stone statue of an angel.

Kind of unexpected.

I knock it over, the rest of what is a wing crumbles, and I drag it to the doorway. I prop it against the wood. I haul ass up the aisle.

I can't say that I feel safe in here; the church is empty and, for some reason, derelict. I know it's old, and although I've never been inside I have a feeling there's more to it than rotted pews and broken statues. Gabriel and Jake had said to come here. Now, I'm not so sure I made the right choice. I glance around. What few pews remain are turned over; tattered hymnals lay scattered on the floor. The intricate stone rafters above are broken and crum-

bling, as are the large pillars lining the aisle. The altar is little more than a pile of stone rubble. What once were beautiful stained-glass windows are now shattered.

There, near the back wall, I see him. The angry kid. Guy. He's no kid. Just a few years younger than me. He's huddled on the floor, staring at me, breathing hard, heart slamming in his chest. All this I hear pounding in my own ears. I hurry over and drop to my knees, and I keep my eyes trained on him. Only then does his breathing ease, his heart slow. "My name is Riley," I say, and he stares back at me.

"Something's inside me," he mumbles. Terror makes his eyes look crazed.

"As soon as I can I'm gonna kick the holy shit out of that thing inside of you." At first he simply watches me, looking innocent. Then those blue eyes turn black again, and he smiles a creepy smile. "Yeah, I know you're still in there," I say, and grab his wrist. "Let's go."

The guy opens his mouth and it stretches, exaggerated, into a crooked yawn just before a high-pitched, screeching scream rips from his throat. I'm new at this—didn't know until now that I could even detect a demon, or a Jodís, or whatever the hell it is, much less beat one's ass—so I'm winging it. Hope to God it works.

I drag the guy, and he's literally digging in with his heels. I'm stronger, though, and somehow I know that there's a big puddle, close to the rubble pile of an altar. A puddle of water. Rainwater? I don't know, but it's inside the cathedral, and I don't see any holes in the roof above. I use my strength to grab the kid by the neck and force his face over the puddle. I push, an inch away from his nose submerging.

He screams again, loud, long, so intense and filled with

pain that I fight not to drop the grip I have on him and cover my ears. Then a big splash. The guy goes limp, and I ease him back. I look at the puddle. Trapped inside the murky blackness, it's there. Screaming. Hairless. Bony. Instead of hands, it has weird, long claws at the tips of a pair of raggedy gray wings. It's clawing at the puddle from beneath it. Screaming at me in a language I don't understand. Not sure I want to. So that's a Jodís.

I take in a deep breath and meet the raging stare of the creature in the water. "Pain, take over."

The creature's expression changes and twists into a deformity that I barely recognize. For some weird reason I don't have it in me to even make a conjured-up creature to suffer. Best to end it now. "Die."

For a brief, split second, the creature's eyes change. I see relief in their black depths.

Then a loud pop. The creature turns to black. The water turns black. Then it slowly dissipates.

Gone. Nothing remains except the stone floor.

The air inside the rectory smells like death, decay, and must, and is as cold as it is outside. With each exhalation my breath billows out in front of me in white puffs. Beside me on the floor is an overturned candleholder; I pick it up, turn it over, and stare at the distorted reflection of my face. A bruised jaw, busted lip, dirt smudges across my forehead. I almost laugh. How the hell did I get those? I don't remember fighting with anyone. Or anything. I look like I've had the shit beat out of me. Maybe I have.

I glance at the candleholder once more, then toss it aside.

Just then, the whispers begin again, loudly, all around the cathedral, and this time I can distinguish what they're saying. Riley. *My heartbeat quickens. Well, as much as it will quicken. It's dead slow as it is, thanks to all the jumbled vampire DNA in my body.*

I turn, grab the guy by the hand, and pull him up. He's confused, blinking, rubbing his eyes and looking around as if he has no clue what's happening. I'm sure he doesn't. I barely do.

We head for the front door.

Above us, the whispers grow to such strength that they're nothing more than a long, hissing hushhh. *The wind stirred by a hundred winged creatures swooshes around us, and we're all-out running now. My sword is heavy. I shove the broken angel statue out of the way and the guy and I stumble out of the chapel.*

I blink. We're back. In real-time Edinburgh. When I scan the street, the tour group I'd pushed through is just stepping up onto the sidewalk. They turn and look at me. They look at the guy with me. I turn and face him.

Large blue eyes stare back at me. I wait for them to turn black. They don't. "Are you okay?" I ask.

He looks around, stares at his surroundings, and I can tell he's unsure. Of everything. He looks back at me. "Do I know you?"

I cock my head. "I don't know. Where were you last?"

"Ian!"

We both turn to see a group of four young guys making their way toward us, coming from just down the Mile. They're all talking ninety miles an hour, and in a heavy brogue I can barely understand.

"Where'd you disappear to?" one asks. He gives me a long look. "Didna notice this one in the club."

"What club?" I ask. I want to know where they last were before the kid was taken over.

"Och, an American," another says. He's tall, pretty cute, with dark short hair. Maybe nineteen. "How long are those legs, lass?" he asks.

Ian slaps his friend on the back of his head. "Shut up, you horse's arse."

I give him a smile. All the guys start whistling.

"Zone Seventy," the other boy offers. "Were you there?"

"Och, damn, I'd have remembered her," the other boy offers, nodding toward my cheek. "Wicked ink."

I look at him. "Thanks. Maybe I was there. Been to several. Where is it?"

"Just up the way. Niddry Street," he answers. "Come on, let's go," he says to the others.

Ian smiles at me. "Wanna come?"

Flattered, I smile. "Maybe next time."

Ian and I share a look just before he and the others take off. I can't tell if he remembers anything at all about what and how a Jodís had taken over him, but I can definitely tell something happened between us. I'll talk to Jake and the others first. Maybe they can tell me something about what just happened.

I watch the guys turn and head down the Mile and turn off onto a side street. Only then do I glance back at St. Giles'.

It's enormous. Beautiful. I'm tempted to peek inside, just to see if it would be all crumbly like I'd seen it . . . before. Whatever that was.

"Riley?"

When I turn, Eli, Tristan, and Jake are standing behind me. I look at Jake first. "What the Hell, Andorra? Something was inside that kid."

Jake rubs his chin. "Aye, I know." The light from the streetlamp is shining behind him, causing his entire face to be in shadows. "Angels. Fallen angels. Jodís. Demons. Evil spirits. Witches." He cocks his head at me. "You do know where you're at, dunna ya? Edinburgh's black past is full of them all, and they come hand in hand. Each have naturally been integrated in Edinburgh's dark past." He shrugs. "We just typically keep them under control."

I glance toward the direction the boys went. "Well, they're not all under control."

"So it seems," Jake confesses. "Many things have changed since the Fallen's arrival."

"Aye, and mayhap we're not as prepared as we need to be," Tristan adds.

"What happened to you?" Eli asks, brushing a thumb over my cheekbone." His expression is at first frightened, then grows dark. "And who did this to you, Ri?"

I touch my cheek. It's bruised. I can feel it. "To be honest, I don't even remember getting hit."

Eli's angry. Pissed. He looks up and down High Street. "I look over, you grab that kid and pull him into the cathedral. Less than a minute later you come back out."

"And you look as if someone knocked the holy Hell out of you," Jake adds.

"Did that lad strike you?" Tristan asks. He turns without hearing my answer and heads after Ian and his friends.

"No, wait!" I stop him. "Tristan, it wasn't the kid."

Tristan turns and waits.

I look up at Eli. "I'm fine. Whatever clocked me, I didn't feel it. And I've had much worse, and you know it." I look at Jake. "I don't think that thing was all demon," I say, then explain its appearance in the puddle. "It looked a helluva lot like a Jodís. Not all features, but some. And the second I grabbed Ian's hands—" I pause as a group of three passes by. "As soon as I grab his hands, everything changes. We're on . . . some alternative plane. Edinburgh, but not. St. Giles', but derelict. Run-down." I glance at Tristan and Eli, then back to Jake. "Abandoned. Inside the church, everything was a wreck, destroyed. And there were wings beating everywhere, and whispers." I take a breath. "They said my name."

Jake stares at me, his features stern. That does not make me feel very good. "Did it see you? The creature?"

"Yeah," I say. "Just before I forced it out of Ian and killed it."

"Jesus, Riley," Eli says.

Jake blinks. "How?"

I think about it. "I . . . don't know. I knew it was inside of Ian. His eyes turned pitch-black, and his voice"—I breathe deeply—"was not his. When I forced him to look at his reflection in the water, it . . . fell out. It was trapped in the water."

"Holy water," Tristan offers. "Had to be nothing else but."

"Then what?" Jake says.

By now the crowds had grown thinner, but people were still walking around us. I lower my voice. "It sort of exploded. Turned the water black, like oil." I look at Eli. "Then the whispers started, I grabbed Ian, and we hauled ass out. That's when you saw us."

"Two minutes, Ri," Eli says. "That's how long you were gone."

I laugh. "Well, in there? In alternative-world Edinburgh? I was gone at least thirty minutes, if not more."

Another walking tour—this one small, only six people—moves toward us. The woman leading the tour is wearing a big black cape lined in deep purple. She has a mass of blond hair piled high on her head. She pauses as she passes me, and our eyes meet briefly. Not sure why, but I don't think it's my inked wings. I bank her features to memory. I'm in unfamiliar territory here. I trust no one. Or anything, now.

We're walking now, up toward the castle. We stop at a slight, supernarrow alley as another small walking tour emerges. "I'm Rob the Foul Clenger, and this is the real Mary King's Close," the man leading the tour announces in a thick brogue. "My job was to clean up the plague victims. Some say to this day those very souls wander Mary King's Close, searching for various appendages that may have rotted off whilst sick."

Two young girls say "Eww" simultaneously.

The group moves on, and I glance down the close. Tightly quartered, it's dark, dank, and reeks of death. Even bygone death. I can smell it. The lamps cast a faint orange hue against the stone.

"All the inhabitants died of the plague. Typhus. Cholera." Jake says and shakes his head. "Nasty times." He looks at Tristan. "Would'na want to go back there."

"Nor I," Tristan agrees.

We continue walking toward the castle. We pass many small passages, closes, wynds—whatever. No way am I ever going to be able to remember them all. There are too many.

"I ran inside St. Giles' and it wasn't St. Giles'," I say.

"That's because you touched a soul taken over by . . . whatever it was. It manipulated you, forced you into its world. Had you entered the church first, it would have been different. And I suspect the Fallen are behind it all," Jake adds.

"Swell," I answer, and continue to note landmarks on my way, various shops and businesses—mostly tourist stuff—along the Mile. Finally, we make our way to the end, and I glance up at Edinburgh's mighty castle, all lit up and majestic.

Yet a heavy blanket of evil veils the area. Everywhere I look, I smell, I sense darkness, lurking in every shadow, close, wynd, and the many ye old shoppes lining the way. If it's this ominous now and the Fallen are on downtime, I can only imagine what it's like when they're full force.

I have a feeling I'll find out soon enough.

We walk the streets a bit longer, and a different sort of people emerge. The tourists, for the most part, pack it in for the night. The tartan shops, cafés, woolen mills, and bakeries close. Nightclubs open. Bars and pubs boom with activity. And along the Royal Mile, the city's youth appear. Mostly in groups and having a rousing good time. Some with ink and piercings. Some Goth. Some all in a class of their own. Some just as ordinary as any suburbanite. Let them carouse. Because Hell is about to break loose.

As we head back to the Crescent, another choking sense of dread overcomes me. I wonder what will happen once the Fallen emerge again with their hideous Jodís, and they realize help has arrived to eradicate them. I think it will be *on*. Us against them. And shit's gonna hit the fan.

I don't wanna be in front of the fan.

Back on Canongate, Tristan and I duck into Bene's and order, well, just about everything. While we wait, I look at Tristan. "So. You used to be a fierce thirteenth-century knight. And a ghost."

He grins. "Still am. A fierce knight, that is. A ghost no longer."

I cock my head. "So how did it all happen? How did you . . . become human again?"

Tristan nods. "Aye, well you see, it all began when—"

"Wait, let me see for myself," I say, and simply touch Tristan's arm.

I see his white smile before the air around me turns pitch-black, and then suddenly I'm in an ancient castle. At least I'm not nauseated anymore.

I'm now Tristan . . .

Tristan tried to rid his mind of everything, save the idiot before him. Quite a difficult task, knowing his woman, whom he'd never been able to so much as kiss, stood no more than twenty paces away. That would soon change.

He breathed at a steady, even rate, his stare fixed as he slowly walked a predatory circle around Erik. Damnation, he could barely believe it. "What does it feel like to come back after all these centuries? After lying beneath that oak with twisted yew about your neck? To be a traitor? To take the lives of those you welcomed in to your hall? Gaining the trust of their fathers. Treating us like sons? Being our leader. Tell me, Erik." *He all but growled.* "I want to know."

Erik, smooth and agile as ever, countercircled. "Feels bloody wonderful, to be truthful. I gave you everything, de Barre. My knowledge, my training skills—everything." *The cynical smile curving his lips made his face appear sinister. He thrust with a vicious strike.* "What did you do for me in return?" *He charged this time, and Tristan deflected the blade with his own.* "You took my only child," *Erik said calmly. He paused, his face blank.* "You took my life."

"Is that what you truly believe, Erik? That we killed your son?" *Tristan said, blade outstretched.* "'Twas an accident, and you well know it."

The pain on Erik's face proved he did not. "Fifteen trained knights, and you couldn't protect one small boy? Nay," he said, his voice cracking. " 'Twas no accident. You allowed it." He arced his blade. "Even seven centuries of being a damned soul isn't enough of a repayment for what you took from me." A smile touched his mouth. "Mayhap your life. Again."

The sickness his foster father suffered pained Tristan, but at the same time, he knew there would be no saving Erik. His mind had turned evil from hatred. But Tristan wanted to know everything, questions answered. He owed it to his men. He continued to circle. "Why Andrea?"

Erik laughed. "Right place, right time. For me anyway." He jabbed at Tristan. Her unfortunate employer happened to be the one to free me from that cursed yew, which allowed me to escape my tormented prison. One, I might add, my own sweet mother placed me in."

Tristan continued to circle, Erik following his lead. "How did you get their swords and helms?"

Erik's face hardened as he followed Tristan's lead. "I gathered them after your men died in the dungeon. I'd already cursed them, you see, but their deaths came more slowly than yours." He smiled. "I'd bound the armor and planned to bury them so no one would find them, but I hadn't realized my own mother's fealty rested elsewhere until . . . later." He thrust the blade at Tristan, who sidestepped. "She followed me out to the hole I'd dug and all but took my bloody head off. Next thing I knew, I was here."

Tristan tapped his blade to Erik's. "You didn't know she'd placed a protective curse on the weapons herself, or that she'd taken my sword, penned a rather useful verse on it, and buried it?" He charged Erik. "Or that your mother's spirit would contact Andi and lead her to it?"

Erik returned the charge. "It doesn't matter now. Does it?" He held up the blade in his hand, turning it side to side. Tristan's blade. "Isn't it odd, Dreadmoor, that you're about to die a second death at the tip of your very own sword?" A smile slid to his mouth. "Thanks to Dr. Monroe, I have my life back. And more."

"Nay, you don't." Tristan moved toward Erik, the arc of his blade swiping the air.

Erik attacked full force, anger turning his face bloodred. With vehemence, he charged.

He waited for Erik to advance, coming within a few inches of Tristan's neck. In a move the Dragonhawk had made famous, he deflected the steel and used his elbow to hammer a stunning blow to Erik's jaw.

Erik stumbled back, shook his head as if to gather his wits, then charged Tristan with a bloodcurdling yell. "I will not yield!"

Tristan remembered the same words in the dungeon more than seven centuries before. Except this time, they were reversed.

Ducking and missing the sword's blow, Tristan fell to his knees and plunged the blade into Erik's stomach. "Aye," he said. "You will."

Their gazes locked, and Tristan watched the pupils in Erik's eyes grow large until he staggered back and fell to the ground.

Dead.

Tristan's breath came hard and fast, winded from the

*battle. Slowly, he rose and walked over to retrieve his
sword. As he bent over, Erik's body began to shake violently.*

"Tristan, move back!" Kail shouted.

They all watched in horror as Erik, being the abomination that he was, convulsed faster and faster, his flesh peeling from his bones, his bones turning to dust. Back to where he belonged.

The bailey fell silent. Tristan raised his head and stared at his men. His knights.

"Someone remove that pile of dust from my keep."

All fourteen knights let out a battle cry worthy of a thousand men. No doubt the village heard.

Then his eyes fell on Andrea. Taking powerful strides, he came to stand nose to nose with her, so close a whisper couldn't pass. Her eyes widened, but before she could catch her breath Tristan swept her up, their lips nearly touching. His body shook, and he briefly wondered if he would fall over with pure joy.

Andi stared at him, breathless, and for the first time, unable to speak.

Tristan, on the other hand, had no trouble at all.

"I love you. I vow you feel powerfully fair in my arms."

She tried to make her mouth move, but nothing came forth. Her tear ducts, on the other hand, worked just fine. Tears slid down her face. She lifted a hand and hesitantly touched first his cheek, traced his eyebrows, then ran her fingers through his hair. The sensation nearly made him drop her. She looked back up and still found her tongue lacking the muscle to speak. Tristan found better uses for it.

He stared down at the woman in his arms. His

woman. *Her warmth spread across his bare chest, making his muscles quiver. Her trembling rocked him to the bone, even as he held her tight. He had dreamed of this moment for what seemed like eternity, and never did he believe it could possibly ever happen.*

And yet he felt the weighty proof in his arms.

He searched her face with his eyes, not wanting to miss a single line, a single freckle—wanting to miss nothing. His own hand shook as he took off his glove with his teeth and set it aside. Lifting his hand to her cheek, he grazed it with the back of his knuckles. He tried to speak again, but found a solid lump in his throat, robbing his breath. He swallowed past it. "Damnation, Andrea, you're powerfully soft." He drew a deep breath, and his words flowed out on the exhale. "I vow I could hold you here and stare at your beautiful face for the rest of my days."

He watched tear after tear slide down her cheek as she stared up at him with those warm hazel eyes. He could wait no more. He bent his head close, his gaze trained on hers as his mouth settled comfortably over quivering lips. So warm and soft, he found himself craving more. He brushed his lips across hers several times, then with strained control, deepened the kiss. When her hand grasped the back of his neck and pulled him closer, it sent him over the edge. He tasted her, deeper and deeper, swallowing her gasp of surprise.

Tristan lifted his head from Andi's but didn't break eye contact. Their lips were a whisper apart, and he could do nothing save stare and thank God and the saints above he had been given such a gift. His breathing panted with the effort of having to maintain control. He wanted her so badly, his insides shook. Suddenly, a loud snort sounded in the bailey. Only when a brave soul tapped him on the shoulder did he remember where he was and who was about.

Tristan turned and glared at the snorter.

His entire garrison formed a half circle around him.

Tristan smiled down at Andi and set her back on the ground. He kept his arm tightly about her shoulder. She teetered a bit, and he gripped her tighter still. She stood, staring, eyes wide. Her lips moved and something came out, but, damn him, he couldn't understand a word. Saints, but he missed his uncanny hearing ability.

Lowering his head, he leaned toward her mouth. Her warm breath caressed his ear and neck, and he all but hit the floor from the impact of it. Shaking his head, he focused on her words.

Her question floated out on a whisper. "How?"

With a smile, he tapped her nose. "Nay, love. We've got time for questions such as that later." His grin widened. "I have another question for you, and by the saints, I must ask it now before my nerve deserts me."

Her gaze remained fixed on his, following him all the way down as he knelt on bended knee. He cleared his throat and grasped Andi's hand, unsure if the trembling came from hers or his own. More likely than not, 'twas both.

"Andrea Kinley Monroe." His voice came out hoarse and scratchy. He hoped she didn't care. "I beg you, wed me. I vow you'll not regret it."

He watched several more tears streak her reddened cheeks. A smile began in the corners of her mouth and crept into her eyes.

"Yes." So soft, he could barely hear her at first, but then she threw her arms about his neck and squeezed. "Yes! I'll marry you!"

Whistles and bellowing cheers from his knights erupted across the bailey, drifting on a North Sea breeze. Tristan looked into his love's eyes and smiled, then stopped whatever words were about to make their escape from her lovely mouth. He, without a doubt in his medieval mind, kissed her good and sound, leaving no question as to how much he loved her.

And would do the like. Forever.

My vision clears and alights on Tristan's handsome face. I smile. "Oh, wow," I say. "Now, that's romantic, for sure. So your now wife read the verse that undid the curse and set you and your knights free. Then once you materialized into human form you killed your murderer, and he turned into a big pile of grossness." I punch the big knight in his arm. "Quite a story, Dreadmoor."

Tristan's sapphire blue eyes twinkle in the light of Bene's streetlamp. "Aye, for a certainty." His stare is intense. "And do not ever forget that, no matter how bleak something may appear, there is always hope." He smiles. "Even hope in the most abnormal of times."

I give him a nod and a smile of understanding. "I will."

With four large white plastic bags filled with batter-fried haddock, chips, and several meat pies that all smell heavenly, Tristan and I step out onto Canongate and into a misty Edinburgh night. A couple passes us at the entrance, and the woman, dressed in a pair of dark tights, a brown wool mini-skirt, and a wool hat, meets my gaze.

I'd already banked her features to memory.

She quickly looks away.

"What is it?" Tristan asks as we cross the street. I glance over my shoulder. The woman is staring at me through Bene's open doorway.

"That woman," I answer. "She's the woman who led the walking tour earlier."

"Ms. Poe, we passed at least three walking tours," Tristan says. "What bothers you?"

We move past Tolbooth Tavern and into the arch-way of the wynd. I turn and glance back. The woman and man are both gone. "I don't know," I answer. "Something about the way she looks at me."

"Well you are a striking girl," Tristan answers. "Might it just be that simple?"

I give a short laugh as we near the Crescent's gates. "I seriously doubt that."

We walk through the gates, and the moment we clear them they begin to close. Gravel crunches be-neath our boots as we cross the courtyard, that ever-present and eerie angel in the fountain spurting water. Inside, the others are waiting for us in what Gabriel calls the common room. It sort of reminds me of Julian Arcos's great hall, with a large fireplace taking up most of one wall, and several chairs, a sofa, and a large center table. On the walls, shelves of ancient-looking books. In the corner, an enor-mous desk with several volumes of . . . something opened. Sydney sits there, her head bowed over one of them.

I find Eli, walk over to him. I peel out of my long overcoat, unstrap my sword, and set them both aside, then plop down on the floor in front of him. Grabbing one of the containers from Bene's, I open it and dig in to a slab of haddock. Bene had already drowned them and the chips with vinegar and brown stuff. I can barely shovel it in fast enough. I glance over at Tristan. He's doing the same thing. Gawan and Lucian both have a container in their laps, too. Jake stands near the hearth with Darius, and he turns to address the team.

"Riley, I've updated everyone on what happened at St. Giles'," Jake says. "Conwyk has a theory."

I glance at Gawan, and he nods. "Aye," he says. "Riley, tell me exactly what happened."

I finish chewing. "This kid, he was screaming, acting freaking crazy on the street, kicking over trash bins, and scaring people. He was holding his head as if it seriously hurt him. I . . . guess I sensed something was up. I grabbed his hands and we were suddenly in an alternate Edinburgh." I took a long pull on my Coke. "I guess I thought to drag the kid into the cathedral because he reeked of death. His eyes"—I recall it in my memory—"they weren't his. His voice, either. And I figured the cathedral was sanctuary. When we got inside, though, the church was all dilapidated and run-down. Abandoned." I shake my head. "Weird."

Gawan glances first at Tristan, then at Gabriel.

"Sounds like the Fallen have initiated a few hench-men from the other side."

"Rather, henchsouls," says Darius. He runs his hand through his dark auburn hair, now hanging loose about his shoulders. He glances at me with his piercing gaze. "You killed it."

"I killed it," I repeat. "Don't know how, or what made me think to drown it out in that puddle, but something lured me there. The moment that . . . thing inside Ian saw itself in the puddle, in it went. Trapped." I make the sound effect of an explosion. "But for a second, before it popped and turned into some oil-like substance, it looked at me. And it seemed, I don't know, regretful. Or something." I shrug and continue eating.

"You didna kill a demon," Gawan said, and in his soft brown eyes I see pain. "You killed an Earth-bound."

I swallow, glance at Jake, Darius, and then back to Gawan. "An Earthbound what?"

Gawan's jaw muscles flex. "Angel."

My heart stops.

"That thing inside of Ian? It was no angel, Gawan. It was evil. Evil as Hell. All except for that one split second."

Gawan nods. The firelight from the hearth flickers shadows over his face. "The Fallen use a curse to change them, which the Earthbounds can't stop. The spells of the Seiagh are too powerful, and the Fallen have saved several to memory. The Fallen trap un-suspecting Earthbounds and use them for their own devices. But you didna kill it. You just sent it to a horrible place."

A lump forms in my chest. "Is there any way to retrieve the Earthbound from wherever I sent them?"

"Yes," Sydney interrupts from her place at the desk. She turns and looks at me. "You have to go in after them."

I immediately feel Eli tense up behind me.

"Can beings other than Earthbounds be sent to that place?" I ask.

Gawan nods. "Aye."

"So Ian's behavior wasn't a demon being evil," I say, finally catching on. "It was an Earthbound rebelling. Trying to get out."

Gawan nods again. "Exactly."

I eye him, and even though I already know the answer after seeing into his memories, I want to hear him say it. "You know all that because you are an Earthbound?"

"Was," Gawan corrects. "For centuries. I'm a mere mortal now, like Dreadmoor."

I'm finally catching on to this twelfth and thirteenth century jive. Not only do both warriors have their given names, but they're also referred to by their home. Dreadmoor. Grimm. Confusing as hell, but I get it.

"I was dead, though," Tristan adds. "A bloody spirit, as were my men, for centuries on and on. Only did my fate change when a young Colonist happened upon my land."

I blink. "You were a ghost for centuries, yes?"

Tristan nods. "Aye."

"Like see-through, mists and orbs, or something different?" I ask.

Tristan laughs. "I appeared just as you see me now, with the exception of my garb. I looked very much alive." He rubs his chin. "I do miss walking straight through walls, and just thinking of a spot I wished to occupy and then just . . . occupying it."

"Do you miss it?" Ginger asks. She's sitting next to Lucian on a long, brown leather sofa.

"Nay," Tristan clarifies. "I wouldn't trade my Andrea for any of it."

Gawan looks at me. "His wife."

I look at Gawan.

I decide my powers are all too useful all of a sudden.

And take a lot less time than verbal explanations.

Slowly, I reach over and brush Gawan's hand with mine.

Now I'm Gawan of Conwyk . . .

Gawan walked close beside her, his arm not too tightly around her, and guided her across the glowing, glittery winter wonderland of Castle Grimm. With the tall, gray Grimm towers, and that giant mouth of a portcullis, it truly did look like something out of a fairy tale. On they walked to the courtyard, where in the spring dozens of flowers bloomed, Gawan said, and the border bumped straight up to the edge of the cliff. The moon hung over the choppy North Sea, and a light sprinkling of snow fell steadily. Gawan had told her how uncanny it was to get snow—and this much of it—at this time of year. Uncanny, he'd said.

For Gawan of Conwyk to find anything uncanny was, well, uncanny.

"Are you sure you want to see this?" he asked.

Ellie stopped and cocked her head. "Are you kidding? Of course I want to."

Gawan guided her to a stone bench set amidst the rose bushes overlooking the sea. "You sit here. I'll need to stand back a ways." He unbuttoned his coat. "Promise me you won't scream. 'Tis overwhelming, the sight of them."

"I won't scream."

He gave a nod, dropped his coat and shirt, and looked at her, just before he walked off. Standing there, the moonlight painting his broad, muscular, tattooed chest in a pale glow, his shoulder-length curls tossing about him in the wind, Ellie appeared taken.

Only she hadn't yet seen Gawan's magnificent yet useless reminders that he'd done something worthy once, several lifetimes ago.

And there, with the tumultuous North Sea roaring behind him and snowflakes falling about, stood Gawan of Conwyk. Born in "a.d." 1115 A.D., died in A.D. "A.D." 1145. Honor bound by his knightly vows; awarded in death a pair of guardian's wings to symbolize his selfless deeds. And as he closed his eyes and said the strange words that carried to Ellie's ears only because of the fierce midwinter's wind blowing directly at her, his wings unfolded from their hiding place within his shoulder blades and spanned nearly twelve feet, tip to tip. They—he—was the most astounding and glorious sight she'd ever beheld.

Not for the first time since meeting the man, Ellie was speechless.

And within the blink of an eye, he'd retracted those wings and was striding closer to her, silently, and when he got to her, she helped him into his shirt and coat, and he embraced her, his mouth buried into her neck.

"I didn't frighten you, did I?" he asked against her skin.

Ellie held on tight. "I'm never scared with you." And wished she could stay there, enclosed within his arms, forever.

"Even that wouldn't be long enough for me," Gawan whispered in her ear.

"Stay out of my head, Conwyk," she said, and he chuckled.

And she cried.

When I focus on Gawan of Conwyk's eyes, they soften. And, he smiles. "Did you find what you seek?" he asks softly.

I nod. "For now." I do know there's a helluva lot more to Gawan and Tristan than what meets the curious eye.

It was a lot to think about. Angels. Earthbounds. Demons. Jodís. Fallen. Vampires. Werewolves. Immortal druids.

And me. Whatever I am.

Weariness is starting to hit me. I'm one of the only souls in the room who require sleep, except for the lupines. Not too sure about the druids. Even I require just a small amount these days.

"Ri, you need to rest for a bit," Eli says. He rubs my head, then explains. "One of the several side effects of her mortal DNA mixing with that of four vampires. She just falls out sometimes. Like a bad case of narcolepsy."

"Go rest," Jake says. "We'll be here when you wake up. We've a lot to go over before Tristan and Gawan leave."

"Why are they leaving?" I ask. "Wouldn't their skills with the sword be helpful?"

"That's what I keep telling him," Tristan says, grumbling.

"Whilst they are the verra best swordsman alive, in my opinion, they are mere mortals. They can be killed. And we're obviously dealing with a lot more than we at first assumed. Not just simply lopping off the heads of a Fallen or a Jodís. I'll not make their families suffer. The both of them have done enough of that in their lifetimes," Jake says.

"Aye," Gawan says. "Dreadmoor already has six children."

"Soon to be seven," Jake corrects. "And you're one to talk, Conwyk. Your bride has been pregnant more oft than not. Five babes now?"

"There is that," Gawan replies, and he nods. "Aye, there is that, indeed."

"I want them out of here before the Fallen rejuvenate. We've one more day left, at best," Jakes says, then inclines his head toward the desk. "Sydney is pouring through the Celtae's old tomes. Only she can read them. Clues are hidden amongst the pages regarding the relics. Then we'll be hitting the streets."

I nod. "I'll only rest for a bit." I push off the floor,

grab my empty container and Coke bottle, and start toward the kitchen. Eli rises and follows me.

I catch the light switch with my elbow as I walk in, Eli behind me. The kitchen is a decent size, with a long wooden block top in the center, a pair of deep white porcelain sinks at the back, and a huge mahogany dining table. It looks old. Modern appliances fill the spaces, a double-sized stainless-steel, side-by-side fridge with a freezer drawer on the bottom, a dishwasher, and a stove. Above it, a mega microwave. In the far corner, the "red" fridge for the vamps. Some smart-ass has placed a magnet of a pair of long, white fangs on the front of the door. Funny.

"Immortals eat a lot," Eli offers. He takes my trash, finds the receptacle, and dumps it. "Almost as much as humans with tendencies."

"Ha ha," I remark, and slide my arms around his waist. His strong arms embrace me, and I feel drowsy just resting against his chest.

"Go upstairs and get some sleep," he says against my hair, then kisses my temple. His lips move to my ear. "You're gonna need it, *chère*."

My heart leaps.

Eli laughs against my hair. "I heard that."

Something hard presses against my abdomen. "I feel that."

He laughs again. "Go," he says, and turns me around and swats my ass. "Go get some rest. You don't want to pass out onto the floor like you did at my parent's house."

"Yeah, that I could've done without," I answer. "Especially with your idiotic brothers watching. Throwing things at me and laughing. So freaking juvenile."

"Don't forget my idiotic sister," he adds. "She laughed just as hard."

"Yeah and your mama scolded you all for it," I remind him.

"Tough woman, Elise Dupré," he says.

To that I fully agree. And I miss her.

I wave good night to the team as I pass back through the common room and head for the stairs. In the foyer, it's dark with only a single lamp burning on a tall, small table. Shadows play on the wall as I go by, and I briefly wonder if it's me causing it or something else.

I climb to the second floor, and only when I hit the landing does a strange sensation come over me. I glance around, but see nothing except dim lights and shadows. I continue on. Stopping by the bathroom, I take care of girly business, wash up, and brush my teeth. I pull my jet-black hair into a floppy bun at the top of my head, and head out into the corridor. I take no more than a few steps before the sensation comes back full force. A whisper brushes my neck, close to my ear, and I whip around. My breath hitches.

At the end of the hall, back at the platform leading downstairs, is that creepy little girl from before. I blink. She's gone.

I half expect her to still be standing there, saying *Come play with me. Forever.*

I stare at the empty space for several seconds. I guess if Tristan can be a ghost for centuries, and I know that to be true, then the ghost of a little girl could be lingering here. Not optimal, since I don't have time for tricks and games and scares, but what the Hell. I turn and head to my room. I pull up short.

She's standing by my door.

I decide to play it cool.

"What's your name?" I ask.

The little girl, with her severely pulled-back hair and white skin, simply stares. She says nothing.

Awkward.

With a sigh, I continue on. My narcolepsy is about to come on full strength. I need to find my bed. Uninterrupted by ghosts.

I stop a few feet from her. "I'm Riley. If you ever decide to talk—"

Again, the little girl's mouth drops down into a crooked, exaggerated *O*, her eyes black and fathomless. But this time the scream pierces straight through my brain.

Then she lunges through me. My insides immediately feel icy.

I jerk around. She's not behind me.

Gone. Unless she's inside of me.

"Okay, well, if you change your mind, I'm not bad to talk to. For an adult. And, for the record, you don't scare me. I kill vampires for a living."

I decide I'll talk to Jake and Gabriel about her after I rest. Sydney and Gabriel both have lived here for a while. Have they had encounters with the little girl before? If not, why me? Why freaking me? I seem to be asking that a lot lately. Right now I feel like I'm about to drop onto the floor. Seriously. I've battled newlings and vamps. My poor neck has been latched on to by Julian Arcos, for Christ's sake. I still shudder at that memory. Saving my skin or not, he's just flat-out creepy. He even asked me to become his wife if things didn't work out with Eli. Really?

Considering all that, I can handle the screaming ghost of a little girl. And, for the record, I did look into her eyes. Nothing happened.

Inside my room, I bend down to kick off my boots.

Only then do I realize I'm too late.

In the next second, I tip over. My body is flush with the floor. My eyes close.

It's as good a bed as any. . . .

I'm walking outside on the Mile, and I'm alone. Although I can't say where I'm headed, I know exactly where I'm going. It's dark. It's raining. And after I pass St. Giles', I turn down a narrow close. Suddenly I'm at a lone door. It's slightly opened, and I enter.

"I'm glad you're here," a voice says from inside. "Come. You're just in time."

"In time for what?" I ask. "Who are you?"

I see a figure ahead of me, crouching by a long, threadbare sofa of blue-and-black plaid cloth. The figure keeps his back to me. He's large. Wearing a dark cloak with a hood.

"Turn around and face me," I say, and he chuckles.

"I cannot. Not now. You won't understand if I do."

I move in closer and notice a middle-aged man asleep on the sofa. On the table beside him, a half-finished pint of beer. The TV is silent, but the screen depicts a UK cop show. I look at the figure. "What are you doing?"

"Watch."

The figure waves his hand over the man's sleeping body, then rises. Although he moves toward me, he keeps his back to me. I slide my gaze back to the sleeping man, and his middle begins to smoke. Smolder. He awakens and yells out and begins to beat his stomach with his hands.

"Help me!" he screams. "Christ, help me!"

I lunge toward him, but the figure grabs me, holds me back.

"Nay, girl," he says. "You cannot stop it."

"The fuck I can't!" I scream. I elbow him in the vicinity of his jaw. I make contact with something. "Let me go!"

The figure laughs softly. "Your valor is impressive. But you cannot stop this." He turns and looks me in the eye, and I blink, staring. His face is . . . perfectly normal. Handsome. Older. With fathomless blue eyes that sear straight through me. Reaching with his cloaked arm, he sinks his fingers into the screaming man's chest and removes his heart. It's still beating. The man's screams intensify, then begin to die down. The smell of acrid smoke and charred flesh fills my nostrils. "And you can't stop me."

I stare into those eyes. "Watch me—"

Strong fingers wrap around my floppy-bun hairdo, and a firm hand grasps my shoulder and shakes me. I jump, gasp, and sit straight up. I take a swing at the man, and he ducks and barely misses my punch.

"Shh, chère," he says softly. "I didn't mean to frighten you."

I'm awake now. It's Eli. I've had enough sleep. I don't know how much time has passed, but it's more than enough. "You never have frightened me, Dupré," I say. "But someone is trying to."

Eli frowns. "What do you mean?"

Rubbing my eyes with my knuckles, I pretend I don't still smell the burning flesh of a human. "I saw an innocent burn."

Eli sighs and pulls me to him. "How? Who?"

I shake my head. "A middle-aged man. Just . . . asleep on his couch. The one there, the one who lured me there . . ." I look at Eli. "I think he was one of the Fallen. I saw him take the man's heart."

"Damn it, Ri," he says, then looks at me. "So the Fallen really don't mind getting their hands dirty after all?"

I shake my head. "We have to stop these guys," I say. "Fast. They have no conscience, Eli. None." I shake my head. "No telling how many more will die. And I think there's a lot more to the Fallen than even Jake and Gabriel, and Darius know." I shake my head. "They can do . . . anything."

"We'll get them, Riley," Eli assures me. "I swear it."

I nod. "I didn't hurt you, did I?"

Eli laughs softly and stands me up. "You missed, so no." He wraps his arms around me and lowers his head. "You didn't even make it to the bed, *chère*. Just fell right onto the floor. And you're still wearing all your clothes, including your dirk."

"Yeah," I answer, burying my face in his neck. I wrap my arms around his waist. "Floor worked just fine. Too tired to take everything off. Good thing I didn't impale myself with my blade on the way down."

His deep chuckle rumbles against my ear. We stand there a second or two, or maybe a minute. I suddenly can't quite get close enough, even after shifting a time or two. Maybe it's the clothing that's in the way?

"Maybe," Eli says. He grabs my hair and pulls gently, forcing my head to tip back, making me look up at him. He lowers his head, his mouth hovering over mine.

"Just being in the same room with you and not being able to have you for hours at a time stirs a need within me so fierce, it literally hurts." He dips lower, his lips brushing mine. Erotic. Inside, I shiver. "Do you understand, *chère*?"

Oh yeah, I sure do.

With light pressure, Eli nudges my mouth open with his, and at the same time he drops the hand holding my hair and grasps one of my hands. He lowers it, pulls it between us, and presses it against the bulge straining against his pants.

I smile and stretch my fingers and palm him, and he groans into my mouth, the sound desperate, hungry, determined.

A total turn-on.

Eli slides his tongue across my bottom lip and pulls it into his mouth, the pressure of the suck light, constant, then a little harder, a bit faster. The erotic, slick movement makes my pulse quicken, my breath catch. The cool metal buttons of his fly come loose under my fingers one by one.

Eli moves his mouth to my ear, his warm breath making my skin break out into goose bumps. He inhales. "You smell good," he whispers. His accent is thicker. Sexy as hell. Another big turn-on, and Eli knows it. I do as he asks. No problem. I mean, this vampire is *mine*. All mine. Eli smiles against my mouth. Our teeth bump together. We laugh. Then Eli's hands slide to my jaw, one on either side. With nothing more than the moonlight slipping in through the window, he locks a profound stare to mine. "I am so in love with you, Riley Poe," he says quietly. He slides his fingers over my left hand and grazes the ring he gave me. "I still can't believe you're mine."

Eli's words wash over me. Funny thing is, I allow it. Revel in it.

And I can actually say it back now.

"I'm so in love with you, Eligius Dupré." I kiss his nose. "It actually took a vampire to claim my icy heart."

"Your heart has never been icy," he answers, and kisses me. He fingers the wings at my cheek. "It was just waiting on me."

Wrapping my arms around his neck, Eli lifts and settles me on his hips. I wrap my legs around his waist, and heat pools low, deep, and I press harder against him. He kisses me and he kicks the door shut behind us.

We fall against the closed door, and my fingers fumble behind me to lock it. The iron bolt digs into my spine, but I ignore it. I all but climb the length of him, digging my heels into his back, pressing the heat growing between my legs against his hard ridge. I thread my fingers through his hair and pull his head back to give me better access to his mouth. I take full advantage of it. I taste his lips. Bite. Lick. Then I kiss him deep, and my heart, surprisingly, beats a little faster. I feel restless inside, and it's growing more difficult to tolerate.

"I can't wait," I mutter on a gasp. "Now, Eligius."

Eli lets me slide from my perch on his hips and pins me against the door. Eyes darkened by raging lust hold my gaze as he tugs the clasps of my thin leather straps and blade sheath, letting both drop to the floor. Grasping my snug shirt by the hem, the material slides over my skin as he pulls it off and tosses it onto the floor. Likewise, I pull his shirt over his head, drop it, and slip my palms over the chiseled muscles of his chest, lower, to his stomach, and around to the smooth contours of his hard, broad back. He buries his mouth against my neck, and I don't even tense up anymore.

Eli has that much control.

Turn-on.

With his fingertips, Eli slides the straps of my bra off my shoulders and unclasps it, and my heavy breasts are free of the silky material. My bra finds its way on the growing pile of clothes on the floor. The cool air brushes my skin, and one of Eli's hands finds my lower back and pulls me closer. He drops his head, kisses my collarbone, and moves lower, his lips dragging over the swell of my breast. Grabbing his hair, I pull his mouth to exactly where I want it. In an erotic kiss, he suckles me, makes my skin flame, and covers the other breast with his hand. I press my groin to his, closer, hot, aching. Shivers of pleasure rack my body each time his tongue and lips rake over the sensitive peak, causing the throbbing pulse between my thighs to pitch. I push my hands through his silky hair and hold on.

His mouth leaves my breast, the chilly air of the ancient chamber cooling my wet skin, and he lowers, kissing with tongue and teeth down my ribs. Goes down on one knee, drags his mouth over my navel, my hip. With adept fingers, he pulls off my boots, socks, unbuttons my dark jeans, pulls them down and off. All shoved away. Wasting no time, he hooks my panties, pushes them down, and pulls them off. Gone. My heart leaps. My breath stills in my lungs.

Those same adept fingers rise to my ribs, one hand on either side, and hold me firmly against the door. He teases first the inside of one thigh, then the other, fire pooling in all my sensitive places. I moan, about to lose my mind, and push his head down.

The moment Eli's tongue slides inside of me I explode, jerking against the cool wood of the door. Eli's fingers dig into the spaces between my rib bones. A sob escapes me. Can't help it. Can barely breathe.

Then he rises and carries me to the bed. The room is bathed in a milky glow, and shadows reach, grasp, and miss. Eli sets me down and moves behind me, and his breath rakes against the bare skin of my neck. "I want you forever," he says. "I always want this." He nips my shoulder softly, causing me to shiver. "You."

Eli's boots, jeans, and boxer briefs are off and kicked away into a dark pile. When he finds me again, he presses the hard, carved stone of his chest against my back and I arch against it, and for a moment, his arms go around me, crossing over my stomach and pulling me close. There is no steady, fast thump of a heart hammering against me, but I feel his body quiver. He whispers *I love you* in French. I feel every ounce of strong, possessive emotion within him. All for me.

Eli turns me, moves over me, his weight resting on his forearm. With dark eyes filled with love, he studies me wordlessly. Then his mouth covers mine. His kiss is erotic, deep, slow. I wrap my legs around his waist, drag my heels down his calves.

Eli groans, and in one move he enters me. He sucks in a breath, stills, and murmurs more French words. They're muffled and I don't understand them.

His hard sex fills every inch of me, claiming its place deep within, and I hold on for dear life. He begins to rock, his hard thighs trapping me and his body crowding me.

A slow arc of pleasure builds and fires, sending shards of blinding light scattering behind the lids of my eyes. A cry rips from my throat as the orgasm racks me, and at the same time Eli's own climax tears from him, over and over as he takes me possessively, claiming me in the most ancient of ways. Uncontrolled. Out of control.

Perfect.

As we both crash back down to earth, Eli remains inside of me, slowly moving, his breath coming in harsh puffs against my neck as his mouth kisses me. His arms are wrapped tightly around me, holding me tightly against him, and I feel more emotion, more love, in that full-body embrace than even the words themselves.

It's that powerful. It's that beautiful.

And I never, ever want it to end.

Part Six

DEMENTED ANGELS

I am never so frightened as when every thing is still.

—*Sir Arthur Conan Doyle,* **The Parasite**

*If anything ever happens to Riley, I don't think I'll sur-
vive it. My love for her has quadrupled since I first realized I loved her. She fits me perfectly, and I want her for
as long as we have together. The thought that something as powerful as a Black Fallen can manipulate her
in her sleep petrifies me. She thinks she can handle herself in all situations, and for the most part, she can. But
with a Fallen? I'm not so sure. They've already homed
in on her. It'll be up to me to keep her safe.*

—Eli Dupré

The thought that I've sent an Earthbound angel to
some godforsaken plane of torture and hideous-
ness plagues me. I can't stop thinking about it. I
know I will have to rectify it. If it kills me, I'll rectify
it. The look in Ian's eyes, the eyes of the Earthbound,
haunts me. It's compelling. Profound. I see it in my
head, constantly.

It pisses me off.

I'm ready to find the Fallen and kick their asses.

The team practices for another day. Tristan and
Gawan's lessons are invaluable. They are truly master swordsmen, and I can only imagine what they
would've been like in their prime. Well, they are in
their prime; neither of them look a bit over their
midthirties. But I mean in their *original* prime.

They're tough as shit, too, and they cut no slack where their students are concerned. Vampires don't sweat, but immortals do and so do the lupines. And so does a human with tendencies. They worked my ass to the bone, both of them. After we went through hours of stances, we were finally given the blades. Not easy. And not nearly as easy as the little blades I'm used to working with. Hell, you aim and throw. Or you stab. With a sword you have to watch your back. And your own appendages.

After, we paired up. At first our mentors took turns with each of us. Tristan is truly a unique guy to engage in swordplay. You wouldn't think someone that big could move so elegantly. He makes it look effortless.

It's a sham. It's hard as Hell.

But we stuck it out, and although we get the fast version of Swordplay for Dummies, we all get the gist of it. In the Crescent's courtyard, Jake has set up several dummies for head lopping. Again, not as easy as it looks in the movies. One big swing and off goes the head. Nuh-uh. You'd better hit that neck at just the precise mark, and you'd better have all your damn weight behind your swing. Or else it'll hang. And squirt stuff.

Not pretty.

And not effective. Apparently, if you don't completely sever the head, the Fallen and the Jodís can regenerate. I almost want to do it just to watch. Sick, I know. But if anything, I'm truthful.

Sydney's the only one missing in our training.

She's already mastered the sword, thanks to a year with Gabriel, and she's been assigned the task of going through the sacred tomes of the Celtae, courtesy of Darius. He's another one that amazes me. It's weird to have seen him, as well as Jake, Tristan, and Gawan, in a time other than this one. It's a surreal occurrence, yet . . . it really happened. They lived in another time, one wilder, untamed—a place where your sword was your protection.

Or, in Tristan's case, not.

I found out a few other things about him. Tristan's wife? Forensic archaeologist. She, after excavating, digging, researching, and falling in love with a spirit, reversed the curse and brought not only Tristan back to life, but all of his knights. One, the youngest, is picking up Tristan and Gawan in a little while, and so I'll get to meet yet another once-ghost. Even saying it inside my head sounds weird. But it happened. Almost as weird as a tattoo artist from Savannah, Georgia, being engaged to an aged vampire.

And Gawan. An Earthbound angel for centuries, he was on the brink of retirement. Was ready to become a full-fledged mortal, live out his life, and die. And just when he was about to retire, *whack*! He found a soaking-wet girl who claimed to be named Ellie on the road near his castle. She turned out to be a girl In Betwixt. Dead, but not. Ghostly, but not always. In and out. Yeah, they fell in love. Of course they did. The story would suck if they didn't. She also happened to be his intended. His soul mate.

I get that. Mine's a bloodsucker.

Gawan had to find Ellie's half-dead real self before she actually expired. He did. Now they're married, madly in love, and have a flock of children.

Blows my mind to hear it. And if all that can happen? Anything can happen. Good or evil. And that makes me know I'd best be on my toes, in tip-top shape. Ready for any damn thing.

We spend the latter part of the afternoon on the streets of Edinburgh. Wet Edinburgh. Wet, cold, mist-shrouded Edinburgh. Still a cool old city. But from someone who is used to the southeastern coast of the United States, it takes a little getting used to.

We move through the streets, the closes and wynds, Grassmarket and Cowgate. Gabriel takes us through the vaults, or the catacombs, of underground Edinburgh. He says we'll need to know the city inside and out once the Fallen have regenerated. The vaults are eerily cold and dark, and throughout most of them only candles, occasionally lit by walking tour staff members, light the passageways.

All at once, I sense it. The others do, too. Another vampire. No sooner does the thought enter my head than a scream pierces the cold corridors of the vaults. In a flash, Victorian races ahead of me and disappears through an archway. He's already morphed. When next I look, so have all the other vampires in my company. We all follow Victorian's lead, through the shadowy passages of the vaults, and the screams grow more intense. I can tell the vampire is young, a girl. And in horrific pain. Like lightning, we fly through the tunnels, and at once we all come to a halt.

We're now in a large chamber. Victorian has a human by the throat, holding him high. Four other humans fill the chamber. And chained to a wall, a girl. Rather, a female vampire. Older than I figured. Maybe twenty. Her merlot eyes are wide, and she stares at Victorian.

"Arcos, don't," Jake instructs Victorian.

"She doesn't deserve this!" Victorian yells. His eyes are latched onto the human in his grasp.

"Put him down or I'll run you through," another human says. She holds a silver dirk, strapped to the end of a long wooden stick. It touches Victorian's back.

Just that fast, I'm there, the silver blade knocked from the woman's hand. I shove her across the chamber and she hits the wall. "I don't think so," I say. "What'd she do?"

"What you murderers all do," another woman, huddled against the wall, says.

I shake my head. "What did she do?" I repeat.

"It's what she will do!" the remaining human, a middle-aged man, says. He steps closer, glancing at the one Victorian has suspended in the air.

"That's not good enough," Jake says. He looks at them all. "Victorian, put him down."

Vic lets the man fall to the floor, where he scrambles up and huddles with the others.

"Now leave," Jake says. And without another word, they all do exactly as he says.

Victorian hurries to the female vampire. "Riley?" he calls.

I go to him, and he nods to the chains. They're made of pure silver. No wonder Vic hadn't broken them himself yet. Grasping first one, then the other, I yank them out of the wall. Then, I pry them off of the girl. I study her. Her eyes are pale now. And she looks absolutely terrified. "She's not a vampire."

"Not yet," Victorian corrects. He looks at her. "What is your name?"

The girl's gaze flashes to all of us before returning Vic's question. Her brows furrow, as if she's thinking really hard. "Abbey," she answers in a heavy brogue. "I think."

"Do you have family?" Gabriel asks.

Abbey shakes her head. "No."

Gabriel nods. "You'll be safe now," he assures her. "Arcos, bring her along."

I watch in fascination as Vic gingerly helps the somewhat-vamp girl out of the chamber. Gabriel turns to Jake. "I know a place to take her. Arcos can accompany us."

Jake nods. "Aye."

Then Gabriel and Vic leave with Abbey. We all follow behind, but instead of leaving out of the vaults, Gabriel leads them down a long passageway in the opposite direction. I stare until the darkness swallows them up.

I glance at Eli. "That was weird."

"Not as weird as you think," Jake answers. "Edinburgh has more than one human group of ghost hunters and monster chasers. They were spot on with this one, though. She's no' far from changing into full-potency vampire. He shakes his head. "We'll have to find out who her maker is."

"Will they be able to save her?" I ask.

Jake's green gaze meets mine. "Mayhap."

Finally, a way out of the catacombs. We enter through an unobtrusive doorway and exit through a pub. Out on the street, the strained sounds of a bagpipe echo off the stone.

I think I have the general makeup of the city engrained in me. No, I don't know each close and wynd, but I see how they work. Just like Savannah runs in squares, Edinburgh runs on the fish spine. I get it.

It rains all day. The oiled canvas coat I wear keeps me dry, for the most part. As the daylight fades, we find ourselves on Princes Street, and the hustle and bustle of tourism and nightlife are just kicking up. The imposing Gothic spires of the Scott Monument draw my attention, and I think before I leave Edinburgh I'd like to do a little crazy free running. If my brother, Seth, could see this place, he'd be all over it.

By the time light fades into shadows, we're back at the Crescent. Gabriel and Victorian have returned and now join us. We all mill in the courtyard. Tristan begins to argue about leaving.

I knew he would.

"My wife would encourage me to stay," Tristan argues. "I cannot in good conscience leave you all here, knowing what you face. What the people, mortals of Edinburgh, face."

"Nor can I," adds Gawan.

"You can use the extra blades," Tristan adds.

Jake pinches the bridge of his nose.

"If we get into a desperate situation, we'll call

you," Gabriel says, then looks at me. "You wouldna argue if you knew the full potential of that one." He inclines his head toward me.

"I know she has multiple senses, mind powers that I do not have," Tristan says. He looks at me. "No disrespect, Ms. Poe, but you simply lack the strength of a man. You are, after all, a female." He glances toward Ginger. "Unlike Ms. Slater, who is lupine—"

Tristan jerks around, because he's now talking to thin air. In the split second it takes him to look away, I have made two leaps. One toward that hideous yet weirdly attractive angel fountain; two, the gargoyle on the far side of the Crescent. I'm now on the ledge of the rooftop, looking down. I'm watching that big, bulky knight look everywhere but up. Bending over, I pick up a loose stone, search for a bigger one, and find it, then throw them both at him. One bounces off his head, the other—the larger—off his ass.

Tristan curses, then spins around. He looks up, and I wave.

"Damn me," he says, low and under his breath. He turns back and faces Jake and Gabriel. "Aye, so she can jump and apparently climb. But— damn!"

Just that fast I leap down and onto Tristan's back. I flip him over, we fall to the gravel, and I land on top of him. He lets out a deep grunt. I pin his massive arms above his head, his tree-trunk legs trapped beneath mine, and I allow him to struggle for a few seconds. I almost can't stand it. I want to burst out laughing.

For a full minute, I let him struggle.

Only when he becomes winded do I grin. "Is that your sword, Dreadmoor, or are you just happy to see me?" I ask.

"Get off me, woman!" Tristan bellows, but his lips twitch.

Before I jump up, I take one more look. I can't help it. Tristan de Barre is just too damn fascinating not to. With a smile, I take his hand in mine. And hold it.

A very small number of people attended the celebration. Live people, that is. Jameson; his son, Thomas, who looked just like Jameson; Miss Kate; her daughter; and Heath, the priest, to name a few. Tristan and his knights, of course. Even Constable Hurley showed up. Dreadmoor had quite a haunted reputation, but there were a few who put their fears aside and dared to come forth.

The remainder of the guests were restless spirits, ghosts from all corners of England, Scotland, and France. They had poured in through the front gates in droves, just to see the arrogant Dragonhawk and his lady wed. The news had apparently traveled fast, because there were knights and warriors of all shapes and ages littering the bailey, the lists, the great hall and chapel—ghosts Andi had not once laid eyes on.

By the time the sun began its descent and the sky turned various shades of purple, gray, and orange, Tristan had threatened to toss her over his massive shoulders and haul her to the kirk. She wouldn't have minded, really. Not one little bit.

As Jameson led her to the staircase, her heart began to pound. That is, until her eyes landed on Tristan. Dragonhawk.

Then her poor heart nearly stopped.

The groom-to-be stood at the foot of the stairs, speaking with his captain. Kail must have announced her, because Tristan's head turned. He stared, a feral glint lighting his eyes, a muscle tightening in his cheek.

Jameson led her down the stairs, and it was a damn good thing, too. She would have surely tripped had he not been holding her steady.

Jameson approached Tristan, gently placed her hand on his arm, then stepped aside and gave Andi a low bow.

The lord of Dreadmoor all but robbed her of breath. He was so big. His very presence demanded respect and authority and power, and reeked of self-confidence. It lingered in each and every knight's eye, whether live or ghostly.

He wore his mail—new, of course—as did the other knights. Dark hose strained to cover his massive calves and thighs, followed by boots and a black surcoat. The mystical Dragonhawk, same as the one on his shield, was stitched on the front, its head thrown back as though issuing a mighty command. Its eye eerily glowed the same shade of sapphire as Tristan's. More of Kate's beautiful handiwork. His sword, now polished and gleaming, hung low on his lean, narrow hips. But something was odd.

The sapphire stone was missing from the hilt. It'd been filled in with a black stone. Onyx?

A voice, deep and raspy, growled in her ear.

"Lady, you're gaping. I vow 'tis immensely satisfying."

The corner of her mouth lifted. "No doubt."

He caught and held her gaze, and the impact alone nearly knocked her over. Love and desire shone bright and intense in his eyes. She couldn't have torn her gaze away had she tried.

Not that she would want to try, of course.

"You are passing beautiful, Andrea. I am the luckiest man in the entire world—dead or alive." He grinned, gave her a quick peck on the tip of her nose, and then lifted his gloved hand to her chin. Tilting her head, he lowered and whispered words meant only for her. Warm breath caressed her ear. "God, I love you." He stared a moment longer, then straightened and tucked her hand in the crook of his arm. "Let's be off to the kirk. I am ready to wed you."

Andi grinned and looked up—ghost medieval knights stared at her and Tristan, some more fierce-looking, a few no more than fifteen or sixteen years old.

Jason, bless his sweet soul, stood close by. He grinned at the pair and led them through the gathering of men. "This way, my lord and lady. Move you, men there, and make way."

Jameson awaited across the great hall, door open and lanterns lighting the path outside to the kirk. They passed through the doorway, followed by Tristan's garrison and no less than one hundred ghostly knights.

A slight salty breeze wafted across the bailey. Andi lifted the hem of her gown with the one free hand she had, so as not to stumble. At the rate at which Tristan pulled her, it was a miracle her feet even managed to light on the ground.

Maybe he was in a big hurry.

Standing now at the front of the small chapel, they turned their attention to the priest waiting for them. He opened a large, leather-bound ledger and began to scribble.

Jameson stood to her left and behind her. Jason took a place beside Jameson. Kail stood on Tristan's right side. The rest of the Dragonhawk knights stood in a line behind them. Kate and her small family lined the wall on Andi's left. The small kirk was literally filled to the brim with the remaining ghostly knights and warriors who'd traveled to Dreadmoor.

The plain, weathered stone kirk suited Andi just fine. Torches lit the room, their flickering flames casting a warm glow. Tristan had her hand tucked safely within his own as they faced the priest. She held on to him so tight, his mail pressed into her skin. Then, before they knew it, the priest began the ceremony in Latin. He turned to Andrea and Tristan, repeating the words in English.

"Tristan de Barre, Dragonhawk of Dreadmoor, how take ye this woman, Andrea Kinley Monroe?"

Tristan cleared his throat, turned, and stared down at her. The dimples pitted deeply into his cheeks, although he didn't smile. There was that intense look, the very one that made her completely senseless. Her knees swayed a bit.

"I take this woman as my own, in the name of our father." His deep voice washed over her like a wave. "Forever."

The priest nodded, then turned his dancing blue gaze to her. "And you, Andrea Kinley Monroe of Virginia. How take ye this man?"

Andi turned to Tristan, and as soon as she looked into his blue eyes, so full of love, the tears started to roll down her cheeks. "I take this man as my own, in the name of our father." She sniffed. "Forever."

Tristan reached a gloved hand and caught the trail of tears with his finger. His heart filled with joy.

The priest turned the ledger around on the table before

them and nodded. Tristan took the pen, dipped it in ink, and signed his name. He dipped it once more and handed the pen to Andi. Her hands trembled as she signed.

The priest nodded. "In the name of our Holy Father and before these witnessing souls, 'tis done." He turned to Tristan. "You, my lord, may now kiss—"

"I know that." Tristan grinned at the priest then pulled Andi into a tight embrace, lowered his head, and captured her lips, then proceeded to kiss her senseless right in front of the entire garrison and gathered ghosts. Shouts and cheers erupted around the small ancient chapel, but Andi barely noticed.

What girl in her right mind would have while at the mercy of a chivalrous knight such as Tristan de Barre? The renowned Dragonhawk.

Her husband.

Tristan broke the kiss, gave her a quick peck on the nose, and grinned. She looked down at her hand.

On her finger sat the most beautiful wedding ring. A wide silver band with a lovely sapphire setting in the center. Her head snapped up. "This is from your sword."

"Aye." Tristan produced another ring, much larger than the one on her finger. "I had this one fashioned, as well." One corner of his mouth lifted in a charming grin. "So we would match."

Andi smiled, took the ring from his palm, and tugged off Tristan's glove. She pushed the ring into place and stared up at her husband. "It's beautiful."

"You, my love, are beautiful."

Tristan swept her up into his strong arms and took off down the short aisle of the kirk, heading for the doorway.

Jameson hurried after them, Kate by his side, grinning and waving at the same time. "My lord and lady, wait!" He panted as he ran. "A feast has been prepared!"

"Well done, Jameson," Tristan shouted over his shoulder. "Have it sent up to my chambers posthaste."

Andi turned and glanced behind her as they left the kirk. Jason laughed, a broad smile lighting up his face. Kail slapped Sir Richard on the back, sending him sprawling. Jameson simply stood in the aisle, grinning. Andi waved and held on to her husband for dear life.

He carried her across the bailey and through the great hall. Even as Tristan held the treasured bundle in his arms, he could scarce believe his good fortune. Andi stared up at him with wide eyes as he climbed the staircase. He flashed her a quick grin.

"Lady Dragonhawk, I vow you'll force me to lose my footing if you do not cease looking at me with such affection. 'Tis unnerving."

Andi giggled. "You're full of it, Dreadmoor."

"Aye, for a certainty. Moon away, love." Tristan reached the top of the stairs and stopped. He studied every inch of his bride's lovely face, from her greenish-flecked eyes to her full, inviting lips. When her hand snaked around his neck and pulled him closer, it was nearly his undoing.

He bent his head and brushed her lips with his. Her sweet mouth trembled, and his poor knees wanted to buckle from the emotions it ignited within him. His throat tightened, so he swallowed. Twice. It did no good. Damn bothersome lump.

With long strides he started up the passageway and pulled to a halt just before plowing into his young knight.

Tristan glared. "Damnation, Jason. How'd you manage to get here first? Move you away."

Jason smiled at Andi and blushed. "Shall I guard your door, my lord?"

Tristan walked past the boy and opened his chamber door. "Aye, and guard it with enthusiasm, pup." He kicked the door shut with his foot.

"Aye, my lord!" Jason shouted from the other side.

Tristan glanced down at his lady, who gave him a bright smile. "He is very sweet," she said.

Tristan shook his head. "That sweet lad," he said, tossing his head in the direction of the door, "has killed more men in battle than you could fathom. I daresay 'tis best he knows you now, instead of when he was alive in the thirteenth century. The pup blushes at the mere sight of you." He grinned. "You would have been the death of him, lady." He brought his head closer. "As you would have me." He brought his lips down to hers. "Do not close your eyes, Andrea of Dreadmoor." His command whispered against her mouth. "I want you to see what you do to me."

She forced her eyes to remain open as Tristan brushed his lips across hers, their eyes locked. He pulled back, then softly brushed them again. Arms of steel tightened around her, his muscles tense. He slowly set her on her feet, his eyes never leaving hers. Large callused hands skimmed her skin as he framed her face.

Her head held captive, Tristan lowered his mouth and kissed her, brushing his lips across hers over and over, his fingers kneading her scalp, tracing the shell of her ear, as he deepened the kiss. Her breath escaped as he tasted her lips with his tongue, softly at first, then possessive, demanding. Reaching up, she entwined her fingers in his long, silky hair and pulled him closer.

A low moan escaped him and, his breathing harsh, he said, "Help me out of this mail, woman, for I vow I cannot do it alone."

With trembling fingers, Andi helped him out of the heavy-gauge steel. Once free, he stepped toward her and in one swift move scooped Andi back into his arms. In two strides he stood at their bed.

Following her down to the softness of the duvet, he kissed her neck, her ears, her throat. Nerves she didn't even know existed tingled with sensation.

Tristan, breathless, lifted his head and held her gaze. "God, Andrea." A rush of warm breath sent a shiver across her skin as his deep, accented voice whispered against her ear. "I cannot get enough of you."

Tristan's large hands shook as he unlaced her gown. The fire in his eyes smoldered as he slowly removed each layer of lace and then, without a word, shed his own clothes, never once dropping his gaze. He came to her, stretched out above her, and kissed her until she couldn't breathe.

Skin to skin, body to body, they moved, and when Tristan claimed her, his gaze never faltered. Watching her intently, his own wonder of discovery turned his eyes a dark, tumultuous blue-gray.

Tears spilled over her lids, and as Tristan brushed a tender kiss across her lips, he whispered against her mouth, his voice hoarse with emotion.

"I would gladly wait another seven hundred years for your love, Lady Dreadmoor." He caressed her jaw with his *callused knuckles. "I love you, Andrea de Barre." He rested his forehead against hers. "I will love you forever."*

When I refocus, Tristan is searing me with a sapphire blue gaze. "What did you find out this time, my lady?"

I grin, jump up, and extend my hand once more. He takes it and stands to his full height. I look up. Way up. "Wow. All that kick-ass knightliness all rolled into a big pile of mush." I exaggerate my sigh. "It's like a fairy tale."

Tristan laughs. "Aye, 'tis, in truth. But keep to yourself the mushy part. I've a reputation to uphold, girl. A fierce one. Not one of a pansy."

I laugh and punch Tristan's arm. "You got it."

"Damn me," he says, and slaps my shoulder. I buck forward. "I renounce my earlier claim. You may fight any battle beside me. Or ahead of me."

I grin. "Thanks. And back at ya." I slap Tristan on the back. "For a mere mortal, you're okay."

Lifting my hand, he drops a light kiss there. "And I believe you're way more than a mere human with tendencies, Ms. Poe."

I give him a slight nod of thanks.

Just then, a pair of headlights bobs up and down over the cobbles at the entrance of Tolbooth Wynd. They stop at the gates to the Crescent. Two short blasts from the horn echo in the courtyard.

"Oy, young Jason is here," Gawan says. He has walked closer to me and lays a hand on my shoulder. "It has been a pleasure meeting you, lady," he says. "I will give you a bit of advice about Earthbounds.

Firstly, the spell in which the Fallen have chosen is a powerful one. Only another spell from the Seiagh can counteract it, which you dunna have." He looks down at me. The light from the courtyard lamp glints off his eyes. "But you've the strength to save them, should you find it in yourself to do so. To go after them, though, is a tricky thing indeed. There's not always a convenient puddle of holy water lying about."

"What do I do?" I ask.

"Not only must you be touching the soul in which the Earthbound has been forced to take over, but you must also be submerged in the conduit yourself. Rather, a piece of you. Hand. Foot. Finger."

"The conduit?" I question.

"Aye," Gawan answers. "Glass. Mirror. Water. Reflections, Ms. Poe. But," he continues, and his expression turns grim. "You must be armed, and you must be careful. Once the Earthbound is trapped inside the conduit, it cannot harm you. It might no longer look like its Earthbound self, but you can tell by the eyes. Their eyes are their own. And as you've seen, they're regretful. Sad. Pleading."

I nod in understanding. "What can hurt me? And what can I take in the conduit to kill it?"

Eli has moved close to me, stands besides me now. I know he hates this conversation. I feel his entire body crowd the space I'm already in. Luckily, I love the feeling. And, thankfully, even though that possessive, protective bone still resides in Eligius Dupré's body, he keeps it tucked there. Unless it absolutely has to come out.

Gawan knows it, too, because he gives Eli a respectful glance before continuing. "You'll be on another plane, like the one you were on earlier with the boy," Gawan explains. "Usually the geography is the same, but," he goes on, "there are things even I don't get the full gist of in there. They hide, and in there they reign, preferably in darkness. And, yes, I am speaking of demons, Ms. Poe. And they're not nearly as easy to tackle as a thirteenth-century knight," he says with a glance at Tristan. "Or even a vampire." He looks at Eli. "They're cunning, there are a lot of them, they toy with your mind, and they want only one thing: your soul."

Again I nod. "And I kill it with . . . ?"

He presses something into my hand. "Prayer," Gawan says, "and this."

In my palm, a cross. It's old. Old as dirt.

"It's Pictish," he says, and pulls up the sleeve of his coat The muscles in his forearm flex as he turns it over, inside facing out. "Just like this one. It will protect you for a time."

I stare at him.

"And you have to repeat this prayer," he says. "In Pictish."

I think about it and nod. "The prayer and cross protect me . . . for a certain amount of time. Anything else?"

"Jason!" Tristan bellows.

"Aye!" a young voice replies. I turn and glance over my shoulder in time to see a young guy—tall, lean, dark hair pulled back—leap from the Rover that just pulled into the gates. He's jogging toward us, carrying something.

"Take that to Grimm," Tristan says, referring to Gawan.

Jason hurries over to us. He has a wide smile and seems excited to see, well, everyone. "Sir Gawan!" he says, stopping just before he plows into the big ex-warlord. "Here you are, just as requested." He hands the thing to Gawan, then looks at me. A sparkle lights his eyes. "Lady," he says, and gives a slight bow. "Jason, presently of Dreadmoor."

I nod. "Nice to meet you, Jason."

Gawan hands me the thing Jason has brought him.

I grasp it and look at it in the lamplight. The team moves in around me. Eli is all but pressed against my back. I turn it over in my hand. It's . . . a gun. Sort of. Looks like a handgun, but the place for a magazine is different. I hold it up and inspect the loading mechanism.

" 'Tis a scathe, lady. Known in our day as a skatha. Made of bronze and modified somewhat, by Sir Gawan there." Jason nods toward Conwyk. "You'll need this, but take care of the points," Jason says, and pulls a handful of clear, heavy glass cartridges the size of a ChapStick tube and places them in my other hand. At one end, extremely sharp and pointy. I look at him, and he seems overjoyed to be giving them to me. He's cute, don't get me wrong. Dead cute. I'm just . . . befuddled.

"They're prefilled," Jason offers as I stare at them. "I've a score more of them in the Rover."

"Of what?" I ask.

"Why, the only thing that will eradicate a demon," Jason answers. "A very strong, very powerful, very magical source," he continues. "Pictish holy water from St. Beuno's Well." He cocks his head. "Have you heard of it?"

" 'Fraid not," I answer. I stare at the liquid in the clear vials, then meet Gawan's gaze. "I trust you. One cartridge per demon, loaded into the scathe?"

"Aye," Gawan answers. " 'Tis mighty holy, Riley. Be verra, verra careful with them."

"I will," I answer.

"Here. I'll show you how to load them," Jason says, then looks down at me. "If you please?"

I don't think in a thousand years I'll ever, ever get used to medieval beings living in the twenty-first century. Never.

"Sure," I answer, and Jason gently takes the scathe and a cartridge and loads it. "Pull back this lever here," he says, showing me, "and just slip it in. Give it a push"—he does so, and it clicks—"and lock the lever back in place. You can load six at once. When you're finished, pull the lever back down." He does, and hands me the gun. "And you're ready."

"Thanks, Jason," I say. "Any suggestions on where to stash it?"

"Oh," Jason says sternly. "You'll not want to sheathe this, lady. 'Twill be best to keep it in your hand at all times."

I glance at Gawan, and he nods. After a quick look around, I see the entire WUP team is watching with intense curiosity. Ginger blinks, a look of astonishment on her face. Lucian simply stares. Noah, of course, is grinning.

Victorian, much like Eli, is frowning. And I can feel Eli's scowl.

"Any questions?" Gawan asks.

"Um, yes," I say. "The prayer."

"I've got that," Jason says, and pulls something from his pocket. He unfolds the paper and hands it to me. "Sir Gawan will translate for you."

"You've got to practice it in Pict," he says. "I've written the words to sound exactly like the Pict words here. On the other side, the English version and the correct Pict version." He smiles. "'Tis the only way."

I nod. "Will do."

Gawan puts a large hand on my shoulder and squeezes. "You're a brave lady, Riley Poe. And I'm afraid you're the only one who can enter that plane and emerge intact. You be careful."

"I will. And thanks," I answer, and meet his gaze. "Now say the prayer one more time. Pretty cool lingo, Pict."

Gawan smiles. "So says my wife."

I return the smile. "I'm sure she does." And then Gawan repeats the verse once more.

"Here are your bags, sirs," Peter says from the front door. A duffel bag weighs down each hand. He makes his way to Tristan and sets them on the gravel.

"Thank you, good man," Tristan says, then looks at me. "Once all of this has been dealt with accordingly, you and your betrothed will have to drive down for a visit," he invites. "We've an annual medieval tournament you won't want to miss." He walks over and takes my hand in his large ones. "'Tis been a pleasure, Ms. Poe. You take great care in your battles."

"I will, and thanks for the lessons," I respond. "We'll kick some Fallen ass and head your way."

"Posthaste," Jason adds. "Lady Andi would truly love to meet you."

"Jason!" Tristan says, already halfway to the Rover.

Jason grins, wiggles his brows, and again lowers his body to a bow and kisses my hand. "Until then," he says, then hastens away. "Coming, Sir Tristan!"

Gawan grabs his duffle. "Godspeed," he says, grasping my shoulder.

Damn, I can't help it. Just once more.

"Gawan, close your eyes for just a minute," Andi said. "I'll wake you up when the doctor comes in."

"Aye," said Tristan, "you can't just sit there, leaning on your knees with your head hanging down. You'll get a bloody crick in your neck."

With a hefty sigh, Gawan leaned back in the chair and scrubbed his stubbled jaw. "I'll be fine." He glanced around.

The waiting lobby was full. Nearly every soul at both Grimm and Dreadmoor filled the place, not to mention the four Morgans. Some stood against the wall; some sat on the carpeted floor, backs to the wall.

Rick Morgan sat, much like he did, forearms resting on his knees, head bowed. Once, he'd lifted his head and glanced at Gawan, and the worry etched into the man's face grew deeper by the second. He'd given Gawan a slight nod and then had gone back to staring at the space between his feet.

Even Nicklesby, Gawan noticed, sat very still in a corner chair, simply staring. Jason sat with Ellie's sister; both were quiet. Everyone looked exhausted.

It had been a night from Hell.

After the medics had all but pried Ellie from Gawan's arms, they'd rushed her to the medical infirmary. After quick X-rays and CT scans of her head and body, they'd rushed her into emergency surgery. While her arms and legs had gained no injury and her head, surprisingly, hadn't suffered any, she had acquired multiple internal injuries that, had she not been found when she had, would have surely taken her life.

The constable had arrived and taken the woman at the farm and her drunken husband into custody. While the man had still been unconscious with drink, the woman confessed everything.

Her husband had struck Ellie with his truck that night Gawan had found her. Fearful of being sent to jail for drunk driving or, worse, vehicular homicide, he brought Ellie to his wife and forced her to take care of her. They'd moved her back and forth from the farm to the kirk, afraid of their secret being found out. Ellie could not have lasted on her own without food, water, warmth. So for that, he was eternally grateful to the woman.

Still, they had no idea why Ellie had been on Grimm's lane. That the man had nearly run Gawan off the road while carrying an unconscious Ellie in the back of his truck made his stomach ache.

And now, she fought for her very life.

They'd been directed to the intensive-care waiting lobby until her surgery was completed. Which, thought Gawan, is bloody taking forever. *They'd taken her at close to five the evening before, and now it was nearly four in the morning.*

For the hundredth time, he rose and began to pace. Shoving a hand through his knotted hair, he rubbed his eyes and walked to the window. In twenty hours, he would have become a mortal again. And while he knew he wouldn't remember later, he wanted to know now that she'd be well and healthy. It was making him daft, the waiting, and the click-click-click *of the minute hand on the old, clunky wall clock echoed so loudly in the lobby, he forced himself not to yank it from the wall and bust it.*

"Mr. Morgan?"

Everyone stood up.

Rick Morgan crossed the floor, and as he passed Gawan, he inclined his head. "Come on."

Appreciation swept over him, for the man certainly didn't have to allow Gawan to listen in on a personal family matter. Out in the hallway, the doctor waited. He looked weary, Gawan noted. And before Gawan could hop into his head, he spoke.

"Your daughter is in critical condition, Mr. Morgan," *he said, meeting Rick Morgan's eyes with a steady, forthright gaze through a pair of spectacles. "I don't know how she bloody made it as long as she did. Her lung was punctured by a fractured rib, and her spleen had ruptured. And with the drastic shock she was in, well"—* *he glanced at Gawan—"it's a miracle she made it."*

Rick Morgan held his younger daughter close. "Is she going to continue to make it?"

The doctor placed a hand on Rick Morgan's shoulder. "This is a critical time for her, I'm afraid. She's young and, prior to this, healthy, so her chances are good. She's stable right now. But given what she's been through . . ." He squeezed his shoulder. "We'll see."

Once the physician left, a nurse dressed in blue trousers and tunic walked up and smiled. "Are you the Morgan family?"

Rick Morgan nodded.

"Two can come back," she said.

"Just two?" Ellie's brother, Kyle, said.

"I'm afraid so. ICU regulations." She glanced around. "Which two? You can follow me."

Gawan locked eyes with her. Five can come in and stay at all times, even outside of visiting hours, if they wish. Let your coworkers know the physician says it's all right.

"Okay," she said, eyes wide. "You can all follow me."

Rick Morgan looked at Gawan and then silently followed the wide-eyed nurse. As they passed the small nurse's station in the center of the ward, Gawan willed them each to let them all stay on in Ellie's room, just for good measure.

Gawan was in no way prepared to see his intended the way he now saw her: tubes, beeping machines, her face pale, and a ventilator doing Ellie's breathing for her. Aye, he knew the names of such machines, and he hated seeing them strapped to her.

Ellie's sister cried and held her hand.

Her brothers, flanking Ellie's sides, just stood there, silent, their hands resting on the covers beside her.

Rick Morgan's face had blanched, and as big as the man was, Gawan noticed the trembling in his hands as he swiped back a bit of Ellie's hair. "Christ, girl," he said, his voice cracking. "Christ."

Gawan stood back near the foot of the bed and watched Ellie's chest rise and fall with each horrible click of that machine. He watched for as long as he could stand it before he simply closed his eyes.

And so it went on like that, all day long. The Morgan siblings went in and out, graciously allowing others to replace them. Only Rick Morgan and Gawan remained constantly. The Dreadmoor knights, they took their turns coming to see Ellie, but none of them stayed long. Only Jason, who, by the bloody saints, looked as pale as Ellie, lingered a while, whispered something in her ear, and then left.

Hours passed by, and Gawan never sat. He could do nothing save stand beside Ellie, hold her hand, and pray she'd make it. Once, when Rick Morgan stepped into the garderobe and no one else was about, Gawan whispered into Ellie's ear, "I mewn hon buchedd a I mewn I 'r 'n gyfnesaf, Adduneda 'm cara atat forever 'n ddarpar." It was a heartfelt verse in his native tongue, and he prayed that even though she was deep in slumber, she may hear it. He supposed he'd never know.

It was hours later when Nicklesby touched his arm. "Sir, are you aware of the time?"

Gawan glanced at the clock. Nearly six p.m. "Nay, not until just now."

"You've only a few more hours remaining," he said, his voice quiet. "I know this is passing sorrowful, Sir Gawan."

"I know what needs to be done, my friend," Gawan said, grasping Nicklesby's bony shoulder and giving a thankful squeeze. "Not yet, though."

"Poor lamb," he said, casting a glance at Ellie. "I'll be just outside, if you need me." Then he left.

By the next hour, everything changed drastically.

He, Rick Morgan, Andi, and Tristan were in Ellie's room when her body jerked. That blasted intubator began to sound its alarm, and within the next second the monitor indicating her heartbeat let out a long, solid scream. Gawan knew well and good what that meant. He and Rick Morgan yelled "Nurse!" at the same time.

The nurse ran in, took one look at Ellie, pushed past Gawan, and slammed her fist against a round silver button on the wall, sending off an alarm overhead.

A code was called.

He was losing Ellie.

The curtain to Ellie's room was yanked, and in a matter of seconds was filled with all sorts of hospital staff, squeezing past one another to get to her. A doctor—not the one who performed the surgery—ran in and yelled, "Someone get these people out of here!"

And then what his Ellie would have termed A Fiasco ensued. Again.

Because, by the bloody saints above, Gawan wasn't going anywhere.

While he didn't want to interfere with Ellie's care, Gawan knew he could not leave. Not for one bloody second. He willed the doctor and other staff to ignore every-one else and simply do their jobs, which they did.

Meanwhile, everyone from the waiting lobby poured out to wait by Ellie's room. Even the Grimm ghosts had shown up.

Gawan paced, glanced over shoulders, and swore. Everything was chaotic, Bailey was crying, Andi was cry-ing, and the men were cursing in various languages.

Gawan lurked in the physician's mind.

She's gone.

"Nay!" Gawan yelled at the doctor. "Stay your course. Do you hear? Keep to your bloody task!" Fury rolled in-side him like a great North Sea wave, his insides burned with it, and as he watched the lifeless body of his beloved laying there, unresponsive, Gawan let out a battle cry he'd not released in centuries.

And as all eyes turned to him, everything, everyone in Ellie's room grew completely silent. No beeping machines, no curses, no commands from the doctor, no weeping. Si-lence.

With his eyes locked on Ellie's face, he released some-thing else. An ancient Welsh verse. Rather, a plea. A barter.

His life force for Ellie's.

And just that fast, without hesitation, it was done.

A white light boomed into the room, and, silently, everyone squinted against its brightness. The stillness was deafening.

Like a bolt of lightning, the memories Gawan had shared with Ellie of Aquitaine flashed through his mind at top speed, yet he saw each one with perfect clarity. And just at that last second, that last breath of a heartbeat, just before

Gawan of Conwyk vanished into thin air in front of the entire ICU, Ellie opened her eyes and their gazes locked.

And then Gawan disappeared.

I blink, and the whole scene washes away, and I'm eye to eye with Gawan of Conwyk, back in the Crescent's courtyard. I cock my head at the ancient Pict warrior.

"You gave your life force to save Ellie's," I say. "Impressive."

Gawan merely smiles at me, those chocolate brown eyes turning liquid in the courtyard's lamplight. "I had no choice."

We both share a smile, and Gawan nods at Eli and strides across the courtyard to the Rover. I know now that I want to know lots more about Dreadmoor and Grimm. Hopefully, I'll get the chance.

With the team behind me, we watch the two big warriors, along with a somewhat smaller warrior, climb into the Rover and pull out of the wynd.

"Nice to see chivalry isn't dead after all," Ginger says beside me.

Eli's arm snakes around my waist, and I lean against him.

"Yeah," I answer. "Nice."

As we all stand there in the light of the Crescent, me clutching my new scathe, I glance around at the souls who will have my back and whose back I'll have. I don't really know them, yet I fully and wholeheartedly trust them. I know that the hell about to break loose in Edinburgh within the next few hours will be unimaginable.

I know we'll all fight together to end it.

The one thing that bothers me, though, and it's something I just can't seem to shake. I hate it. I wish like hell the thought didn't exist, but it does.

One of us won't make it out alive.

Despite my DNA, I'm still the most vulnerable. It may very well be me.

I don't want to hear you think that again. Ever. This from Victorian. Moving my gaze to his, I stare. The furrowed dark brows, the narrowed eyes, and pursed lips all express fierce anger. Even a little fear. *Nothing will happen to you. Do you understand me?*

I give a slight grin. *Whoa, step back, my crazy Romanian bodyguard. I'm just being realistic. Keeps me on my toes.* I frown. *And get out of my head. You promised.*

To my surprise, instead of a smart-ass remark, or, more Vic's speed, a dirty remark, he stares. Scowls. Then turns away.

Silence.

I mentally shake my head and sigh. Without thinking, I scan the Crescent, up the aged stone of the former school until my vision rests on a window. My window.

The little white-faced girl stares back at me.

Although my initial reaction is anxiety, it's over in an instant. I'm not scared of her. I don't know why, but I'm not. Something about her intrigues me, and I have a strong feeling she's probably the same creepy kid who scared the life out of that professor so long ago. I wonder what she wants. I have to remember to ask Gabriel about her later. There has to be a reason why she is seeking me out over all the others.

I hold her gaze for a moment more. I think we might be having a staring contest, and since I've had several with not only my baby brother but also with my dog, Chaz, and won them all, I'll see how I hold up with a naughty, creepy Victorian kid spirit.

Several moments later, she disappears.

Riley, one. Creepy little dead girl, zip.

The creaking of the Crescent's gates draws my attention, and I notice they're closing. Peter is hurrying to a side door and quickly disappears inside. As a group, the WUP team begins to move toward the front entrance. I glance up at the dark sky. Clouds shift, stretching across the half-moon, and a few stars shine through. A coldness drifts across the courtyard and whisks in through the doorway behind us.

And with it, that thing I'm starting to recognize more clearly. It's actually becoming a nuisance.

Dread.

And that's when I hear it. Softly, at first—so barely there I almost think I imagined it. Then I hear it again. It sounds like it's coming from the street. By Bene's, maybe? Close. It's a kid's voice. A boy. Teenager. He's whimpering. Without a thought, I stand, listening.

"Ri, you coming?" Eli says from the doorway.

"Yeah, just a minute," I answer. I glance at him. "I'll be right in."

Eli stares at me for a moment, then cocks his head. "You okay?"

I smile. "Yep," I answer. "Just gathering my thoughts. I'm coming."

More stares, then a nod. He follows the others inside and closes the door. Eli learned a long time ago to allow me space. This is one of those times I need it.

I hear the whimper again, and I turn my gaze toward the gates. I focus on the boy's voice, and everything silences but him. The gates are crystal clear, and I head straight to them. In one leap, I'm over the wrought iron and am hurrying along the cobbles to the street. The boy's voice, his whimpers, is closer. Clearer. I turn left and jog up the sidewalk. Another set of gates come into view, and, glancing around, I leap those, too. It's a church. The whimpers are coming from behind it. I hug the wall, easing around the old stone building. A cemetery stretches out behind the church, and across the graveyard I feel it. Another presence. With the boy. No heartbeat, though. Not a good sign. At least I hear the boy's heart. Fast, but strong.

Hurrying across the graveyard, I slip over the ground soundlessly. I see shadows coming from a hollowed-out tomb. Peeking inside, I find the boy crouching in the corner. Alone. His eyes widen when he sees me, and I press my finger to my lips, shushing him. The boy shakes his head, and his eyes dart behind me. I glance. Almost too late.

I leap high, bounding off the wall of the tomb, and land in a crouch several feet away. Before me, bathed in moonlight, an otherbeing. I'm guessing a vampire. Tall. Wearing dark jeans. Black T-shirt. Black jacket. Gray skully. Maybe midtwenties. At least, that's how old he looks.

"Plus a few hundred years, darlin'," he says in a heavy brogue. "You're a nice surprise."

I glance at the boy, still crouched in the corner of the tomb. "Run, kid. Get out of here. Now."

The boy doesn't move. He's quivering in his shoes. And from the smell of it, he's peed his pants. I use a stronger suggestion. "Get outta here, kid. Now. Go home to your family. Stay off the streets."

This time, the kid scrambles out of the tomb and hauls ass out of the cemetery. When I turn back to the guy, he's right in front of me.

His face suddenly blurs, shifts form, and his fangs drop. Not just two incisors. All of them. Jagged, sharp fangs that look like they can bite a head off.

He grabs for me, but I duck, leaping out of his grasp and rolling across the stone and rock. I jump to my feet and he's staring at me. His eyes are opaque. And before I can blink, he's got me by the throat. My toes leave the ground.

"Think you can escape me, little human bitch?" he says smoothly. He slams me on the ground, then pushes his foot into my chest. "You cannot." Dropping to one knee, he draws close to me. "This will be . . . interesting." Lightning fast, he kicks my jaw. My head snaps to the side. He's damn fast. And he's grinning at me. Pissing me the fuck off.

My hand slips to my waist, and I pull out my blade. Pressing the tip to his spine, I smile. "Yeah. It will—"

He's suddenly off of me, his body slamming into the trunk of an old tree. Eli is completely morphed. "Babe, your blade?"

I leap to my feet, aim my blade at the newcomer, and throw. Hard. It buries to the hilt. Eli backs up, just as the body begins shuddering. The vamp drops to the ground. Dead.

Walking over, I kick my blade out of the vampire pile and pick it up. I wipe the blade on my pants and glance at Eli. "He was about to kill a kid. I heard him whimpering from the Crescent."

Eli drapes an arm over my shoulder and we quit the cemetery. "I'm guessing he got away?"

I lean into him. "Yeah. He was scared shitless. But he finally ran." We're under a streetlight, and I look up into Eli's face. "I had him."

Eli chuckles. "I know you did. I might give you space, darlin', but if you think I'm going to just let you run off into the city to fight bad guys alone"—he kisses me on the nose—"you're crazy."

Much later, we're all in the study, going over maps of Old Town. In front of Eli and me, an intricate layout of the vaults. An entire network—no, an entire town—once existed beneath Edinburgh.

"With poor or virtually no ventilation and at times inhuman living conditions, many inhabitants died there," Jake says. "Candlemakers, whiskey merchants, shoe cobblers; they all had businesses below the city. As I said before, the plague wiped out most of them, and the vaults were left untouched for centuries. Superstitious lot, the Scots, and for good reason." He grins. "All those cold wisps of air and hair-raising spectral shoves are, in fact, real."

I just stare at him.

"There are any numbers of places to hide down there," Darius adds. "But we've a suspicion, based on what we know about these particular Fallen, that they use the vaults strictly as a place of torture," he says, his face solemn. "For their victims."

I shudder at the thought. "So where will we find them?" I ask. "And how do we keep them from knowing who and what we are?" Although one, I believe, already knows me.

"Once you're spotted the first time, that's it," Jake says. "They already know of Gabriel, me, and Ms. Maspeth," he says, inclining his head toward Sydney, who still pores over the old Celtae tomes. "Your element of surprise won't last long." He looks at me. "Use it wisely. As for us," he continues, "Gabriel has charmed this place. They can't reach beyond our gates."

Well that's a relief.

"Their tastes run exquisitely high," Darius adds. "And in their search for the relics they seek out high-priced antique auctions, among other gatherings."

"Charity balls, for example," Gabriel says. He looks at me. "For the women."

"If you are part of the brethren who killed the Celtae in the first place," asks Ginger, looking up from her map of Old Town, "how is it you can't read those tomes?"

Darius sighs and shoves his hand through his

hair. "Because despite our daring overtaking of the Celtae, they were wily," he says. "They used the curse of illiteracy against all of us." He looks at Sydney. "The only way I could counteract it was to target Ms. Maspeth's fate as the Archivist." His gaze moves back to me. "She unwillingly sacrificed her entire life to become one of us. Left her home, her family, her job."

"It is what it is," Sydney says without looking up. "This is what I do now."

Darius nods. "We've all sacrificed. Without it, mankind would be in peril."

"You mean 'serious shit,'" Noah says, looking up from his own map of the city. He scratches his ear. "I'm restless," he says, stands and stretches, and crosses the floor to stand next to where I sit. "I need to go for a run." He thumps my head and looks at me. "Ri?"

"Yep," I say, and look at Eli. I crack my knuckles. "How 'bout you?"

"I need Miles to stay," Jake says. "Gabriel and I have a few things to go over with him."

I stand and pat Noah on the head. "Sorry, old boy," I grin. "Maybe next time."

Noah growls under his breath.

I look over at the lupines. "How 'bout you guys?" Then at Victorian. "Vic?"

"Pass," they all say at once.

I shrug. "Suit yourselves." I grin at Eli. "Race you to the monument?"

"Winner gets ice cream," he says. "Vittoria's." A grin stretches his face. "Found it earlier."

"You're on." I glance at my clunky boots. "I gotta change."

"Me, too," Eli says.

We both head up the stairs and are ready in two minutes. I pull on what I wore to train in, except I secure my silver dirk beneath the waistline of my Lycra pants. I pull on black Nikes and braid my hair into a long tail on the way down the steps. Just before we come into view of the hall, Eli pulls me to a stop. His body crowds mine, and I lean against the wall. With a knuckle he tilts my head upward to meet his stare. He says nothing, just . . . stares. Then he lowers his head and brushes his lips over mine. A shot of fire stings my veins as Eli's tongue caresses mine and his hand slips behind my neck and holds my head in just the right position. He kisses me slowly, with intent. When he pulls back, I'm breathless.

"I love you, Riley Poe," he whispers, and brushes a finger over my cheek. "My soon-to-be wife."

I smile at him, slip my arms around his waist, and fall into his embrace. "I love you, Eligius Dupré." I grab his ass and squeeze, and he laughs into my hair. "Forever."

"I'm literally going to throw up this time."

With a start, I turn. Noah stands at the bottom of the steps, his arms crossed over his chest. That crazy mass of dreads is pulled back into some sort of a ponytail. Contained anyway. "Jealous?" I ask, and bat my eyes.

Noah's mercury eyes shine. "Absolutely." He looks at Eli. "Lucky fu—"

"I suggest you take a left out of the gates to Parliament, then cross over to Carlton, then to Waterloo, past Waverly Station," Jake interrupts Noah's swear. "And stay to the shadows if possible. Too much gossip about a pair of crazed free runners may cause unwanted attention."

Eli gives him a nod, then looks down at me. Wordlessly, he inclines his head toward the door. "We are masters at hiding our free-running talents."

"Good," Jake states. "Make sure it stays that way."

"You wanna go, Andorra?" I ask, smiling. "Test your skills against a little ole human with tendencies?"

Jake grins. "Another time, Poe."

I feel not only Noah's eyes on me as I leave, but Victorian's, as well. Worrywarts. Neither will ever get used to the idea that I can handle myself. Eli worries, too, but he's learned to keep most of it to himself. Besides, I'm with a vicious vampire. When provoked, he's as rabid as a sick badger on crack.

"Flattery will get you nowhere," Eli says outside.

I give him a smile. "You know what will?" I say.

Eli cocks his head and grins. "What?"

I sink my elbow in his ribs. "That!"

I take off.

Eli takes off after me. Swearing. In French.

"Shall I open the gates, lass?" Peter calls from behind me.

"No, thanks!" I reply, and take one leap to clear the tall, wrought-iron monsters. Landing in a crouch in the shadows, Eli drops right beside me. He glances at me and grins, and we both turn left at a normal run. A mortal run. A few people are still on the streets—late-night revelers, college kids.

We make it almost to Parliament, where it's darker, and turn left onto Carlton. Not much activity, so we pick up the pace. I look over at him. "To the top of the monument," I clarify. "The pointy part."

Eli simply grins.

Its two thirty a.m., and even the black cabs have thinned out. Much of Edinburgh is quiet, including Vittoria's, which means no ice cream tonight. For the most part, though, this street is safe. Staying close to the stone buildings, the shadows, we free run. Bounding off walls, garden gates, and tree trunks, we move swiftly, silently, at speeds a mortal can't possibly conceive. I can barely conceive it. I'm pretty positive that even if we do pass a mortal, their eyes couldn't follow our movements. Not enough to actually see what they think they saw.

Eli has trouble keeping up with me, and I fight not to laugh out loud. My body feels good, healthy, strong, and I stretch the strides a bit more. My skin and the Lycra feel one and the same. Wind must be moving through my lungs, because I am a mortal, after all, yet I'm not winded. Not one bit. It's as though I'm standing still, unmoving. Or flying.

We hit Waterloo Place and really open up. In the heart of the city there are plenty of shadowy places to hide, and we take advantage of them. I'm ahead of Eli now, and I'm determined to reach the top of that damn monument before he does.

Waverly Station comes into view and I head

toward it. Pass it. Hit Princes Street and slow down long enough to find shadows again, then turn up the speed. The monument is, like, right there—tall, spindly, and stabbing the sky—and after a few leaps onto the aged stone spires, I'm climbing. Hand over hand. Faster. Jagged stone scrapes my palms as I ascend, closer to the top of the spire.

I grab the point and brace myself against the wind whipping me. At this height, I can see the whole city. Exhilaration fills me, and I want to shout but I don't. Instead I look down, readying myself to have my ankle yanked by Eli.

Eli isn't here.

My eyes scan the spire and farther down the monument. The street below me is empty. I don't see him anywhere. Shit! *Eligius Dupré, where the hell are you?*

For a second, no answer. My heart skips, and I descend the monument. From twenty feet I drop to the ground and stay in the shadows of the aged arched stone, waiting. Adrenaline fills me—a condition that has begun since my heart now beats so slowly. A frantic feeling is slipping inside of me, and I call again.

Eli, goddamn it! You better answer me. Swear to God, this isn't funny!

No answer. My eyes scan Princes Street and back toward Waverly Station. The more I see nothing and the more Eli doesn't answer me inside my head, the more frantic I become. It's not like him to be silent. Especially when it comes to me. And especially when he knows we're facing unknown shit in Edinburgh. I begin to move through the streets. Closer to the train station.

It's not quite three a.m., and Waverly's insides are dark and closed up. The station itself is huge, and I've already watched a security car go by twice. I'm in the shadows, and no way do they see me. Something is drawing me here, and I can't identify it other than gut feeling.

And it's not a good one.

Eli, if you're fucking with me, I will not forgive you. Swear to God I mean it.

No way. No freaking way is he screwing with me. Something's up and I know it. My insides feel icy with fear. This is completely out of Eli's character.

I stop a second, lean my back against the stone wall, and think. Concentrate. *Get your head together, Poe.*

Listen.

Inhale.

I smell it first. It's coming from inside the station. And that's where I'll be in five seconds.

Slipping into a place as big as Waverly Station in the heart of Edinburgh isn't easy. Looking over, I see the reddish stone main building of Waverly rising skyward, complete with its clock tower. I make my way closer. I get to the closed and locked outer gate of one of the station's car entrances, leap over that gate easily enough, and jog down the paved ramp and through the underground tunnel. It's dark, with only a few lamps casting a little light ahead of me. The main entrance is locked. Too bad metal doesn't work the same way a soul's mind does, or I'd force it open. Instead I place my palms against the steel, press my weight against my arms, and push. *Hard*.

Hard enough to bend the steel hinges. I push until it gives—a large-enough gap for me to squeeze through. Inside the station, it's dimly lit and vacant. Store merchants are closed down, roll cages in place, lights off. The big arrival/departure board is black. The stench is nauseating. The silence is nearly deafening. At least until I tune in.

A voice—in a language I'm completely unfamiliar with—vibrates in my ears. Rather, in my mind. It barely sounds human. So what the hell is it? There *are* no human words, not in this station anyway. I fine-tune my hearing by concentrating on my immediate surroundings, so the sounds from a mile away, up the street, in people's homes, the pubs, the police department, don't filter in. I turn my head. It's coming from . . . closer to the tracks. Hugging the wall, I ease silently on the rubber soles of my shoes, through the shadows. As I near a sign that says PLATFORM 11, I slip over the bar, and move closer. The incoming track is empty; a vacant train waits on the other track, lights off. When I look left, toward the exit, the tracks disappear into the darkness.

That's when I see them. At the end of the platform, where concrete meets tunnel wall and eventually, blackness.

They're with Eli. But it's not what I expect.

My heart drops.

There're seven of them. Punks. As far as I can tell,

just mortal older teenagers. Maybe even a gang. Why the hell aren't they saying anything? And what's that stench?

They speak.

"You'll leave here wi' us, freak," says one to Eli. The guy's tall with short-clipped dark hair and multiple piercings, and dressed in dark jeans frayed at the bottoms and a dark wool coat. "Dunna know how you got here, but you ain't stayin'." He shoves Eli square in the chest. Eli stumbles backward. "Ya ken, freak?"

Ken? What is that? Edinburgh slang? I don't understand most of it, but the meaning is there and universal. He wants to kick Eli's ass. And Eli must be dragging every ounce of strength he has not to drop fang and rip the kid's head off. *Eli, move away from them. Do it now.* I wait after the suggestion, but Eli doesn't budge. Why isn't it working on him?

The kid says something to the others, who've remained silent, over his shoulder. Again a language that I can't understand. I can't even mimic it. It's that odd.

There's a body on the ground at Eli's feet, unmoving. I tune in past their voices and listen. The faint whisper of ragged breath slowly escapes that body. The thready thump of a pulse. A slight groan. Beaten, maybe? Hopefully, that's all. Had Eli tried to help the kid on the ground?

I remain in the shadows, observing, but that's not what I want to be doing. I want to charge them, fight, and shake Eli until he snaps out of his wordless daze. *Eli, why don't you answer me? What in Hell is happening?*

Eli ignores me. He doesn't look at me. Doesn't answer me. Doesn't even flinch at my silent call. That scares the hell out of me.

The stench is overwhelming, yet I can't determine where it's coming from. I don't sense that the boys are Jodís; something about them is all wrong for that. But they're *something*.

I've had enough. My body hums with adrenaline, fear, and fury. Power collects in my muscles, my joints, bones, and just before I lunge out of the shadows, I hear it. Overhead. The sound of a hundred wings beating. The wind picks up on the platform and pushes me against the wall. I fight it, push back. My eyes find Eli and I call out. Again he doesn't move, just stands there, looking dead at the kid in front of him. Doesn't even acknowledge me or the beating wings and wind. Then it happens. So fast, I can't process it until it's over. My body freezes. I can't move.

Eli remains motionless.

I concentrate on the punks. *Move away. All of you. To the far wall, across the station.*

Every one of the guys back up. Swearing and looking around, they continue to back up.

Eli still doesn't move.

In the next second, three men emerge from above. Sweep down. They surround the pack of kids, push them forward. Again that noise, that speech that makes no sense, fills my head, and it's coming from the three. Shadows flicker and keep in sync with the deafening sound of beating wings overhead. I can barely see Eli now, only in quick flashes of light. But I see enough. Hear enough.

In the distance, the screech of metal against metal. Train wheels on tracks. My eyes dart to the tunnel and I see a light advancing.

Eli, run! Turn around and run. Toward me. Eli's legs, move!

Nothing happens. Eli stands there as though in a weird trance.

Then two of the three men move so fast my vision can't keep up. In patches of flashing light and shadow, like I'm in some freaky disco club, one by one the boys are flung across the platform to the opposite wall. Their screams fill the tunnel, echo and sink into my insides. The crack of human skulls hitting concrete walls sickens me; their bones fracture loud enough for me to hear them splinter beneath their clothing. Blood is everywhere. The walls. The floor. They're all dead. Dead humans.

Just that fast, Eli changes. His jaw extends, fangs drop, and his body quivers with silent fury.

But he still doesn't move.

Soon, silence. The one who stands closest to Eli bends over and picks up the boy lying crumpled on the ground. He holds him effortlessly, suspended in midair, by the back of his neck. Only then do I recognize the boy as Ian, the one I'd saved from the alternative St. Giles'. He is limp, head hanging, arms and legs like sacks of boneless gel. I also recognize the man.

He's the cloaked and hooded Fallen from my dream. The one I watched burn that human.

Then the other two turn to Eli. They're speaking in that fucked-up language directly to Eli, and acting as though his vampiric state isn't very impressive. Eli just stares at them, unblinking. Quivering, like his body is fueling. *Eli! Snap out of it, goddamn it!* I yell silently to him, but he still ignores me.

The one holding Ian turns his head in my direction. The flashes of light and shadow are so rapid that I can't get a good visual on his features, but it's definitely the same one from my dream. He's as tall as Eli. Solid. Older.

I stare at him. *Pain, take over his body. Nerves, seize. Tendons, cinch up. Unmoving. Completely still.*

A chilling smile stretches across his face, and he cracks his neck and looks me square in the eye. My power of suggestion doesn't work on Fallen. Jake was wrong after all.

A presence approaches. I whip around, my heart leaping from my chest, but relief drowns me. Noah stands beside me in the shadows. His face is drawn tight; his mercury eyes, illuminated by the flashing lights, are filled with fury. They lock on to the scene before us. His hand reaches for mine, squeezes, and drops.

Then everything happens at once. So fast.

So fucking fast.

A train approaches the tunnel, and it's not slowing down. The screech of steel on steel all but deafens me, but that train isn't braking. It's flying into the tunnel, heading straight for PLATFORM 11. Then, in the midst of that blinding flash of light and shadow, the one holding Ian also grabs at Eli.

Just as the train approaches.

Just as the other two speak. One Fallen points at the tracks. Eli stands perfectly still. Frozen in place.

I scream and lunge, and Noah grabs me. Pushes me behind him and lurches forward. I grab him. Hold fast. He allows it.

The Fallen throws himself at Eli, and they both fly in front of the train.

The vociferous sound of the train squalling through the station drowns out my anguished cry. All air leaves my body. I'm numb, in shock. Sick to my stomach. The wings are still beating furiously overhead, but their sound no longer rises above the screeching train. I try to move, try to speak, but nothing comes out of me. I barely feel Noah's arms around me, keeping me upright. My larynx is paralyzed. Breath sticks to the lining of my lungs. I'm frozen in place against the wall in the shadows.

Eli! Eli, please! Answer me!

Then, all at once, the train passes through and the wings cease, as does the incessant flashing light and shadow. Everything around me is a dull gray. The train disappears into the darkness, and I free myself from the choking fear, push out of Noah's arms, and stumble to the platform's edge. *Eligius! Please!*

Nothing. I hear nothing. I see nothing. No remnants of their bodies, no . . . nothing.

Impossible.

My eyes scan the tracks. My mind screams for him. Only silence. Only shadows.

Only Noah and I are left on the platform. The others have disappeared. Noah looks at me, kisses my forehead, and takes off up the tracks. He's moving so fast, I lose sight of him in the next blink.

I leap down off Platform 11 and onto the tracks. I begin to run, forgetting momentarily that behind me, on the platform, stands a . . . being. I don't care.

I don't fucking care.

As I run, I scream for Eli in my head. My feet move swiftly over the tracks, and once outside the tunnel I follow them far, to Edinburgh's city limit. I don't know how far I go or how long it takes me. Suddenly, though, I slow, then stop. I'm standing on a lone track, and behind me, way behind me, is the tall clock tower of Waverly Station.

I feel a chill inside of me, something too close, in my space, and I whip around.

The one who'd been holding Ian stands there. No more than two feet away.

He's alone. A Fallen. Tall. Too shadowy to see features. Even two feet away, he crowds me. Fear escapes me. Fury replaces it.

"Tell me where he is," I demand. He knows I speak of Eli. No need to explain.

In the darkness, he cocks his head. Studies me. Remains silent.

I find it hard to turn away.

"Tell me!" I scream to the top of my lungs. That voice doesn't even belong to me. It belongs to someone who has lost her mind. Fury brews just below my skin's surface. I feel like I'm going to combust at any second.

Wordlessly, he extends an arm, fist closed, facing down.

Hesitantly, I hold out my hand.

When his fist opens, a medallion falls into my palm.

Eli's medallion. His family crest. I know it before I even look at it. I can feel the particular ridges in the pattern. My heart sinks to the bottom of my soles. I know what it means. I know what it's supposed to mean. I can feel it.

But I refuse to acknowledge it. I fucking refuse.

I lift my gaze to stare at this demented asshole angel . . . whatever and whoever he is. After a moment more, he turns and walks away.

I blink. He's gone.

I mean, goddamn *gone*.

Jogging up the track a bit, I search the area. A mist rolls in from the Firth of Forth and creeps across the tracks. The air is boggy with the scent of sea life, so thick it's like soup. Gulls scream overhead. At least I think they're gulls.

There isn't the first sign of that guy. Of Eli. Or of the other two.

Did Eli just . . . I squeeze my eyes tightly shut, feel the strength go out of my legs. "No," I say, slipping to the ground. Rough gravel and stone bite through my Lycra and dig into my knees. "No . . ." I can barely even say the word. It's like there's something stuck in my throat and I'm unable to breathe. Unable to speak. Someone has their hands around my throat, choking me.

Noah is beside me now, crouching down, his eyes locked onto mine. Never have I seen his face so stern. "Ri," he says calmly. "We have to get out of here." With his hand he pushes my loose hair back, off my face and out of my eyes. "Now, darlin'."

I stand, looking around. I scan the tracks. No way what just happened, happened.

No way. It just didn't.

Noah's hand grips my shoulder. "Now, Riley—"

"Let me go, Noah!" I say angrily, and take a few steps up the tracks. I see nothing but grayness and mist. In the distance, a train rumbles. Steel against steel. A sound that now jabs my heart.

"You don't know what we're up against," Noah says behind. "We can't do this alone. Not just the two of us. Maybe not all of us."

I turn and stare at him. Pissed. "The hell I don't, Noah." I glance in the direction of the train. "It's not real. It didn't happen." Again, air sticks in my lungs. "Those kids." I turn and look at him. "Eli, Noah." I shake my head, dig my knuckles into my eye sockets. "It didn't fucking happen!" As I'm standing here, arguing with Noah, I feel my legs turning rubbery again. Swear to God, I don't think I can walk.

"I'll carry you outta here if I have to," Noah says. "But you're the strongest soul I know, Riley Poe." He tilts my head, knuckle to chin. Eyes filled with a mix of rage and pity stare at me, pleading. "And we gotta get the hell outta here. Now."

I stare across the tracks at the tall gray buildings. The mist is even thicker now than before. The heavy scent of brine fills the air. If there's a horizon, I can't see it.

I'm completely numb inside. I don't even know what to do. I just want to sink to the ground.

"I'll help you," Noah says, both hands on my shoulders. He squeezes. "But we have to get back to the Crescent."

Eli's medallion weighs heavy in my hand and I glance down at it. I'd been gripping it so hard, its imprint rests in my palm. With a deep breath I nod and slip the medallion over my neck. I glance at Noah, nod again, and begin to run. It's still dark out, but the mist rolling in makes even the shadows hazy. It feels like a spray of fine water against my skin, and I inhale it into my lungs. The air is chilled, salty, and for a second it reminds me of Savannah. Of the salt marshes. Of home.

Only this place isn't home. Home is where Eli was, safe. Fearless. Top of the food chain. No predator could confront and win against a vampire. Impossible.

Yet I can't even say the words I know in my heart are true. I'd watched it. Witnessed every move. I saw it happen. I know it happened.

Edinburgh houses a brand of evil I can't seem to grasp.

I just encountered it. I know it with all of my heart.

At Old Tolbooth Wynd, I swing through the arches, run up the narrow path, and leap over the Crescent's iron gates. Noah is right behind me.

Jake has to know something. Darius. Gabriel. One of them has to know what to do.

As I hurry up the steps, the weight of Eli's medallion burns into the skin of my chest.

The Black Fallen just fucked up.

I'm going to make them wish they'd never fallen from grace.

Or I'll die trying.

Part Seven

UNINVITED

Evil is like water, it abounds, is cheap, soon fouls, but runs itself clear of taint.

—Samuel Butler, 1835–1902

The change in Riley now is like mist to black vapor. It is as obvious as a knife plunged into the heart. She won't accept her mate's fate. Will not. I can see it in her eyes. There's a fury there that is chilling. For the first time since arriving in Edinburgh, I feel like the Fallen have no chance in Hell of surviving. Not Riley Poe anyway.

—*Lucian MacLeod*

"Riley."

The moment I walk through the door, Victorian is there. Noah immediately steps in front of me, blocking the Romanian vampire from me. Noah says nothing. He simply stares at Vic, who only returns his hot glare for a second before turning his brown gaze to mine. *What is it? Talk to me.*

Noah's hand grips mine and leads me through the foyer to the library. Everyone is pretty much where we left them.

Where Eli and I left them.

I feel my knees go numb, my body begin to crumple.

Noah grabs me, holds me up. Victorian, despite the glares and threats from Noah, is at my other side.

"What is it?" Jake says, striding toward us.

"The Fallen. They got Eli," Noah says. His voice is laced with fury. Eerily calm, barely contained fury.

"What do you mean, 'got him'?" Jake asks.

I look up and meet Jake's green gaze. The memory of what I saw rushes back, hits my gut like a brick. "I'm gonna be sick," I say, and pull from Noah's grasp. I bolt for . . . anywhere, stumbling, my hand over my mouth. I'm lost, trying to find a bathroom, a trash can. Plant. Door. Anything.

In my next breath I'm swept up and Jake is running through the Crescent. I close my eyes because my head is now spinning. He eases me to the floor, kicks the toilet lid up with his foot, and holds my hair back. I wretch and wretch until I cough.

Coughing turns into sobbing. I break. I can't help it. I try not to but . . . it happens.

I totally break down. Even while it's happening, I know I'm allowing myself this one weakness. This one snap. I'll let it all out, then be done. None of it will help bring Eli back.

At the sink, with Jake still holding my hair back, I throw water on my face and rinse out my mouth. He hands me a hand towel and I dry off, then our eyes lock in the mirror. Even Jake's face seems ashen.

"It canna be," he says, his unusual accent washing over me. Comforting me somewhat. "Tell me."

With my hands propped against the sink, my head drops forward and the tears fall. Pain surges up from my insides, seizes my gut, my throat, and escapes on a noise even I can't define. Wailing cat. Singing whale.

Mourning human with tendencies.

Uncontrolled sobs rack my body, my shoulders shake, and I feel myself sliding downward again. And once more Jake scoops me up and I allow it, just this once. Wrapping my arms around his neck, I bury my face into his chest and he rushes . . . somewhere. I don't know. Don't care. He's using more strength than he probably realizes to hold me close, because I'm barely able to breathe. Again, don't care.

Jake lowers me onto a bed. As he sits beside me, his weight presses the mattress down and he pushes my hair from my face. I look up at him through hazy, teary eyes.

"Rest," Jake says. "We can talk later."

Inside, I'm shaking. "No," I say, my voice quivering. "Now."

Jake studies me thoroughly, then nods. "I already know what happened," he says gently. "After Miles arrived. But I need to know what happened before that."

Need, he says. Not *want*, but *need*.

I draw a deep breath. "We were free running, racing to the monument. I got ahead of him," I say, and Eli's image flashes before my eyes. "And just kept running. I was to the top of the monument before I even noticed Eli"—saying his name out loud physically hurts me—"wasn't with me." I stare at Jake. "I called to him in my head, but he wouldn't answer." I close my eyes. "He never would *not* answer me, Jake."

Jake is silent, his gaze remaining on mine, patiently waiting for me to continue.

"He always answers me, no matter what. I felt inside that something was wrong. Then I smelled it," I continue.

"Smelled what?" Jake asks.

I shake my head. "That awful stench. It's hideous. It smelled like a Jodís." I look at him. "I followed the smell to Waverly Station. When I got there, the station was closed up, but I could hear voices inside," I say. "But the language." I shake my head again and look at him. "I can't even explain it, Jake. Nothing I've ever heard before. It almost . . . hurt to hear it."

Jake's angry gaze locks with mine. "That's the language of an angel. No one can understand it or mimic it."

"When I found them, I saw Eli just standing there," I continue. Tears spill over my lids, and Jake wipes them with a fingertip. "He was surrounded by several punk kids, and one was lying on the ground." I look up. "It was that kid I followed into St. Giles'."

Something flickers in Jake's eyes. Recognition?

"I used my suggestion to make them back off of Eli, and they did. But then the three showed up." I look at Jake. "The Fallen. I knew right away it was them. I try first to make Eli run. It doesn't work. And neither does it work on the three. The one . . . he just smiled at me."

"Continue," Jake encourages. He pushes my hair off my face.

"I yell and yell to Eli in my mind, but he ignores me. Then beating wings, and flashing light and shadow," I say, "and in a blink, Eli changed—complete vampiric change—and just . . . stood there. Two of them," I recall, "literally tossed the punk kids across the tunnel, and their heads smashed against the concrete wall." The vision makes me squeeze my eyes shut. "Dead. They were all dead." I open my eyes and look at Jake. "Except for Ian, on the ground. The third Fallen picks him up and holds him, suspended in the air. Then another Fallen grabs Eli and they both fall in front of—"

Jake presses his fingers gently against my lips, shushing me. "I know," he says, and scrapes my tears. "I know that part, Riley."

"It happened so fast," I continue, my voice cracking. "I couldn't move, couldn't speak out loud—nothing. Powerless. Just like Eli." I close my eyes and rub. Hard. "It's like . . . all these damn tendencies I have? Worthless, Jake." I shake my head. "Nothing I have is worth shit now. Don't you get it?"

"One Fallen is bad enough," he says. "But to stand alone against three? Impossible even for one of us," he says. "It's why the whole team is here."

I shake my head. "I don't understand. They were supposed to still be regenerating. They came out of nowhere." I reached into my shirt and grabbed Eli's medallion. I hold it up to Jake. "The one Fallen, who held the kid up? He gave me this after. It's Eli's."

Jake stares at it. "You saw no trace of neither Eli nor the Fallen who took him?"

I look at him. "Took him? He threw him in front of a train, Jake."

Jake nods. "Aye. So it seems." He squeezes my hands in his. "We'll figure this out, Riley. I vow it."

Tears scorch my eyes. "I can't," I shake my head. "I can't do this anymore."

"We'll wait to inform his family. This has to be settled first," Jake offers.

A surge of pain beats inside of me at his words, and I squeeze my eyes shut. "I hate this, Jake. This isn't me. This isn't *right*." I feel Eli's medallion against my chest. The ring he gave me on my finger. "It's not. I still feel him here," I slap my chest, above my heart. "He isn't gone. I just know it."

The weight of Jake's hand on my cheek makes me open my eyes. He's studying me, his stare just as profound as Eli's. "Do you want to go back home?"

Part of me does. Part of me wants to curl up into a fetal ball and die, go back to Eli's family, my brother, Nyx, Preacher, and Estelle, and mourn. Confusion webs through my brain.

"Let me think on it," I say, turning onto my side. I close my eyes. The tears start again.

Jake silently rises and leaves the room. The door clicks behind him. I'm alone.

Alone. Without Eli.

Pulling my knees to my chest, I wrap my arms around them, clutch them tightly, and silently sob myself to sleep.

Something I should've never done.

I can't determine the exact moment my body gave way to narcoleptic sleep, but I last recall Eli's image.

He's close to me, staring down with those intense cerulean eyes that are the Dupré trademark, and it's kind of weird to be able to see so much love in those eyes, but I do. I can vaguely even remember sometimes that he is . . . what he is. But then he smiles, moves toward me, as if for a kiss or an embrace, and suddenly shadows swallow his features and I can't see him anymore. He pauses, cocks his head to the side as if studying me, and continues to move toward me.

Only then do I realize it's no longer Eli. He is male, though. This I know from the shift in his posture, the change in his movement, and the aura between us. There's a surge of power emanating from this new being, and it's . . . overwhelming. It's almost inexplicable . . . it's everywhere, in the air, and I breathe it in as if an inescapable vapor. Yet not a vapor. Not a mist and not just air. It's him. Almost suffocating.

And highly intoxicating.

Then he moves again, the shadows recede, and his features are illuminated by candlelight. I vaguely notice my surroundings: stone walls, not all intact, dark, damp, cold, and ancient. All I can do is focus on him. I'm entranced, unwillingly so. Swear to God, I can't help myself. It's like I'm being forced, but . . . not. Curiously, I study him.

Tall. Broad shoulders. Hair is light, long, and wavy, and some of it hangs loose about his face, brushes his jaw, catches on his full bottom lip. His nose is straight, jaw strong, throat masculine with pronounced columns and

Adam's apple. Perfect brows arch over exotic eyes, wide yet almond shaped at corners that slightly tip upward. They study me with such intensity, I want to look away. But I can't. They're light in color. I can't tell what color, though. Too dark in this place. Hazel or green, if I had to guess. Mesmerizing, without a doubt.

Then he smiles. It's a sensual, wide, almost shy smile, and it hits me square in the chest. Straight, even white teeth, his incisors just a slight bit pointed, but not vampire pointed. His gaze holds mine.

"You are even more beautiful up close," he says, and his voice is not too deep, not high at all, and a little raspy. His brogue is heavy, ancient, the word close *sounding more like* cloose. *Slowly, his hand lifts to my cheek. "Be strong," he says, and his eyes follow his knuckle, then return to me. "I will watch over you. I've been assigned to do so and I will until my dying breath. And in the end, when all is over, you'll know. And you'll choose. And you will be content. I vow it."*

"Who are you? I'll choose what? And where are we?" I finally ask, finding my voice but startled to hear that it's soft, unsure, and hesitant. When did I become such a wimp? What I should do is kick the guy in the balls, grab him by the throat, and sling him against the stone wall. Maybe even give him a little door prize for our meeting, like a nick on the cheek with one of my blades.

That doesn't happen. None of it does.

He smiles again and moves a step closer to me. The candlelight flickers at his movement, causing shadows to shimmy across his face. With a crooked finger he lifts my chin, and I wait as his head bows closer to mine. Electric-

ity soars through my veins, unwanted, uninvited, but there all the same, and his lips pass by mine so closely, they nearly touch. Instead, though, his mouth moves to my ear.

"Soon," he answers, hovering close to me for several seconds while I stand there shivering. "Verra soon."

When he pulls away, his face, his body, is encased in shadow once more.

"Wait," I say, waiting for him to step back into the light.

He doesn't. A soft, deep chuckle emerges from his out-line just before the slow, strong beating of a single pair of wings meets my ears.

"Please, love, wake up."

"Eli!" I gasp, and bolt up in the bed. It's dark, and although my eyes scan the room, I'm dazed, it's hazy, and I'm confused as Hell. Long shadows stretch across the floor and walls. I have no idea how long I've been out, but it seems like forever.

"All day you've been fast asleep."

My heart is beating hard. Freaking hard. Not faster, as it doesn't do that anymore, but *hard*. So hard I can feel it through my shirt. It feels as though someone is pumping a syringe of adrenaline straight into my artery with each heavy thump. *Who the hell was that?*

A hand finds mine and cool fingers link through my warm ones and grasp gently. "Shh. Calm down, Riley. It's me. Victorian." A lamp at the bedside turns on.

"Vic," I say. I'll worry about the dream later. Just

a dream. Not real. And it wasn't Victorian. No one I know.

Then it all rushes back. "Oh, God," I mutter. It really happened. It's real.

Pain crushes my chest and doubles me over, and I draw up my knees, press my forehead to them, and try to breathe. I don't cry, though. I think my tears have dried up. I just . . . grunt. Groan against the pain. It almost sounds ridiculous, and I can't even help it.

Victorian's hand moves over my back, then to my neck. "Riley, don't," he says quietly. "I may not have had any love for your man, but I did respect him. I respected how he cared for you inevitably. And I know Dupré would insist on your strength in overcoming this. It will get better," he says in a soothing tone. "All things eventually do." He pushes my hair aside, strokes it. "You were talking in your sleep, love. To whom?"

It comes back to me. That . . . person. Man. In the dream. I know I've never seen him before. I would've remembered. Yet there was something familiar about him at the same time. It doesn't make sense, and I shake my head. "I have no idea," I answer, and I cross my legs. I look at Victorian, who sits close to me on the bed. His beautiful face is illuminated by the glow of the lamp. Only now do I realize I'm not even in my room. Victorian's dark brown eyes catch the light and shine as he studies me in silence.

"This is impossible, Vic," I finally say, and shake my head again. "I don't understand how it happened. How something like this can happen," I say, staring at him, "to one of you."

Vic watches me closely. "The Fallen have powers beyond us, I fear," he says. "More so than any of us expected. You will have to be guarded much closer. After all, you're still only a fragile human, regardless of your incredible strength."

Something about that just doesn't sit right with me. Even before the tendencies, I was far from fragile. "Jake wouldn't have brought me in if I was just a weak human, Vic." I push off the bed and turn to look at him.

Now I'm pissed.

For a flash second, I think I see a slight grin on his face. *Prick.*

Not waiting to see if he follows me, I head downstairs. To the others. My team.

Inside, I separate myself into two people. The woman who now has her heart ripped in half and mourns the loss of her fiancé. I shove the pain aside, and I actually feel it as it recedes into the darkness of my too-recent memory. There'll be time later for mourning. For tears. For heartache. *Not now.*

Because I'm also the woman who not only has a personal score to settle, but my own race to protect. I'm far from average. I can run. Jump. Fight like a wildcat.

I can kill. And I can make almost anyone do anything with my mind.

And I won't stop until all of the Black Fallen are nothing but fucking dust.

As I ease down the corridor, I allow the shadowy, eerie halls of the Crescent to consume me. There's something here, and I feel it. I allow myself to be enveloped by it. I become shadows. Aged darkness. Callous. Edgy. Treacherous.

Just as I near the landing to the steps, I see her again. The little girl. She emerges from a small recess in the wall, an alcove.

Our eyes meet; my green ones to her yawning black ones. With her skin illuminated, she almost glows. Instead of slowing down, I pass right by her. Before I take the first descending step, she disappears.

I don't know why, but we connect.

I'm sure I'll find out what she wants soon enough.

Downstairs, I slip through the darkened halls and chambers of the Crescent. I find the others still in the library. As I enter, I pull my loose hair back into a ponytail. I shake myself mentally, ready for the fight.

And inside of me, I will not give up on Eli. Until I know for absolute, positive sureness that he's dead, I'll not give in to it.

I have a Pictish scathe, holy water cartridges, and an ancient verse for protection.

And I'm going to fucking use them all.

"Riley," Noah says, rising to meet me. "Sydney found something."

His eyes lock with mine, and we share a long look before I acknowledge. In Noah's face I can see he understands that I've compartmentalized my feeling. What I've done to see this through. "What is it?" I ask.

I glance over and see Jake, Gabriel, and Darius all hovering around Sydney. She looks up.

"I'm pretty positive it's a clue to the location of the first relic," Sydney says. Her blond hair hangs straight past her shoulders, and she glances back down at the aged tome she's been searching through. "If my calculations are right and they coincide with the paragraph I found, it lies somewhere beneath the medical research center at the university." She looks at me. "The morgue."

I blink. "Beneath it?"

"Aye," Darius answers. "At one time that ground was hallowed. Catacombs run below Old Town and below the university as well, although many are either filled in or haven't been stepped into in centuries."

"How do we move through the city now?" Noah asks. "The Fallen know we're here."

"We can't be certain that the attack on Eli wasn't just a random thing," Jake says. "They could've noticed nothing more than that he was a vampire and wanted to toy with him. But thanks to some potent root doctor magic, we've something to help shield us," Jake says, "from the Fallen." He looks at me. "For a while anyway."

I already know what he means. Potions. Similar to the ones I took for so many years to mask the heavy scent of my blood. Preacher must've sent some with us. "Let's go," I say, anxious to get moving. I have nervous energy now—energy that needs to be spent. Pacing, my eyes are on Jake. Waiting.

He watches me closely. As do the others. I already know they have reservations about me because of what just happened to Eli.

I shake my head. "I'm fine. Yes, I'm dying inside," I say, and meet their gazes. "But if you think I'm just gonna sit around while you guys fry the Fallen, then you don't know me very well." I meet Gabriel's gaze, then Darius's, then Jake's.

Victorian, now standing behind me, puts a hand to my lower back. "I'll stay by her side—"

"The hell you will," Noah says angrily, and stands and moves directly in front of Victorian, meeting his hard gaze head-on. "I still don't trust you, Arcos. Eli never did, and I damn sure don't trust you with my dead friend's woman." He steps closer. "So back the *fuck* off."

When Noah gets pissed, it's something you have to witness for yourself. Usually a flirt, a jokester, when he's pissed off he is a force to be reckoned with. In that quiet, crazy, Mel Gibson in *Lethal Weapon* kind of way.

I put a hand on Noah's arm. "I'm fine. Seriously." I look at Vic. "I can handle myself without a babysitter."

"Riley, you'll be with Miles, Gabriel, and me," Jake says, making the final decision. He looks at Vic. "Arcos, you're with Darius and the lupines."

"What about Sydney?" I ask.

"She stays and continues her research through the volumes," Jake says. "Gabriel has a protective ring surrounding the Crescent. She'll be safe for now."

Just then, old Peter bustles into the room.

"Come get your magic juice!" he calls out with a chuckle. He reminds me of Tootles from the movie *Hook*. And, yes, I truly believe he has lost his marbles. He has two pots of steaming something on a large tray. He sets it down on a side table, then bustles back out. Moments later he returns with another tray, this one loaded with cups. A paper sack, top rolled shut, sits beside them. One by one, he sets out the cups and fills them with the hot liquid. My root doctor grandfather's art at work.

"Drink up," Jake says, and steps over to grab a cup for himself. He takes the paper bag, opens it, and pulls something else out. A smile touches his mouth as he loosens the object, and a small silk satchel attached to a leather cord dangles from his fingers. He hands one to each of the vampires and the lupines, and even though I don't believe it will work on me, I take one anyway.

"Preacher says this is just in case our blood or venom won't accept the potion," Jake offers.

I slip mine over my head, bring the pouch to my nose, and sniff. Immediately, the inside of Da Plat Eye, Preacher and Estelle's potions shop, rushes to my memory. For a second, I'm so homesick I can feel my stomach actually hurting. Dried jasmine, crushed sand dollar, burnt saw grass, and a few other scents I don't recognize. All of it, I'm sure, is blessed with one of Preacher's root-doctor charms. It rests against Eli's medallion on my chest. I grab a cup, bring it to my lips, and drain it.

You know I am just a thought away, Riley. If you need me, call. I will come.

That from Vic, and I shoot him a quick glance and nod.

"Let's get out of here," I say, anxious to move. Anxious to ash the bastards who took Eli away from me.

Everyone drains their cups. Those who have Preacher's talismans slip them on. Noah doesn't think twice about his. Ginger and Lucian, the lupines, both sniff it, make a face, and tuck them beneath their shirts. I think about taking the scathe, but I decide it's not time yet. I leave it stashed in my room. Soon we're all geared up, swords hidden beneath dark coats, and talismans filled with an ancient Gullah charm, and we head out into the misty Edinburgh night.

Darkness had fallen again since I'd returned from the streets this morning. God almighty, I'd spent all day sleeping and dreaming. Before we take off, a hand finds my arm. I turn to find Ginger standing there, her eyes wide.

"I'm sorry," she says, and doesn't take it further. "If you need a girl to talk to, I'm here."

I give a short nod. "Thanks, but I'll be ok."

Ginger looks at me with a solemn gaze, returns the nod, then finds her mate, Lucian.

If I give in to that, to spilling my guts to another female, I'll lose it.

I can't afford to lose it. Maybe later, but not now. Hell, no.

Jake stands before me, his impossibly hulking figure throwing a shadow completely over me. I glance up.

"Can you handle this?" he asks. He's not condescending, not sympathetic. He's matter-of-fact.

I nod. "I got it."

He watches me a few seconds longer, then nods. He addresses the others. "Let's go. We're headed to Teviot Place, at the university."

The groups separate once more, and Darius takes his one street over, to Cowgate, and we slip into the sidewalk crowd and head up the Royal Mile, toward the castle. I walk fast, one hand in my coat pocket, the other against the hilt of my sword. Locals amble up and down the Mile, some heading to pubs, some just getting off work. Jake is in front of me; Noah's behind me. *Eli should be beside me. . . .*

Riley, get it together, babe.

I turn and shoot Noah a look. *You get it together.* Noah stares, waiting for a decent answer, I guess, but I give myself a mental shake and push Eli back to the shadows of my mind. Noah's right. Gotta have my head fully in this. Fight now; everything else, later.

Weaving through people carrying steaming coffee from the local grind, others moving fast, head down, hands shoved into their pockets, and others—youth—moving in groups, loud and raucously, we finally turn left at George IV and head toward the university. The mist is heavy now, not only visually, but also the scent of the Firth of Forth hangs thickly inside of it, filled with rotting seaweed and sea life, saltwater and God knows what else. Taxi horns blast every once in a while, and as I glance up, the lights illuminating Edinburgh Castle form a beacon to the city. Voices fill my head, and they're the voices all around me, in front of me, behind me.

Meet me at the Mercat Cross in thirty minutes.

I'm no' feckin' tha' bitch! Are you feckin' daft, girl?

Vinegar and brown sauce?

Give me a pint, aye?

I concentrate, push aside the voices, and filter through the mass of people's random conversations until the only sounds surrounding me are those of my footsteps, of Noah walking behind me, and Jake and Gabriel walking ahead of me. There's something else I hear, too. I'm not sure what. I can only describe it as a low, subtle hum. Almost like an electrical buzz, but even more faint than that. It's weird. No matter how much I try to push it out of my senses, it stays. It won't clear out. Soon, we cross Candlemaker's Row and onto Teviot. University goers mill about, and a young couple passes us. The guy has a cigarette dangling off his lips, and he's walking with his arm draped around a pretty girl dressed in head-to-toe black, with a bright purple scarf wrapped fashionably around her neck. The girl looks at me as they pass, her eyes darting to my inked wings. "Feckin' ripped," I hear her whisper to her guy friend, who gives me a curious look. "Aye," he answers her. But just that fast, they move away and into the other passersby meandering along the walkways.

Jake leads us down a narrow close—I don't even catch the name of it—but it goes down a long, even narrower flight of aged steps. The walls are close and smell of wet stone, and not a soul is around. Just us. Ahead of me, I look at Jake's wide, broad back and shoulders and wonder how in Hell he and Gabriel can walk straight through. Then they stop and half-turn to us. I throw a look over my shoulder. Noah is behind me, and Darius, Vic, Ginger, and Lucian have joined us. Jake's eyes catch a slender beam of light pouring in from the streetlamp above us.

"We're beneath one of three medical labs in this section of the university," he says. "They're side-by-side, as are the chambers through this entrance. "It's dark as Hell in here, and passages you don't even think exist, do." He looks at me. "Easy to get lost. I've done it. Many times."

"So this is just another entrance to the catacombs?" I ask.

"Aye," he answers. "They virtually run course beneath all of Old Town. Some are caved in; some are easy enough to navigate." In that beam of light I see Jake's eyes narrow. "But be careful. They can be treacherous even for the experienced." He inclines his head to my pocket. "Use your torch, lass."

"What are we looking for, Andorra?" Lucian asks.

Jake glances over my head to stare at Lucian. "According to Sydney, a stone embedded in the corner wall of a chamber. The stone will have a tilted impression of a cross. By now 'tis barely visible, so it won't be easy to spot. Once we find the stone, we have to wedge it out. Whatever the relic is, 'twill be there."

Lucian's silence signals an okay to proceed.

My hand goes for the mini flashlight I carry in the pocket of my coat.

With a final glance at us all, Jake pushes open a rickety old wooden door and ducks through the entrance. I turn my light on and follow.

"I'm right behind you," Noah says in my ear. "Don't do anything stupid."

I jab his gut with my elbow. "You mean like that?"

Noah's grunt is the only response I get. Along with a nice swear word.

My eyes try to focus in the dark, but they don't. Can't. It's an absolute pitch-black abyss down here and the only thing I can see is what my flashlight beam alights on. It's crazy. The floor is stone, some loose pebbles, and dirt. Uneven. Good thing I wore my Nikes, or I'd surely bust my ass. This is worse than the cobbles on River Street back home.

We're in one big chamber right now, all of us, and Jake shines his flashlight to his face. "We need to split up and check out these other rooms and be done with this place. I dunna like it."

I don't like it, either. Feels like . . . death. Old death. Like plague-riddled death.

"We'll break into twos. Search the walls near corners for a misplaced stone. You'll have to feel it with your fingers for the cross, more likely than not. It's been here for almost a thousand years."

"Come on," Noah says, and grabs my elbow. "You're with me."

"I'm the one with the flashlight," I answer, and yank my arm free. "You're with me."

Noah chuckles. "That's my girl."

We head off down a ribbonlike corridor to another chamber. Noah has to turn sideways to wedge through the narrow gap of rock. Inside the chamber, I arc my flashlight, the beam sweeping the stone room. "Let's start on opposite sides of the room and feel with our hands," I say. "You take that corner; I'll take this one."

"Yep," Noah says, and moves across the room.

Within minutes, we're done. "I don't feel anything," he says.

"Me neither," I answer. "Let's go into the next chamber."

We do, and again find nothing.

The *tink-tink* of water dripping and hitting something reverberates in my ears. It's weird how stone has a scent, but it does. It smells like cold and wet. And something else. Years. It smells like lots and lots of years.

Then, I hear it. It's louder now. That annoying hum in my head. It's almost like a ringing in my ears now. Borderline painful.

"What's wrong?" Noah asks.

I shake my head and glance around. "I don't know. I . . . hear something—"

"Whoa!" Noah yells, and pushes me aside just before something flies straight at me. I stumble against the wall and look up.

"Riley, run!" Noah yells as he morphs into a full-fledged vampire.

I rub my eyes and look. Old decaying cherub statues have loosened from their places, only they're not sweet little fat-faced babies. They have long, jagged teeth, and there's at least a half dozen of them flying straight at us. What the hell?

"Riley, damn it, run!" Noah hollers.

I take off down a dank passage, running as fast as the narrow, low-ceilinged corridors will allow. I take turn after turn, those freaky little fanged cherubs crashing into walls as they chase me down. Further back, I hear Noah swearing.

I stumble into a chamber and immediately notice it's different in here. Not the same. Am I in an alternative catacombs now? How the hell did that happen? Everything is in sepia, overgrown with moss, darkened by shadows. A light flickers. When I blink, Eli is standing there. It's him. I see his face. "Eli!" I yell. I try to run toward him, but I can't. My feet won't move. Slowly, though, he steps toward me. I knew he wasn't dead. "Eli, hurry!" I call to him.

Then, his beautiful smile drops, and dozens of sharp pointed teeth lower from his gums. He's moving straight toward me. "Eli! Goddamn it!" I try to run, but I can't even lift my foot. I think to grab my silver blade, but my hands won't budge, either.

A figure flies past me and slams into the alternative Eli. Both hit the wall, and when one rises, he flies toward me so fast, I don't have time to blink. It's Noah. I know his scent. He grabs me and rushes me out of the chamber. Through darkened passageways we race, my feet barely touching the stone flooring. Finally, we stumble into another chamber. I drop to my knees immediately. That humming sound. It's so potent in my ears, it's making me sick.

"What happened?" Jake is there, asking. The ringing in my ears is so loud, I can barely hear Noah's words as he explains. "Riley?" Jake is shaking me, then helping me up. I cup my hands over my ears. The pain is searing into my brain.

"What is wrong with you, girl?" Jake yells at me.

"Got it," I hear Ginger's voice in a distant chamber. "I think I found it."

Noah, standing right next to me, grabs my hand holding the flashlight and points it at his face. "Are you okay?"

The ringing is overwhelming. I take off running. Blindly. I don't even know where I'm heading. Just . . . away from that sound. I think I'm moving toward the exit of the catacombs, but even as I hear Noah's swears softening behind me, I duck into another chamber. The ringing isn't quite as loud now. I must be near the street side. I see a door. I move toward it.

Riley, wait. Don't go.

I stop in my tracks and tune in my hearing. Only that dripping water sound. The other WUP members in another chamber. The wind, squeaking in through some miniscule cracks, and it's almost a whine or a moan. Not a voice.

This way. Please.

My body turns toward the voice, and I arc my light across the room. Empty.

Left.

I shine my light left, and it falls on a small passageway. Something is drawing me that way. More than the voice. A familiar sensation comes over me, and the first thing that pops into my head is Eli.

Hurrying now, I squeeze into the passage, and it empties into a long threadlike hallway of stone. I move as quickly as possible, my flashlight providing only a small patch of light to keep me from stepping into holes or tripping over loose stones. Far ahead, a light flickers.

You're almost here. Hurry.

Eli. All I can think of is Eli. It might be him. How, I don't know, but it might. I have to find him.

I step into the chamber with the flickering light, and all at once it extinguishes. A force—not a hand, but a force—knocks the flashlight from me. It clamors to the stone floor and goes out, leaving me in total darkness.

All at once the sensation of being crowded envelopes me. Warmth. Sensual arousal penetrates my rock-hard senses, and I feel weak. It's like a drug, and my body involuntarily moves toward it.

"I've not been able to think of anything else, save you," a seductively raspy voice says. "I had to see you again."

I blink in the darkness. "I can't see you now. Who are you? And what . . . are you doing to me?"

"I'm not who you think I am," he answers. His

voice is oddly ancient, with a medieval accent, sort of like Darius's. Yet different. "I have no intentions of harming you, Riley." He gives a low, soft laugh. "Trust me. That's anything but my intention."

"I didn't ask if you were going to harm me," I say, forcing my eyes to remain open, even in the pitch-darkness. "Who the hell are you?" I'm not physically restrained. Yet . . . I can't seem to move. Except closer to him.

"That doesn't matter right now. I just . . . had to see you," his words brush my jaw, my throat, and it's intoxicating. I can't help it. I lean into it. Into him. "I will watch over you," he whispers, his lips grazing mine. "I vow, nothing will happen to you."

"Riley!"

An arc of light sweeps the cold, dank room, and immediately my body is released from the shackles even I can't detect. I shake my head a few times, just long enough for Noah to reach me. I look at him, and his face is angry.

Seriously angry.

"What the hell are you doing?" he says, and looks me over. "Where did you go?"

"Well, apparently I went here," I answer. "I thought I heard something."

"So your best course of action is to find that something instead of alerting the rest of us?" he answers. "Come on. Let's go."

Meet me, Riley. Beneath lights, so I am no longer a shadow to you. In three days, at the Marimae House, in New Town. Seven p.m. Dress formal. I'll find you. And come alone. I don't wish to share you with another soul. . . .

Quietly, I push the seductive voice out of my head and follow a fuming Noah, who has confiscated someone's flashlight out of the chambers. That humming, ringing in my ears is strengthening again, and its pain rips into the side of my head. I almost drop to my knees. I stumble along, following Noah. We wind through the passageways of the catacombs until we meet up with Jake and the others. Ginger is pointing her light toward him. In his hand, Jake holds a small, old-as-dirt-looking cross. Part of it is broken off. He looks up at me. "Let's get out of here."

That's when I notice the shadows.

All at once, medieval shit hits the fan.

"You'll not take that anywhere, I fear," a voice says from the darkness. It's a voice I don't recognize; poignant, refined, and sophisticated. He almost sounds apologetic.

"I fucking damn well will take it," Jake says, not quite so refined. Even in the darkness, I can hear the tone and pitch of his voice change. He's morphed. Ready for a fight.

Someone, I think Ginger, arcs her beam in the direction of the voice.

What the light illuminates is somewhat shocking. Even if for a second.

A woman. Midthirties, maybe, with an abundance of blond hair. Suddenly I recognize her. She's the tour group leader in the long cloak. I'd also seen her outside of Bene's. She's wearing head-to-toe black—

I can't make out exactly what, other than the color. She looks dead ahead at Jake and pulls a knife. Silver. Sharp.

And smiles.

Hey, Blondie. Ease on out of the chamber. Now. I say to the stranger, in my mind.

She stands there, still smiling, but slowly starts to back out. She doesn't see me, though, and that's a good thing. *That's right. Keep going. When you're on the street, head to the castle. Don't stop until you reach the front gates, and then shout to be let inside.*

The woman says nothing as she continues to back out of the chamber and into the close. She's almost ready to turn when behind her emerge four more figures from the close. They're big. And I'd smelled them before I'd seen them.

Jodís. And the one in front grabs the woman and in one movement rips her heart from her chest. The ringing in my ears now is deafening. I can't hear anything else. The woman's scream dies on the misty night even before her body hits the stone, jerking and kicking. It sort of shocks me. I'm not ready for it, and it's shaken me up a bit.

Pull it together, Riley, Jake says in my head. After a deep breath, I do.

Only a small stream of light from the lamp on the close shines through, just enough illumination to see the Jodís lunge toward us. I hear Noah curse. Lucian says something. I don't know what it is. Gaelic, maybe.

"Riley," Ginger calls, inching closer.

"Right here," I answer her, and we're back to back now. Lucian wants her as far away from him right now as possible. I hear her heart racing. "Stay with me," I say, and I reach for my sword. God almighty, I hope I lop off the right head. Ginger has reached for her sword, too.

Then it begins.

One Jodís lunges toward us, and I use the point of my sword as a brace, rear back, and kick both feet into its chest. Hard. It falls back but bounces right up and lunges again. Another lunges at the same time, and I hear Ginger's sword make contact. Then we're separated.

I'm fighting one alone now, and from the sounds going on around me, everyone has their own Jodís to fight. I concentrate on mine alone, and the ringing in my ears is getting harder to ignore. It's confusing me, and my balance if thrown off. Still, I fight. I wait, weigh, calculate; then it charges me, arm reaching out to grab my throat. With an uppercut, I swing.

One Jodís head rolls across the stone.

The aftermath of a dying Jodís is just too nasty to stand by and watch. I've seen it once before, when Sydney touched me. They melt into this screaming, gross puddle of white pus. The screaming has already begun. I seek out the others.

Another head hits the floor, and from Noah's curse, he did it. Two more soon follow, and the squirming piles of Jodís are just too much to take. I literally fall out of the catacomb entrance and onto the close. Only then do I notice something.

The woman's body has disappeared.

"Where'd she go?" I ask, looking around. I shove my sword back into its sheath.

Jake's face has not returned to its human form. His eerie eyes, now white with a pinpoint dot of red, scan the close.

"They weren't here for us," Gabriel says. "They came for her," he says, referring to the woman. "I know who she is. I've encountered her before. She's one of the Gemini." His gaze finds mine. "A small sect of modern-day monster hunters determined to take back the city of Edinburgh. Just like that group of humans from before. They know of us. They know of the Jodís. And they probably know of the Fallen." He searches the area once more, then inclines his head. "Let's go."

Thank God, because that freaking hum in my ears is so loud now, I think I'm going to pass out. We all separate and head back to the Crescent. The humming is weak now. I can still hear it, but it's tolerable. Maybe I've got an ear infection or something . . . human like that? Who knows? The activity on the streets has slowed to a drag, only a truck or two still out along with the cabs. People still mill about, locals leaving pubs and heading home. We're almost to Old Tolbooth Wynd when a woman's scream breaks through the misty night. My ears pick up a muffled whimpering. It's one lane over from Old Tolbooth. And the stench is unmistakable.

Another Jodís.

The kirk. I run toward it, not waiting to see who

follows me. I hear Noah swear and say my name under his breath, and he's probably right behind me. The girl . . . her pulse is fast. Her breaths are faster. The distinct sound of fingernails clawing at gravel cuts through my senses, and I hurry. Although a lamp illuminates the churchyard, it's empty, and I make the black wrought-iron gate in an effortless leap. Crouching as I land, I scan the area. The kirk's front is adorned by a circular glass window at the top and flanked by a pair of oblong windows with a crest in between. No lights are on. No one is here. Her heartbeat, so slow now it barely beats, is coming from around the back of the church. Then the beating stops altogether. Silence.

Through the darkness I run, *haul ass*, around the ancient stone structure and into the shadows. Abruptly, I halt. There in the gravel is a woman's body. I fall to my knees, and even though I can't hear her heart beating any longer, I still feel the pulse at her throat. Nothing. That's when I notice the gaping hole in her chest, heart *gone*.

That's also when I notice her lifeless eyes staring wide, frightened, up at me. Lips slightly parted. Lifting one of her hands, I notice her fingertips are scraped and bleeding. She might be twenty years old, if that.

And I'm too fucking late. Reaching over, I close her eyes.

"Let's go, Ri," Noah says beside me. "Nothing you can do."

"Yeah, I know that," I answer angrily. I rise and

just walk off. Noah's right behind me, and he leaps the gates a few seconds after me. Together we cross the street and head through the arches of Old Tolbooth Wynd.

"The only way to stop this is to stop them," Noah says, and I know he's right. "Stop the Fallen."

Because apparently I can't even detect when an innocent is having her heart ripped out of her body until it's too frickin' late.

My arm is grabbed and my body swung around, and Noah is standing there, holding me in a tight grasp. "Let it go, Ri. You have to. Let that girl go, and let Eli go. For now. You've got to focus." His mercury gaze sears me. "I'll be here for you. After. Okay?"

I stare at Noah's beautiful features in the moonlight, and the slender dreads that have escaped the leather band holding them back. He looks nothing like Eli, yet he reminds me of him every time I look at him. Reminds me of what I have to do now. "Yeah, I know," I answer. "I will."

Noah play-slaps my cheek. "That's my kick-ass girl. Now let's go see what the relic says. Jake took it up to Sydney."

Giving Noah a nod, we continue up the wynd near the Crescent gates, and Peter must have known we were coming because the gates are open. The ringing in my ears grows louder and louder again. Damn, I might have to get that checked out. The closer we move to the front door, the louder it grows in my head. At the doorway, I stumble to my knees and cup my ears.

"Ri, what's wrong with you?" Noah asks. He's kneeling down, his hand on my back.

"I don't know," I answer. "I think I have something wrong with my ears," I push my palms tighter against my head. "This humming is nonstop."

Noah helps me stand. "Well, come on. Let's get you inside, human," he says.

I concentrate once more on siphoning the sound out of my head. It takes more concentration than before, but I do it. It's still in there, and it still hurts, but it's dull. Dull enough for me not to be babied and carried to my room. "I'm okay," I assure Noah. "Let's find the others."

Inside, we find the others gathered in the library.

Jake looks up when we enter. "I'm sorry, Riley. I could've told you what you'd find," he says solemnly. "No matter how fast you are, if a Jodís gets there first, there's virtually no hope for the innocent."

"That's pretty obvious," I say. "I used top speed to get there and still didn't make it."

"The Fallen may have created the Jodís with the power of shifting," Gabriel says, his deep voice and odd accent breaking the air.

"Shifting?" I ask.

"Aye, space. From here to there," Gabriel says. " 'Tis an ancient, magical way of transportation created by the Fae, back before Scotia was even Scotia. If 'tis a verse they can recall, they'll use it."

"Then why don't they just shift the entire body?" asks Lucian. "Why take their heart? Why so brutal?"

Gabriel rubs his jaw. "I can only imagine they're working with verra little in the form of common sense and intelligence with the Jodís," he answers. "They're conjured creatures, dunna forget. 'Tis easier for them to comprehend short commands. Like to bring just the part they need."

"Okay, I've got it," Sydney says from her corner desk. On it, lying atop a soft cloth, she has the aged cross Ginger found in the catacombs. Sydney stares through a large magnifying glass eyepiece. She lowers the piece and looks at us. "It reads—" Then she reads the inscription out loud and the language almost hurts to hear it. It's completely incomprehensible. Dolphins might as well be talking. It's that odd. I almost cover my ears.

"Basically it says, *Wherein the hallowed ground of the remnants that battled the painted warriors from the north, in the center of such a mass grave of bloodshed, lies what you seek. No matter time, 'twill remain the same until the one who reads it releases it.* Oh— ouch! Shit!" Sydney drops the relic onto the table and blows on her fingertips.

The moment the last word leaves Sydney's mouth, the cross turns red like embers, and as it lies on the table, it literally bursts into flames. Suddenly, the vicious humming inside of my head weakens. I take in a deep breath. The pain is gone. The humming is still there, but so faint, I can barely hear it. Sydney jumps back, and Gabriel grabs her by the arm and pulls her away from the table.

We stare as the cross turns to cinders.

"I hope you have that memorized," Noah says, then shakes his head. "Damn."

"Yeah, I do," Sydney answers. "And I wrote it down." She looks at Gabriel. "Didn't expect that."

"Nor I," he returns. He looks at Jake. " 'Tis a puzzle that requires more searching. Edinburgh is an ancient city, and before the castle was built, battles raged and lives ended." He looks at Darius. "We've got to find the spot where the Caledonians battled."

"Who are the they?" I ask.

"The early Picts," Darius answers. "Savage fighters, they tattooed their faces and bodies to terrorize their opponents and make themselves seem more brutal." He half grins. "Gawan of Conwyk is such. As am I."

"Then you should know precisely where to look." Victorian, who sits quietly in a far corner, is listening. He glances at me, his eyes warm and somewhat sorrowful.

"I know where to start," Darius claims. "Much has changed over the centuries. The landscape, the construction—while ancient in truth 'tis still changed from back then." He glances at Jake. " 'Twill take some time."

Sirens from Canongate blast through the night, and I know the girl's body has been found at the kirk. It sickens me. A family's lives will forever be changed as they mourn the loss of their loved one. All because some selfish bastards want to remain on earth forever.

On the far wall, the flat screen is on a local news channel.

"Hey, turn that up," I say, and Noah takes the remote and turns up the volume. Moving closer, I sit on the arm of the sofa next to him and watch.

"Edinburgh's streets are in peril after the discovery of yet another body found earlier this evening," the reporter says. "A young male, approximately age nineteen, was found on the banks of the Firth. His identification is being withheld until all family have been notified. This makes the fourth young person in two weeks. Meanwhile, near Niddry street, another person has been found completely reduced to ashes. Is there a curse on Edinburgh?"

"Five," I say under my breath, thinking of the poor girl who was just slaughtered in the kirk yard. "Seriously? A curse? They have the balls to say that on TV, with family members watching?" I shake my head and pace. "Fucking idiot reporters."

The reporter continues. "Is there a serial killer running amok in the streets of Old Town? The police are out in full swing to catch the person responsible for these heinous acts."

I stare at the flat screen and fixate on the video coverage. A black body bag is being hauled up the banks of the Firth by officers. Inside lays the heartless body of an innocent. Another one.

Weariness sets in, and I can feel my narcoleptic sleep about to kick in.

"I'll walk you to your room," Noah says beside me. He grins. "I can see it on your face. You're about to go out."

"I'm okay," I answer, and rise from the arm of the

sofa. "I can make it alone." I put my hand on his shoulder. "Thanks, though." I cock my head. "You're kinda sweet when you're not being a prick, Miles."

Noah shrugs. "What can I say?"

I shake my head and start across the library. As I pass Jake, I stop and look up at him. "I'll only sleep a few hours. We gotta end this. Fast."

His green gaze sweeps over me. "I know. Go rest."

With a slight nod, I leave. No sooner do I hit the staircase than a presence is felt, and I immediately know who it is.

"What if you fall out while walking the stairs?" Victorian says. "You could hurt yourself."

I stop, turn, and stare up into Vic's brown gaze. "Nice try. I've fought and killed rogue vampires. You think a little tumble down a staircase will hurt me?"

With a shrug, Victorian places his hand to my lower back, and gives a little pressure to urge me to continue up the stairs. With him. He grins. "It's the only thing I could think of."

"Right," I answer, and begin the climb. The staircase is lit with muted amber lamps that cause shadows to dance on the walls as we pass. It's drafty, cool, and eerily quiet. We're almost to the landing to the second floor when I go out.

Like a light. Bam.

I vaguely remember arms around me, my body lifting up and seemingly floating down the corridor. Then all is still. I'm in darkness.

For a while.

When my eyes open next, the room is engulfed in heavy

shadows. I'm being held, suspended in air in a pair of strong arms. Confusion webs through my mind as I focus on the person carrying me. Well-known. Closeness. Yet . . . not. A man. His features are obscured by darkness. But other things make me want to stay; the feel of him seems . . . familiar. At least I think so. I'm unsure. I pin him with a hot stare and a frown I can only hope he sees in the dark. "Let. Me. Go."

Moonlight shifts into the room, and only a shade of his features is revealed. Something flashes in his darkened eyes briefly, and then it disappears, replaced by raw, male desire. Just seeing it makes the uncomfortable ache inside of me grow. He lowers his head, his lips touching mine. "Don't leave. Please." He sets me down on the floor, his body crowding me close to the wall. I try to push past him, but again he begs me. Pleads. "Don't go."

Releasing my hands, he drags a forefinger across my forehead, down the bridge of my nose; traces my jaw. His eyes follow his finger, as though amazed with each place he touches, and as though he's never done the like before. Then he holds my jaw and tilts my head.

And his mouth descends.

As soon as his tongue touches mine, I lose control. I have no explanation; no reasoning. Only a strong sense of familiarity that makes this feel unstoppable. It's Eli. As soon as I shove my fingers into his hair and pull him closer, this man, this . . . shadow Eli man loses control.

More than passion fuels his movements—I can feel it. It seems more like starvation, a primal, uncontrolled drive to satisfy basic needs, to mark what is his and to make sure no other dare try to take it away. That's what it feels like.

My lips are soft, pliable, and desperately seeking. They all but consume him. The urgency in my touch surprises me; the scrape of my nails through his shirt nearly drives him mad. He grabs the hem of my shirt and lifts it above my head, flinging it to the floor, his hands replacing the soft cotton as he moves them slowly down my arms, my ribs. "I want to feel your skin against mine," he whispers. Feather light, his fingertips trace the dragons trailing down both of my arms. "You're so beautiful," he says, and I find I don't have the strength to answer him back. Sensations overwhelm me, every nerve ending is on fire, and there's a place deep inside of me that is dying to be satisfied.

I watch him watching me in the darkness, and without thinking, I lift a hand and stroke his jaw, his lips. I feel his body shudder beneath my touch. He allows me to unbutton his shirt and push it off his broad shoulders. Taut skin is found beneath my seeking fingers, as are corded muscle and prominent, healthy veins. Large hands. Strong biceps. I still see nothing more than a silhouette, yet I want him so badly it hurts. It literally aches inside of me. I understand none of it. Neither can I stop myself. This is Eli. But why can't I make out his features? Why?

As he peels the clothes from my body, I can hear his heart hammering against his chest. His hardness pushes at his groin and against my hip. With nimble fingers he unlatches the small metal front clasp of my bra and pushes the silky material to the side. His breath hitches in his throat as he stares at me. Then he turns me around. He says nothing, but his hands grasp either side of my ribs, then slowly begin to explore the intricate markings of my inked dragon. Callused hands slip around my stomach as his mouth finds my shoulder, kisses then my neck, then ear. "You're the most exquisite creature I've ever encountered," he whispers, and pulls my lobe into his mouth. I shudder, and he turns me to face him. With his eyes fastened to mine, he sweeps me up in his arms and carries me to a bed, where he follows me down.

Moonlight streaks in through the window in a single beam, and that beam casts just enough illumination for me to see the outline of his features. He's . . . not Eli. He's breathtaking. I don't know him. Yet . . . the familiarity of him stuns me, urges me to touch him, return his kisses, and arch into his embrace. I can't stop. Is this Eli? My heart tells me it is. Yet my eyes reveal differently. The moonlight bathes his skin, making it strangely luminescent in the small hours of the night. He's stretched over me. Somewhere we both lost our clothes and are nothing but skin against skin. I arch into him and reach for him, my hands slipping over his muscular chest, then around his corded neck. It makes my skin tingle, my nerve endings sizzle. Blood pounds through my veins and rushes to my groin as his fingers trail my stomach, smoothing the feminine muscles there, tracing my ribs.

My own nimble fingers trace the muscles in his back, down his sides, and between us, where his thick hardness pushes heavily against my thigh. I grasp it—soft, hard, velvety—and a low growl emanates from his throat. Lowering his head, he brushes his mouth across mine, tasting with his tongue and holding my jaw still with his hand. His kiss is . . . internal. Exploring. Soulful. I never want it to stop. . . .

He's wedging hips between my legs, his weight braced on one forearm. The firm peaks of my breasts brush his chest, and he shudders. Staring down, his eyes sadden. "This wasn't supposed to happen," he whispers, and kisses me. "I'm not . . . Forgive me."

My body is alive with more sensation than I can handle, and my mind won't process his words. Not now. All I want is feeling.

All I want is him. "Eli, please," I whisper.

With anxious fingertips, I trace his spine from his neck to his waist, counting each vertebra, lining each muscle as they tense under my touch. Slowly I lift my legs and pull my heels against his buttocks, hooking them around his hips.

I can feel his heart slam against his ribs, and I know he can take it no more.

Lowering his head, he takes my mouth as though savoring every inch of my lips, tasting with his tongue, and I kiss him back with desperate fervor. Skimming my hips, my stomach, he cups one breast and deepens the kiss, our tongues entwined, and the intensity of the dual contact makes his arousal push hard against me. Inside, my body is wrenching for release.

Again I arch and push against him, then grab his neck and pull his head down to my bare chest. He tastes the soft rise of my breast, dragging his mouth erotically over it, tasting the aroused peak. I think I'll lose my mind.

My breath catches and I moan—a soft whimper that doesn't even sound like me. I can't help it.

With a hard yank, I pull his head to my mouth, where I kiss him, sweeping my tongue across his bottom lip, then gently take it between my teeth. "Now," *I demand on a hoarse whisper.* "I want you now, Eli. Please."

We stare at each for the space of a second, eyes locked. This . . . figment of my imagination shifts his hips and fills me in one slow thrust. I moan out loud as my wet heat envelopes him, holds him, forces his eyes to close, and he shakes with aroused need.

"Christ, Riley," he mutters against my throat as he starts to move inside me, reaching for a destination singularly his, the wild need to claim it growing with each powerful, primal thrust.

The mounting eruption within him grows at an uncontrollable speed and I can feel it, just as I feel my own, and he drives into me with furious passion.

My own savage response shocks me, and I desperately claw at him, matching his every move, pushing him over the edge until my name tears from his throat as he explodes inside me, over and over as he buries himself deep inside of me, his body seizing, shuddering.

My breath catches again and I hold him tightly as my own climax peaks and consumes, my feminine muscles contracting around him with each pulse of my orgasm. I bite his shoulder as its intensity heightens, little gasps escaping my lips; then slowly, with each breath, my body relaxes.

He rests his forehead against mine as our ragged breathing returns to normal. My arms go around him and pull him close. It's not right. I can't stop. Can't move away.

Pressing his lips to my damp temple, he smoothes back my hair; kisses me long, deep, taking his time to savor my mouth; then moves to my side and gathers me close. "I am never far from you," he says softly. "Even when you don't know I'm there, I am. And don't forget about my invitation. I look forward to seeing you there. Alone."

"Ri, wake up," a voice calls to me. A hand caresses my cheek. "Riley?"

Slowly my eyelids drag open. I feel as though I've been run over by a truck. I blink several times, and only after a few moments do I realize I'm completely naked. "What the hell?" I say, then turn to the voice awakening me.

"Vic, what's going on?" All I can now remember is the incredibly erotic dream I've had. And especially the fact that I didn't think it was a dream at all. I thought it was freaking real. I thought it was Eli. Yet . . . now I'm not so sure. I stare at the Romanian vampire. "Tell me you didn't take my clothes off." I pull the sheets up to my chin.

Victorian Arcos, in the hazy light of my room, stares down at me with liquid brown eyes. And says nothing.

"Poe, Jesus Christ, when are you gonna—"

Noah bursts into my room and abruptly stops when he sees Victorian. I know he doesn't like the Romanian and will probably never trust him as I do, but he tolerates him. To a certain degree. Noah turns to me, plops down on the bed, the mattress sinking under his weight and making me roll toward him. He thumps me on the forehead. "How long are you gonna sleep, woman? It's been almost twenty-four hours now."

I bolt up, barely remembering to take the sheet with me. The last thing I want to do is flash these two pervs. "What? What the hell?" I say. How could I have slept so long? "Move, Noah. Actually, both of you get out of here. I need to dress. Without an audience."

"Damn," Noah mumbles, and rises from the bed. "Jake said to let you sleep, that your body probably needed it."

Not wanting to wait another second for either of them, I crawl out of bed, dragging the sheets with me and around me, and walk over to the trunk where I have my clothes stashed. Lifting the lid, I grab a pair of panties, a black tank, and a navy pair of cargo pants. "Why did you listen to him?" I answer, holding the sheets now with my chin and yanking up my panties. Dropping the sheets I turn around, back to the boys, and pull on my tank top. Turning again, I glare at Noah. "I have a hard time believing you just . . . listened to him. You know I don't want to just . . . sleep!" Grasping my cargoes, I step into them and pull them up. Only then do I notice the wide-eyed expression on Victorian's face and the ridiculous, pervy, wolfish grin on Noah's. "God almighty, you two." I shake my head, punch Noah in the arm as I walk by, and grab a clean pair of black footie socks from the chest. Pull them on, followed by my Nikes, and gather my hair into a ponytail. I head for the door. "Coming?" I ask the two.

"Almost," Noah says, then laughs at himself.

I shake my head. "Jesus," I mutter, then head to

the bathroom in the hall. Just as I reach the door, with Vic and Noah not far behind, I remember. Everything. That sexual dream. Is it just my conscience missing Eli?

But the invitation. That was real.

The erotic dream and the invitation to the Marimae House are from the same person. And guilt claws at my gut about both. I wanted that dream to be of Eli. Not of some . . . stranger. What does that make me? In the dream, I was completely willing. A sick feeling washes over me, and the empty void left by Eli aches as though someone has jammed a knife into my heart.

I duck into the bathroom to wash my face and brush my teeth. I need to tell Jake about this . . . whoever he is.

And now.

Part Eight

FALLING

The angels are so enamored of the language that is spoken in heaven that they will not distort their lips with the hissing and unmusical dialect of men, but speak their own, whether there be any who understand it or not.

—Ralph Waldo Emerson

Riley looks calm, even at most times acts calm, but I can tell what lies just beneath the surface. A simmering, almost boiling fury that will unleash on anyone whom she finds responsible for her mate's death. No' that I blame her. But a storm is brewing, and she will be leading it. The Fallen will never know what hit them.

—Darius

I find Jake and Gabriel upstairs in the dojo, working the swords. It's early—seven a.m. Both are bare to the waist, hair pulled back, ferocious as hell. They look like they're trying to kill each other, hacking, swinging. Warriors. I stand quietly by, watching and admiring. It's odd to think that they both once swung those weapons as a means of survival so many centuries ago.

"Amazing, aren't they?" Sydney says, suddenly beside me. I glance at her. Leaning, back to the wall, hands crossed over her chest, she stares at the pair on the mat with admiration gleaming in her blue eyes. She looks at me. "I'm so sorry about Eli," she says, and admiration is replaced by sorrow. "I can't imagine losing someone I loved like that." Her gaze immediately shoots to Gabriel. "It must be so painful."

"Yeah," I answer, "it is. I miss him every second."

Sydney looks at me, and I don't know if it's something in my voice or something else that causes her to. I continue. "He totally changed my life. And in my book, he's not dead. Something has happened to him, but he's not dead."

After she holds my stare for a moment, her gaze returns to Gabriel.

I'm uncomfortable talking about Eli. It makes me realize he's not here for me right now. To talk to. To touch. I turn at every corner and think I'll see him, and I don't. I crave him. I know he hasn't been gone that long, but it feels like it. Just as it feels like he's been in my life forever. What really sucks is that finally, finally I trust someone with my heart . . . and I lose him. It's not fair. It's just not fucking fair. And I'm going to find him. Even if it kills me.

"So, what about you and Gabriel?" I ask, wanting to quickly shift the conversation off of me and Eli. "What's up with you two?"

Sydney gets a faraway look in her eyes before answering. "I'm the key to this whole thing, that's what's up," she says, and I hear remorse in her voice. "Without me, the Seiagh can't be found or destroyed. I was born to become the Archivist. To do this very thing we're doing now. To save mankind. Gabriel protects me." She looks at me. "That's it."

I stare at her for several seconds. My brows furrow. "Bullshit."

Sydney's cheeks actually turn pink. "Yeah. Bullshit it is." She gazes at Gabriel. "Unfortunately, it's a one-sided deal."

"What do you mean?" I ask.

Sydney's quiet for a minute, watching the two swordsmen. I join her, and, yeah, it's more than amazing. Jake and Gabriel are pretty equally matched when it comes to brawn. They're about the same height, too. Gabriel seems, though, to be more at ease, or as one, with his sword. As if he's been wielding it a lot longer. He probably has. The muscles and cords in his back bunch and tighten as he arcs his blade, and when it connects with Jake's, both men make a grunting, guttural sound that reminds me of a pair of Vikings fighting. Jake's biceps . . . ridiculous. Veins popping everywhere, despite them being void of blood.

"He's never faltered with me," Sydney says. "Not even once."

"What do you mean?" I ask.

She shrugs. "He's never made a move on me. Never even showed me once that he, I don't know, wants me. Or even cares about me, Sydney Maspeth. It's like he's all business. Protect the Archivist. Blah, blah, blah."

"Meanwhile, he sets your skin on fire," I add.

"Is it that obvious?" she asks sheepishly.

"What? That he rocks your world? Yeah, girl, it is. To me anyway." I drape an arm over her shoulders. "Don't worry. Your secret is safe with me. Although," I say, turning my attention back to the guys, "you may be way off on your assumption about Gabriel's feelings for you."

Sydney lets out such a long, lonesome sigh that I

have to fight not to laugh. "Not holding my breath, Poe."

I grin at her. "You sound like my brother. Besides. Wouldn't matter if you did. You're immortal, silly. Now," I say, inclining my head toward the rack of swords against the far wall of the dojo. "Wanna go at it?"

Sydney lifts a brow. "Might as well."

"Good," I answer, and we hug the walls of the dojo. "I need to burn off some steam."

Sydney works my ass off good. She's strong as hell, and her training has paid off. She may not look it, but she can kick some serious tushy. I concentrate on my moves, everything that Tristan taught me. Where to put my weight before I swing, and how to thrust, jab, and hack. Sydney's face is pure business as she weighs me, studies my moves, and swings at my head. I'm breaking a furious sweat by the time we call a stalemate.

"Impressive," Jake says as he and Gabriel watch from the edge of the mat. "I think I'm in love."

"You're our boss," I say, catching my breath. "Sexual harassment. Ever hear of it?"

Jake grins. "Never."

"You've improved," Gabriel says, sheathing his sword. "De Barre is a fair teacher."

"De Barre is a kick-ass teacher," I correct, then nod. "You're not too shabby yourself."

Gabriel merely gives a slight nod of acknowledgment. One day I'd love to see what his already-gorgeous face looks like in a full-blown smile. He really is something else. No wonder Sydney has fallen for him.

Gabriel's eyes seek out Sydney, and I'm looking at him the moment he spots her. Yeah. He's hiding it, all right, but that is one immortal otherbeing head over heels with Ms. Maspeth. All business, my ass. I can see it in his eyes. There's more to that hawklike, intense stare than just merely keeping the Archivist safe and sound.

I turn my attention to my employer. "Jake," I say, and incline my head. "I need a word."

Jake sheaths his sword and swaggers across the dojo. The man towers over me and stares down at me with an unbendable look. "Aye?" he asks.

"I've been issued an invitation," I begin, meeting his gaze. When he doesn't say anything, I continue. "By someone who can speak to me inside my head. And apparently have sex with me in my head, too." I sigh. "I thought it was Eli."

Jake raises a brow. From the corner of my eye I notice the rest of the WUP team entering the dojo.

"Nice of you to share info, Poe. Do you recognize this person?" Jake asks.

I shake my head. "I don't think so. I haven't seen his entire face." I leave out the part about the erotic sex dream that still brings me shame. "I don't really know who he is—"

"It's a man?" he asks.

"It's a male," I clarify. "Obviously an otherbeing, if he can speak to me in my head."

Jake nods. "So true."

"So that's all he did was give you an invite some-where?" Noah asks, walking up to stand beside me. "Out of the blue?"

I eye Noah. "Watch that jealous tone, spud," I warn. "And no. He seemed . . . familiar to me. And with me. Yet I'm sure I never met him before."

"Where did he invite you to?" asks Darius, joining in. His hair is loose about his shoulders, and he's pulling it back from his face as he speaks. He gathers it with a leather band and awaits my answer.

I look at him. "Some event at the Marimae House. He says it's—"

"In New Town," finishes Gabriel. "Still an old home. They host several charity events a year. Edin-burgh's elite turns out, as well as many Londoners."

"He's lookin' for something," Jake says. Then gives a slight grin. "Besides you, of course."

"Who is he?" Ginger asks, and she comes to stand by Sydney. She's wearing head-to-toe black training gear.

"Mayhap another of us," Jake answers, meaning vampire. "He obviously either saw Riley or senses her presence."

"Then he may sense our presence, as well," Victo-rian adds. "Riley's not safe."

I glance at Victorian, and his expression is dead serious.

"Riley can handle herself," Jake says, and looks at me. "Am I right?"

"Yes, you are," I say without hesitating.

Jake nods. "Good. Now, what exactly did he say to you?"

I shift my weight. "He wants me to meet him at the Marimae House at seven p.m." I have to think. "Since I lost a day to sleeping, I guess that'll be tomorrow at seven p.m."

"And what else did he say?" Noah prods.

"Well, he did say to come alone." I look at Noah. "And that he couldn't wait to see me."

"Fucking creeper," Noah mumbles. "You're not going alone, Ri. Forget it. We don't know what he is." He gives Jake a challenging look.

"You're absolutely right, Miles," Jake answers. "She won't be going alone." He turns and glances at Sydney and Ginger. "The other girls are going to join her."

Lucian gives a low growl. I think I'm the only one, besides Ginger, who hears it. Ginger places a hand on her mate's arm and looks at Jake. "I'm in."

"Me, too," Sydney says. "I can't stay cooped up in here one more day."

"'Tis a formal event," Gabriel says. "We'll have your attire ordered."

Jake glances at first Sydney, then Ginger. "A four, a four." Then he looks at me. "And an eight. In black." He grins at me.

Prick, I say to Jake in my head.

Tsk, tsk. I'm your boss. Sexual harassment. Ever hear of it? he responds back.

I simply smile. *I'm flipping you the bird. Here. In my mind.*

Jake laughs out loud.

It suddenly reminds me of Eli. The thought that there's a chance, no matter how slight, that Eli is . . . somewhere, and not dead, gives me strength. Courage. And lightens me. I feel energized.

"Right," Jake says, and turns to everyone. "Since the Jodís move during the night and the Fallen are, as far as we know, down again to recover, we should spend the daylight hours training. So partner up."

"And tonight?" asks Ginger.

Jake gives a slight grin. "Tonight we hunt."

"Hunt Jodís?" asks Victorian. He slides a glance my way.

"Hunt . . . everything," Jake corrects. "Unless Syd finds another clue."

For the rest of the day, we train. Swords. Hand-to-hand. Dirks. You name it. All the while, though, my thoughts remain on Eli. I see his face every time I blink. In my head, I even hear his voice. How can someone like Eligius Dupré come into my life, change it so drastically, then . . . leave? It doesn't seem real. I still expect him to walk around the corner any minute. Sometimes I glance up. Hoping. I even hear his voice in my head.

It doesn't happen.

"Shit!" I yelp, and jump back. My thoughts rush to the present, and my vision focuses on what's in front of me. Lifting my hand to my shoulder, I cover the trickle of blood caused by Jake's sword with my palm. I stare hard at him.

"Pay attention," he warns. "Your mind has to be

in this, Riley. It could mean your life." He inclines his head to the rest of the group. "Or one of ours."

I wipe the sweat from my brow. "Yeah," I answer, frowning. "Gotcha." By now the sun has started to drop, and I need a little alone time. Maybe a short run before darkness totally falls. My pride is a little stung, having been chastised with the tip of a sword in front of the whole WUP team. I need to blow off a little steam.

Again. Seems I have a lot of that built up lately. But that's the way I handle things. I don't sit around and cry or mope. I run. Or kick the shit out of something. Usually my training bag at home. Since I don't have one of those here, I'll just run.

Replacing my sword in the rack, I slip out of the dojo as the others are sparring. Peter is in the kitchen doing . . . something. I hear plates and silverware clanking together. The Crescent's hall is shadowy and dark, the lights extinguished downstairs all except the one lamp in the foyer. I ease out the front door and into the cool, briny Edinburgh evening. The sun is not fully extinguished yet, so the sky is a myriad of purples and pinks. No sword to weigh me down, I've only one dirk tucked into the inner belt of my black training pants. Wearing a long-sleeved black tee to cover up the dragons, I take off, leaping over the Crescent's black wrought-iron gates and onto Old Tolbooth Wynd. I'll be back before it's time to head out into the city.

At Canongate, I turn left and jog toward the Palace of Holyroodhouse. Behind the old palace is

Holyrood Park, and from what Gabriel says, it's something like six hundred acres. The Salisbury Crags slope up to one of Edinburgh's landmarks, Arthur's Seat. Gabriel says it's a little over eight hundred feet high. That's a pretty sick steam blower, if you ask me.

So, that's where I'll head. Out of the city, and a place where, especially at this time of evening, I can wide-open run. No one to notice but the wildlife.

Jogging down Canongate, I pass the kirk where I found that poor girl the other night. Slain by a creature concocted from dark, ancient magic. I glance over and see a middle-aged couple and a younger boy, maybe fourteen, standing near the very place I found her. I slow to a walk. The woman has a small collection of wildflowers bunched in her hands, and she bends over, lays it on the ground, and turns to the man beside her and sobs. The boy looks . . . helpless, hands shoved in his pockets, and he glances around. His gaze catches mine. *Yeah, kid. I know the feeling. I'm sorry as hell you have to go through it.*

The boy blinks and stares at me for several seconds, then leans into his father.

I continue on.

The streets are damp from the afternoon's rain shower, and the dark gray cobbles take on a slick shine in the haze of evening. There's still enough light to see, so I take it easy at first, keeping my pace to a leisurely, humanlike jog. The blast of a horn cuts through the air, followed by another. I dodge a store clerk locking up his business for the day. FISHMON-

GER, says the painted sign on the window. The man looks at me. "Aye, lass. Are ya headed up to the Seat, then?" he asks.

I stop. "Yes, I am," I answer. "Why?"

"Och, a Yank. Here on holiday?" he continues. He's short, with a bulbous red nose. The man obviously likes his whiskey.

I smile. "Right again."

His eyes, crinkled at the corners, graze over the inked wings at mine. "Right. Well you might want to bear right just up the way and take the Radical Road. 'Tis a rough track that'll take ya straight up to the Seat."

I give a nod. "Thanks."

"Aye," he responds, and turns to finish locking up the door.

With a wave, I jog onward. At the end of the block I bear right, and sure enough, around the palace, which is pretty impressive, is a rough road. Radical Road. I take it and, after seeing no one around, open up.

Even at top speed I can't help but notice how wild yet gorgeous the landscape is. The grass is still green, even in October, and stretches out toward the sharp hill that juts up—Arthur's Seat—and the beauty of it takes me by surprise. I have to remember that just because there is evil invading Edinburgh doesn't mean the city itself is evil. It's . . . stunning. And I wish more than anything Eli could be here to see it with me. One day, again. Soon.

Before I know it, the sun is dropping fast, but I

don't care. I can still see out, and I'm determined to make it to the top of the Seat. A sweet aroma—different from the city's brine—hits my nose. Clover? Whatever it is, I like it. It soothes me. Pushes me harder. Soon I'm at the foot of the Seat and I start the climb. It's not straight up, so I run at an angle, and at one point I'm bent over, using hands and feet to gain the top. Sharp rock, spongy stuff that I can't identify, and clumps of faded brownish-purple bushes that I think are heather are all over. They're not soft to the touch. Neither are the thistles. I ignore all of that, though, and scrap my way over and up. As a full-fledged human it would've taken me, I don't know, probably an hour or two to climb. Now? Let's just say I left the Crescent about fifteen minutes ago and I'm nearly to the top. I notice how fast the sun drops out of site, and the purple-and-pink-streaked sky has become gray and dark. It's not pitch out yet, but it's getting there. I'd better hurry or I'll miss the view.

In less than three minutes I'm at the top. The city's lights are on now and the castle is illuminated, a guiding light in its gray center. Tall, dark spires that look like jagged shadows jut skyward. I can hear tires splash through puddles. Doors scraping the wood floor as they close. Grease sizzling as battered fish and whatever else is being fried. Conversations merge, and I have to block them all out because trying to decipher the different dialects and accents makes my head hurt. I breathe in, long, deep. That clover smell is potent up here, almost like someone's just cut the grass and run over a giant pile of, well, clover. And some other things I'm not familiar with. Makes you think nothing could ever be as wrong as they are down in the city.

But they damn sure are.

Since going down has to be even easier than going up, I know I'll get back to the Crescent in minutes. Just as I start down, I jolt to a stop. A dead halt.

A lone figure stands twenty feet away. His face is cast in shadows, and I see nothing but his silhouette. My heart leaps.

"Eli?" I say out loud. Jesus Christ, it looks just like him. At least I feel it does. His height, body shape, broad shoulders. Even the way he stands. I move slowly toward him. He's saying nothing, yet I feel . . . something. A familiar presence about him. "Eli, is that you?" I know it sounds absurd that I even think it. I saw what happened to him at Waverly Station. There's no denying what happened. Yet . . . I still have doubt. *Eli! If it's you, you'd better goddamn answer me!*

I'm almost to the figure now, and he's not moving. He's not speaking.

He's not breathing.

I hear no heartbeat.

I freeze. Standing my ground, I do nothing but stare.

The image blurs, shifts, and disappears.

Blinking, I gape at the empty space. I rub my eyes with my knuckles and look again. I look around. I'm on the Seat, totally alone.

And I must be losing my frickin' mind. Now I'm seeing what I think is Eli? Shaking my head, I start down the Seat once more, and in a couple of seconds I'm at a full run. I cross the park, leaving the path and going straight across the grassy field, and pass a small body of water. A loch. Maybe one day I can return and enjoy all of this to its fullest.

I circle the palace, and the second my feet hit the grounds of the ruined abbey, a body hurls from the shadows and knocks square into me. I go flying sideways and land under its weight. "What the hell?" I mutter, and with two hands easily shove the body off me. I jump to my feet. "What are you doing?" I say to the kid pushing up off the ground where I threw him. From the shadows of the abbey, five more emerge. Six guys in all, and in this light I'd say they're between the ages of eighteen and twenty-three. Youth. Probably punks.

Shit.

I don't have time for this.

"Where ya goin', lass, in such a feckin' hurry?" one says, and he steps closer to me. The others fall in behind him. One by one, they fan out. Circling me.

"What are you?" another says. "We watched you run from the Seat. You ain't normal."

"I'm very normal," I say. "Now move. I've got somewhere to go."

One bold one takes a few steps up and pushes me backward. "You ain't goin' nowhere, miss." He cocks his head, his face half in shadows. "What's with the ink?" he reaches out and tries to touch my cheek.

Bad move.

I grab his arm and in a second have it twisted up and behind him. The others loom toward me, and I yank his arm higher. He curses and yells. "You're feckin' breakin' my arm, bitch!"

I tug a few more times, and he yelps. "No," I say, in his ear, calculating. "You've still got a little more give before the bone snaps."

"Ge' off me!" he yells, his accent heavy.

The others advance. And without hesitation.

I look at the one in the lead. *Fall to your knees.*

He does with a yell. "Feck!"

The next one's already looking at me. *Down on your side, grab your balls, and scream like a girl.*

He does, but the screaming is so annoying and loud that I put a stop to it. *Scream silently.*

His mouth is wide open but nothing's coming out. Perfect.

The rest, all wearing dingy clothes and T-shirts with jackets, fall in the same manner. Squirming on the ground in silence. I walk the one standing, my hand still jacking his arm up behind him, toward the ruined abbey wall. I look up and notice the darkened sky peeking through what once was a grand window but now is a gaping mouth in stone. I shove the kid against the wall, face into stone. "Do you seriously not have anything better to do than jump, or try to jump, women in the park? Really?" I shove him harder, and he grunts. His hair is cut close, or I'd grab a handful of it and yank him hard. "Stop being a useless piece of shit for society and go do something. Get a job. Whatever." I lean close, my mouth to his ear. "But be careful who you fuck with."

I give him one last push into the stone wall. He grunts again.

Now drop to your knees, be quiet, and don't turn around for five minutes.

I let him go and he drops to his knees.

With a glance at the rest, I shake my head and take off back to Canongate, wondering the whole time not who that group of punk guys could've potentially raped or beaten if I weren't there, but what exactly I saw on top of the Seat.

And why I thought it was Eli.

The streets are dark now, lamps burning and shining on the wet cobbles, and people are hustling about. The wind has picked up and it's brisk against my cheeks. I barely make it to Old Tolbooth Wynd before I almost run smack into Noah. His face is glowering, almost illuminated, in the lamplight.

"Where've you been?" he asks.

"Lose the 'tude, Miles. Jesus. I went for a run," I answer.

"Alone? Without telling anyone? Seriously?" he says angrily. "Goddamn, Riley. Use your head."

I stare at him, bewildered. "I like the old Noah better. You know, the one who eggs me on at a vampire fight club?" I frown. "Where's that guy?"

Noah's eyes soften in the lamplight as his gaze locks onto mine. "He left the minute Dupré did." Sun-streaked dreadlocks shift over his shoulder as he shakes his head. "Eli made me vow to watch over you if anything ever happened to him. And I take my vows seriously, Ri."

We start walking up the wynd and toward the Crescent. I glance at Noah. "Well . . . thank you. I appreciate it. But I can—"

"Handle yourself. Yeah, I know." He grins. "Eli said you'd say that. A while back, in Savannah. Before we left."

I smile again. "Yeah, he would." Inside, though, my heart is ripping just thinking of him. "Noah, up on the hill back there. I . . . thought I saw him." I look at him. "Eli."

Noah's face hardens. "Who was it?"

I kind of laugh and shake my head. "That's just it. It was . . . no one, I guess." My gaze meets his. "He . . . blurred, faded, and disappeared. No one else was around except, well, that was later, by the abbey."

Noah grabs my arm and we both jerk to a halt. "What happened at the abbey?"

I snatch my arm back. "Listen, vow or not, you can't be Mr. Overprotective all the time. Good Lord." I shake my head. "Humans. Kids. Punk kids. I took care of them."

"How many?" he asks.

"Six."

"God, Riley," he mutters. We get to the gates, and the others are already waiting. "What'd you do to them?"

I shrug. "Nothing much." I smile. "Promise."

"So you've found your way home again," Jake

says. "We're going to hunt in sections, teams of three. Miles, Gabriel, and Sydney. Darius, you're with the lupines. Arcos, Riley, and myself. Keep to the shadows. It's what they prefer. Royal Mile upward way, the castle gardens below, the clubs on Niddry Street, around the kirk yards. My group will take first Tron Kirk, St. Giles', and Greyfriars, and the university. And any close or wynd in between. Darius, your group takes Niddry Street. Gabriel, castle gardens, Scotts Monument, Waverly."

Noah gives me a furtive look. *I hate not being beside you. Fucking hate it. Be careful, and don't do anything stupid. Got it?*

Yeah, I got it, Mr. Grumpypants. Keep your mind in the game. Sydney, above all else, needs her back watched. It's why you're with them tonight. I told Jake what a kick-ass fighter you are. And don't worry. I'll be safe. Pinky promise. I smile and nod, despite the scowl he gives me, and join my team.

Through the darkness, old Peter comes hurrying toward me across the Crescent's drive. "Here ya go, miss," he says in his heavy accent, making *go* sound like *goo*. Ya canna forget these now. Can ya?" He hands me my coat and sword.

I grin and take them. "Thanks, Peter."

"Aye," he answers, bobbing his gray, cap-covered head. "Be safe now, the lot of ya."

I pull my arm through the leather strap, buckle it at the waist, and sheath the sword. Victorian helps me into my coat.

"I know you're in pain over your man," Victorian

says close to my ear. "But even I agree with Miles. Get your head in the game, Riley." He turns me around and looks me in the eye. "I couldn't bear to see you harmed. In any way." His gaze deepens. "I won't bear it."

I stare at him. "Okay, okay, Vic. Chill. I promise. I will be careful."

He continues to study me, as if he doesn't believe a word of it.

With good reason.

"Okay, let's go," Jake calls. We all disperse.

We immediately cross over to Cowgate and head toward George IV Bridge. There are a few cafés still open, a bakery, and a few chip shops. Several restaurants. Traffic on the streets has slowed, almost as much as foot traffic has on the sidewalks. We reach Candlemaker's Row and head toward Greyfriars. We slip into the shadows, hug walls, and keep a critical eye—and nose—out for Jodís. I see and smell nothing unusual. We move in and out of alleyways, behind businesses, and into any small, shadowy place evil would lurk. Nothing. Finally, at Greyfriars, a guided ghost tour is just leaving the kirk yard as we pass. The guide, a big guy with a head full of dark hair and a black cloak, stares hard at us, but continues on with his group.

Inside the kirk yard, we separate and slip around the many stone crypts and headstones filling the ancient hallowed yard. The cemetery is neatly manicured, with paved pathways among green grass. Ahead I hear something. A heartbeat. Alone. I back into the shadows and wait. Soon a young woman appears on the path coming in through the front gates of Greyfriars. Why she's alone, I have no idea. It's well after nine p.m. She must've slipped away from the tour group. She's dressed in a black pea-coat, with her hair all tucked up beneath a cream-colored knitted cap. She has her hands stuffed into her pockets and is walking fast. So fast, she walks right past me without noticing. I follow.

Where are you? Victorian calls to me inside my head.

I don't know. By a crypt. There's someone in here. Human. She seems to know where she's going. I answer.

And where's that? Vic asks.

Then the smell hits me. Stronger than usual. That means there's more than just one.

Jodís, Jake, Vic. Get over here. I can smell them. I'm near a wall of graves. So gray, some almost look black. And there's a woman in here.

No way in freaking Hell is another Jodís going to kill an innocent with me this close by. I hurry behind her, my eyes darting in the dark. No Jodís yet. Hopefully, we're here in time. I ease back into the shadows as I follow her. I don't want to scare her and I don't want the Jodís to see me. Not yet anyway.

Then I see them. Rather, their shadows. Shit, and no sign of Vic and Jake. *Where the hell are you guys?*

No answer.

So I handle things alone. My way.

I look at the woman's retreating back. *Turn back around and run. Back to the front gates and into the first open establishment you see. Or rejoin your tour group. Do it now.*

The woman turns right around and starts hauling ass up the paved walkway.

That immediately draws the Jodís out.

As soon as the human runs past me, I draw my blade and step out into the path. It's dark as shit in this place, and only a faraway glow from a nearby yard lamp shines in my direction. I'm just outside the arc of light. I turn to the Jodís and watch four of them emerge from the shadows.

Shit.

You in the front. Drop to the ground.

Nothing. Nothing at all happens. Except they all begin to hiss like fucking Sleestaks from Land of the Lost and edge closer. Three begin to circle around me. Guess they're creations of magic, and my quadruple-vampiric mind wizardry just doesn't work on them.

Double shit.

That means I'll just have to hack off their ugly heads.

Quickly, I shrug out of this suffocating long cloak and kick it out of the way. Not so restricted, I can move better now, and I face the first Jodís advancing on me. They're tall, gray, and leathery, with exaggerated mouths that don't close all the way. And they stink like a rotting hog carcass. Yes, unfortunately I know what that smells like. You'd think a creature of magic could possibly be more . . . becoming. Not the Jodís.

The one in front of me lunges, and I crouch, roll, and jump up behind him, my sword raised. With a heavy swing, I take his head. *Off.* It rolls on the paved walkway and into the grass, where it turns into white mush. The screaming starts, the white gross liquid stuff the Jodís turns into begins, and I'm facing the next one. *Where the Hell did Vic and Jake go?*

Scratch that. Two more facing me, one circling behind me. Hissing. Their mouths open and hissing. Long, spindly fingers with ragged claws reach for me, and the only thing I can think to do is knock one down and hack at the other one. I do just that. With one leap I bound off the chest of the one facing me, swing midair at the other's head and connect. The head rolls, and I land in a crouch. The one I knocked down is already up again, advancing.

I'm grabbed from behind. A cold, leathery grasp around my throat. It literally lifts me off the ground. The other two are advancing still, and I slam the tip of my sword down and into the top of the foot of the one holding me. It screams but doesn't let go.

Then a crack of glass, the lamplight extinguishes, and darkness falls upon the whole cemetery. I see nothing. The grip tightens around my throat and I choke, and with my elbow I slam into the ribs of the Jodís. Lightning fast, over and over, I hit it, but still it holds me.

Then wings. Dozens of beating wings. I can't see them, only hear them, and they're overhead and furious. So close now I can feel the air stirring against my skin. A shrieking noise, more wings, and a turbulent

wind picks up. I'm dropped. Rolling, I find my footing and spring up, stay low, and peer into the darkness. It looks as though a cloud of shadow swirls
through the cemetery, and the cries of the Jodís fill the
night air. Then, just as swiftly as they arrived, they
cease. Silence fills Greyfriars. The Jodís are no more.

Question is, Who killed them?

*I told you I would watch after you, Riley. No matter
that you were left to defend yourself alone. I might not be
physically there to help you, but I'm always here. I look
forward to tomorrow evening. Until . . .*

"What happened?" Jake says suddenly, running
up the paved walkway. Victorian is just behind him.
Both look as bewildered as I feel. "Where'd you go?"

Confusion webs my brain and I give Jake a puzzled look. "Where'd I go? Where did you two go? I
called you both and neither answered."

"Yes, I did," they both answered at once.

"You said you had followed some human out of
Greyfriars gates and onto Niddry Street, into a club,"
Jake says.

"When we couldn't find you inside, Noah and the
lupines went to fight a few Jodís just up the block.
We went there to help, thinking you were there, too."

I am completely perplexed. "That's not what I
said," I tell them. "I said to come here."

Both shook their head. I nod. "Well, then, the
Fallen have one up on us." I look at Jake. "They've
figured out how to manipulate us without even
being physically here. They told you to go to a different location."

"What happened?" Jake asks, looking around me at the bubbling piles of Jodís goo.

"I sent the human out," I say, and that sounds funny to my ears, as if I'm not still human. "And I stayed behind to fight off the Jodís. I got two out of four."

Jake looks around. "Where'd the other ones go?"

I shake my head. "I heard the wings overhead again, and the light went out." I point to the yard light in the corner that is still extinguished. "And next thing I know, the one holding my throat lets me go, and . . . something kills them all."

"Shit," Jake says. "Why would any of the Fallen send aid to you?" He shakes his head. "Doesn't make sense."

"My thoughts exactly," I answer. "It was that voice, though. The one who gave me the invite. I recognize it." I look at Jake. "He says he won't let anything happen to me."

"Well," Victorian says, staring me down. It's dark, but I can vaguely see his silhouette. I know those liquid brown eyes are shooting daggers at me for being careless. "There won't be any more splitting up. From now on, I don't budge from your side."

Just then, a church bell tolls eleven.

"Let's hit the other side of Old Town," Jake says. "We'll hunt until dawn."

And we do.

We slip through every nook and cranny of Old Edinburgh, through the closes and wynds, in between ancient establishments and even inside a few.

There's a small slice of time when the city is still; no black cabs, no trucks, no merchants, and no tourists. That time is now, and it's about an hour before the day breaks. Out in the Firth, seals bark, and the breaking of surf against rock invades my senses. A mist rolls in, sweeping through the aged stone and embracing the spires and architecture that make up Old Town Edinburgh. That white vapor slips through and wraps its long, spindly fingers around every surface, every rock, stone, mailbox, and parked car. It even weaves around my ankles.

We're all in Niddry's Pub, not on Niddry Street but a pub just the same, and the owner knows Gabriel and Sydney well enough to give them a key. We're at a large table in the corner, lights turned low, and I'm sipping a dark lager.

"A total of seven Jodís were killed tonight," Jake says. "I don't think one innocent soul was lost this eve."

"Two of those were killed, courtesy of the Fallen," Darius says. "I dunno about you, but I think Riley has an admirer," he says, and looks at me. "One of the Fallen."

"Same one who gave her the invite to tonight's charity," Noah says. "I'd bet a bag of fresh blood on it."

"We'll see tonight," Jake says. He looks at me. "And if you think for a second you girls will be there alone . . ." He gives me a slow grin. "Then you just don't know us very well."

I pull long on my lager, looking at Jake over the

bottle bottom. I finish and grin back. "Yeah, I know that. Kinda used to it by now."

"You should be," Noah says beside me. His stare is a little more profound than usual. "And don't think to get un-used to it."

"Any of you," Lucian says, pointedly to his mate, Ginger.

My gaze immediately goes to Gabriel.

His immediately goes to Sydney.

But he says nothing.

Chickenshit.

I've got half a mind to use my control and force him to tell her how he really feels.

Gabriel's gaze turns directly to me. And stays. For several seconds.

Point taken.

I smile.

Just as darkness wanes, and the light takes over, we file out of Niddry's and head to the Crescent. In a mansion full of vampires, werewolves, and immortal druids, I'm the only one who has to have real sleep.

There's still a lot of work left to be done. Darius, Gabriel, and Sydney scour the history books, old tomes passed on from one clan of people to the next, in search of battles fought according to the inscription of the first relic. While they do that, I crash.

Hopefully not for twenty-four hours.

"Oh, I'm ever so glad to see you all safe and sound," Peter says, greeting us at the gates. It's early morning, mist is sweeping our ankles, and old Peter is wearing his tweed cap, dungarees, and a woolen coat. His nose is bright red, and his eyes twinkle with genuine happiness. What a cute old guy.

"Yeah, we're pretty happy about it, too," I say, and smile at him.

"Do you care for a full Scottish breakfast, lass?" he asks me, then looks over the other members. "Anyone?"

"Ooh, I'm for it," Ginger says.

"Aye," Lucian, Gabriel, and Sydney all chime in.

"Excellent! It shall be ready posthaste!" he says, then bustles off to the main entrance.

"Walk with me while I have a V8?" Noah asks, knocking me in the shoulder.

"Riley, a word before you go to sleep?" Victorian interrupts.

I smile. "Sure. I'll call ya."

He nods and heads inside.

I give Noah a sidelong look. "Are you clinging to me just to piss Vic off?"

Noah almost chokes. "Clinging? And no. Make that hell, no."

I grin. "Okay, then. Just for a sec. I'm beat."

His mercury eyes study me far longer than necessary. "Something's up with you," he says. "You never used to sleep so much. And what about the ear ringing? Is it better or do you need to see the doctor?"

"It's better, I guess. Still there but not so intense. Probably just a head cold brewing."

"Nice try," he says.

"Well, then, I have no idea. I was just thinking it myself." I look at him. "Maybe because I've gone from slightly eccentric yet full-blown human, despite what others might say, to human with tendencies. Maybe it's all . . . catching up to me." I shake my head. "I don't know. But, damn, when I fall out, I'm out."

"Yeah, I know." He opens the door for me, and I walk through. He follows, we cross the foyer, and he pulls me aside, into the sitting room just off the main entrance. Only a slight light shines through a crack in the drapes not yet pulled for the day. His stare finds mine and holds it. His body is close, and he brushes loose hair back from my face. "It's dangerous, Ri. Too dangerous for you to be alone. Ever."

I let my head fall back and I close my eyes. "Noah. For God's sake." I lift my head back into position and look up at him. "What is so freaking big-deal special about my safety? Not that I don't value my own life, but . . . damn. Everyone is so worried about keeping me safe." I grab his hand and squeeze it. "None of us are impervious to death here. Even the immortals can die. All of our safety is at risk, not just mine."

"Yeah, well, you're the only one here I vowed to keep safe," he threads his fingers through mine and squeezes hard. "And I keep my goddamn vows."

Lifting his hand, Noah scrapes the pad of his thumb over my lip. "I keep them, Riley Poe. You're important to me."

The sincerity in his unusual eyes gleams true,

even in the haze of an early-morning, nearly dark-ened room. Emotions come from nowhere within me, and I suddenly feel so vulnerable, so . . . weak. I miss being embraced, being cherished. I know it sounds ridiculous, but . . . I can't help it. I lost someone I loved with all of my heart. And it was a helluva long struggle to give that hard heart of mine away.

Noah's eyes soften. "Your heart is far from hard, woman." He brushes my cheek. "Never has been."

Out of nowhere, I get the hugest sensation to just . . . fall into Noah's embrace. But I don't. Instead I squeeze his hand and smile. "Sure it has. I promise to be careful. You have my permission to watch over me mercilessly." I start out of the sitting room and look over my shoulder. "See ya in a few."

Mercury eyes stare silently at me as I leave.

I'm halfway up the stairs when Victorian is sud-denly at my side. "You didn't call me."

I jump on the step. "Jesus!" I look at him and elbow him. "I'm sorry—I forgot. Don't do that again."

"I don't trust Miles," Vic blurts out. We hit the platform on the second floor and start up the corri-dor. "I don't like him, either."

I laugh. "Well, trust me, the feeling's mutual." I look at him. "Why don't you trust him? You mean with me?"

Victorian nods, and walks with his hands behind his back. "Now that your man is gone."

"He may think the same of you," I say. Truthfully, I've always felt a reaction from Noah. I just brushed it off as powerful vampire sexuality. Maybe I was wrong.

"He has good reason to," Victorian answers bluntly, and stops at my door. "I know you mourn your man," he says, looking down at me with those dark brown eyes. "And I know you ache to be held, to be comforted," he says, and lifts my hand and kisses it. "I am here for you, love. If ever you want me."

I blink. "Not much for beating around the bush. Are you, Vic?"

He gives me a slight grin. "I suppose not."

"Well," I step around him and open my door. Over my shoulder, I look at him. "I appreciate the offer," I say. "And you'll be the first to know if ever I want to take you up on it. Good night."

I shut the door, but not before I see a huge, ridiculous grin spread across his handsome face.

Good Lord.

"I will win you over one day," Victorian mutters in Romanian on the other side of the door.

"I know what you just said," I say back in Romanian.

Vic swears and leaves the hall.

Finally, my bed.

I peel out of my clothes, kick them onto the floor in a pile, and crawl into bed with only my bra and panties. Within seconds, I'm asleep.

At least before the dreams plague me again.

Part Nine

HEAVEN AND HELL

It was night, and the rain fell; and falling, it was rain, but, having fallen, it was blood.

—Edgar Allan Poe, "Silence—A Fable"

I see the pain in Riley's eyes, and I feel so sorry for her. To have lost her mate, Eli, and in the manner in which she lost him . . . it's unbearable to think of it. But, damn, she's a fighter. She hides her anguish well, and puts the team and innocent lives over her own pain. I've never seen anything like it. To be frank, I'm glad to be on her side. She hasn't exactly warmed up to me yet, but she will. I hope.

—Ginger Slater

I'm in a place so deep, so dark, and so heavy, it takes all of my effort to breathe. I'm not sure what it is—whether it's the place itself or my company. I thought I was alone. I thought I was in my bed.

I'm definitely not.

In an instant, a slight haze filters through the clouds, and it barely illuminates my surroundings. I'm at a lake? Some body of water. I glance down. I'm wearing nothing more than my bra and panties. It's October, yet I'm warm. Not cold at all. Actually, it feels like a summer's day back home in Savannah.

"I thought you'd never wake up."

I jump, startled, and turn to see who has crept up on me. Familiar, yet I don't recognize the silhouette. Male. Tall. Broad shoulders. Long hair pulled back. Muscular. The slight haze of the moon doesn't give me access to his features. His accent, though, is . . . unique. Appealing.

I almost can't help but be attracted.

"I'm . . . sorry. I just couldn't wait," he says, and steps closer to me. I allow it, and I don't know why. Again, I can't seem to help myself. Butterflies stir inside of me, and I take a deep breath to try and dissipate the feeling. It doesn't work.

He—I have no idea who he is or what his name is, and, for some reason, I don't even ask—stops a breath away from me. With that hazy moonlight behind him, I can't see his face. I just know the allure he has hits me in a place I'm not used to being hit. Only Eli gets me there. I think this is Eli. But is it? I feel him. Sense him. Yet . . . he's different. I'm confused as hell. Again a deep breath. Again it doesn't work. Useless.

Next his large hands grasp my jaw on either side and his lips brush against mine in a whisper. "I'm going to kiss you, Riley," he says, and uses the slightest pressure to urge my mouth open. He angles his head and presses into me, taking in a long breath as he kisses me.

My own breath hitches and I drown in the slow, erotic brush of his lips, shoving my fingers through hair that feels like heavy silk, and taste him back.

His hands graze my sides, then move upward and cup my breasts through my bra. Quickly, he unsnaps the front clasp and pushes the silky material from my shoulders. It drops to the ground below. With callused hands, he caresses me, and my eyes close from the feel of it. His mouth claims mine, and the warmth from his hands against my breasts makes me sink into him, but he makes no further moves—only deep, possessive kissing.

Then he stops.

Resting his forehead against mine, he slides his hands around my back and pulls me close. Why do I want him so badly? Who is he? Why is he so familiar? And why am I so out of control right now?

I push his hair aside and move my mouth to his ear, brushing the lobe with my tongue. When he shivers, I whisper, "Please don't leave me, Eli. Not yet. I can't bear it."

He stills, pulls back, and looks at me. I can't see his eyes, only a dark glare, but I know he's studying me. Contemplating. Wondering what the hell I'm doing.

"I . . . Jesus, I need you, Eli. So much it hurts," I say, my voice a broken whisper.

Without another word, he does as I ask.

"Are you sure? I . . . don't think I can stop if I start."

"Yes," I whisper, my breath ragged. "I won't want you to stop."

He then lifts me in his arms and begins to walk toward the water. "I can smell you—almost taste you, so potent are your needs." He keeps moving, his long fall of silk hair brushing my bare shoulder, making me shiver. He lowers his head and sniffs my neck, an animal on the prowl. "I have dreamed of tasting you fully, of feeling you explode against my tongue. Never did I think you would have me . . . like this." He sets me on my feet, and the warm water rides up to my waist. He circles behind me and stops, his head bent close to my ear, his whisper a deep purr, yet still not touching, sending vibrations of pleasure across my wet skin. "I'm going to bury myself deep inside of your tight wetness, feel your woman muscles grip my hard length as you take all of me in," he says as he licks my lobe, his warm breath caressing my cheek. "But first," he says, his raspy words vibrating against my throat, making me shiver with excitement, "I'm going to make you lose control right where you stand."

Every nerve ending in my body hums with power, ready to unleash the energy simmering in my veins. So erotic are his words, his voice, his promise, that damned sexy accent, I have to clench my muscles to keep from coming right then. I reach for him.

"Don't touch me. Just feel."

He moves behind me again and brushes my hair to the side. His mouth hovers over my skin, his warm breath coming in light puffs, and then the wet velvet of his tongue strokes me where his breath has just been. He trails my spine with his fingertips, making small circles against each vertebra, and I clench my fists, aching to touch him, but I manage control and keep them by my side. Heated liquid pools between my legs, making me pulsate with desire. "Please, Eli . . ."

Finally, he touches me. His wet hands skim my sides, down my ribs, over my hips. Hooking my panties with his thumbs, he slides them down and I step out of them. He reaches down, grabs them, and throws them to the shore.

"Christ, you're beautiful," he whispers close to my ear, sending another wave of shivers through my taut body. Slowly he kisses me again, and it's so painfully slow and erotic that I nearly explode right there. Again I don't. But I can't control the moan of pleasure that escapes me.

I don't miss his sharp intake of air.

I don't know how much more I can take.

I want it to go on forever.

His large hands close over my breasts as his mouth claims that portion where my neck meets my shoulder. His thumbs brush the hardened, sensitive tips, and my head drops back to rest against his chest.

He moves his leg between mine. "Settle back against me."

I do, and the full erection pressing into the small of my back makes me moan again.

He kisses my jaw, then moves his mouth to my ear. "I want to see how ready you are for me, love. Can you stand it?"

Between breaths, I shiver and whisper, "Can you?"

A low growl rumbles deep in his throat. "Be very still."

Keeping one hand possessively cupped over my breast, he slides his other hand over one hip, over the flat of my stomach, then farther, closer.

The moment he touches me, an uncontrolled growl tears from my own throat.

"Christ, woman," he says, holding his hand still against my wetness. His whisper turns hoarse. "Now." He dips inside of me with one finger, holding me tightly against him. I suck in a raw breath and hold it, squeezing my eyes shut, fighting not to explode against his hand.

It doesn't work.

A gradual climax, one pulse at a time, increases with each beat, with each movement of his hand against me, until I turn my face against his shoulder, taking his flesh between my teeth as the orgasm claims me. Slowly it subsides.

With his arms encircling me, he walks me forward, the flesh between my thighs still quivering from pleasure.

I tread water and welcome its tepid temperature to somewhat cool the fire he has caused within me. Yet . . . I'm somehow not satisfied. I hadn't wanted to explode, but, damn it, I couldn't help it. I wanted it to go on forever.

Bathed in the milky glow of the moon, this enigmatic

male, Eli, stands tall, thick, muscular, and powerful. Volts of energy shimmer off his body in sizzling waves. His hair, silver from the moonlight, hangs loose to his waist, making him look wild, untamed, and I easily drum up a vision of him standing on a craggy Scottish sea cliff, a bolt of plaid draped over one shoulder, sword strapped to his side, a fierce wind whipping his hair. The beauty of it sucks the air from my lungs. And I have no idea where that vision comes from. Eli isn't Scottish. And he's not a Celt.

He releases me for a moment, ducks under the water, swims a ways off, and rises, hair soaked and dripping down his chest. He holds out an arm.

"*Come here.*"

I swim to him, eyes locked, something more than lust propelling me. Inexplicable. I push it to the far corners of my brain and just . . . accept.

We both tread water as we meet. "Look at me," he says.

I do. I still can't see his face. Not completely anyway.

"*I can only offer you this moment," he says. Regret underlines his words.*

I draw in a deep breath. "Don't be silly, Eli," I whisper. "We're engaged. Remember?"

"*Hold on to my shoulders," he whispers.*

Hard, thick muscles jump under my fingertips as I hold on. With one hand under the water, he pulls me against him, his fingers digging into my lower back. His thick arousal crushes against my belly. My throat tightens.

With the pad of his thumb, he traces my lips, hooking the corner, then lowering his mouth to mine, urging it open. Our tongues meet, slow, exploring at first, and then he breaks the kiss, angles my head, and moves his mouth over my throat. Sensations ripple through me, the brackish water lapping between us, mixed with his unique taste settling on my tongue, making me crave more.

He gives it.

Treading me backward, his eyes, still two dark orbs not fully visible, lock with mine and he turns, lifts me around his waist. Biceps muscles flex. "Hold on to me, love. Lock your legs around my waist."

As my legs encircle him, he slides into my slick wetness with one swift push, burying himself. I gasp, moaning as my feminine muscles stretch and accommodate the invasion. I almost come again.

"Put your arms around my neck," he commands.

When I do, his mouth claims mine, devours me, his tongue tasting every corner. He moves his hips, pulling himself almost all the way out, then thrusting back in. His motions mimic his tongue, both making love, and I hook my ankles around his waist and move with him.

He thrusts faster, once, twice, a third time, and I close my eyes as jabs of heat flash across my skin and light erupts behind my eyes. And then as waves of powerful orgasm break over me, the feminine muscles contract, pulse, and squeeze in an unstoppable rush. A moan rips from my throat on a ragged breath.

His body jerks as his own climax convulses him, the muscles in his stomach flexing with each thrust, the vein in his neck thick, the columns of his neck prominent. His movements slow, yet he remains inside of me.

Wrapping his arms around me, he kisses my mouth in a slow, erotic movement of possession. Under the water, his fingers dig into my buttocks, pulling me closer still.

He kisses my throat, making my head tilt back, and he gently bites the small hollow of my pulse.

Opening my eyes, while his mouth makes love to my neck, I stare at the sky, at the tiny flashes of starlight glittering like a trillion blinks of camera flash. It's surreal. This whole thing is. This moment is.

With one hand, he palms the back of my head, bringing our mouths a whisper apart. He stares, the moonlight glistening against his wet, slick skin, and he kisses me deep, then brushes whispered words against my ear in an ancient language, words I have no understanding of. I don't dare ask their meaning.

The haze begins to fade, darken, and soon the moonlight is completely obscure. Once more that oppressive feeling comes upon me, and I have no idea what time it is, where I'm at, or who I'm even with. I don't care. I'll worry about it later.

All that matters at this time, this place, is the man holding me close.

He lifts his head and looks at me, a flash of light appears from nowhere, and a silver gaze meets mine, and I gasp . . .

Awareness of my surroundings floods me, and I open my eyes. Adrenaline propels me and I bolt from the bed. I'm standing, naked, in my room at the Crescent. The drapes are pulled, but there is a fading light creeping in through the crack. Still daylight.

The dream. Highly erotic sex with . . .

Those eyes. Not Eli's. Not Eli at all.

Fury builds within me, begins low in my gut and fires up into my chest. I start for the door, remember that I'm buck-ass naked, then turn, go to my chest, grab sweatpants and a hoodie, yank them both on, shove my feet into my Nikes, and fly out the door.

Everything is coming back to me now.

Everything.

Every. Last. Detail.

I'm on *fire*.

Flying out of my room, I storm out into the corridor. The moment I start hurrying down the hall, I hear steel clang against steel overhead. I change directions and climb one more set of stairs, sweep into the dojo, and eyeball my target. His back is to me as he rests, bare chested, the flat of his sword against his shoulder. He's talking to Jake.

I cross the mat, yank Noah around, rear back, and punch him square in the jaw.

His sword falls to the mat.

"Shit! Ow!" he says, holding his jaw, although I know it didn't really hurt. I just surprised him. "What the hell, Riley?"

"Outside, Miles. Now!" I say, and turn and head back out of the dojo without waiting on him.

I know he'll follow.

Meanwhile, I hide that I think I just broke my hand on his steely jawbone.

Right now, I don't give a crap. I'm mad as Hell.

I fly down the corridor, down the steps, and into the receiving room. Then straight out the front doorway. Down the steps I go, and wait. I don't have to wait long.

"What is wrong with you?" Noah says, his sandy brows slashes above angry mercury eyes. "You know you didn't hurt me with that punch. Your hand is probably broken, Riley. What the hell?"

I round on him. I fight to keep from whacking him again. "I trusted you," I say. "Completely. And now . . . how could you, Noah?"

Noah's brows furrow closer. He's quiet for several seconds. "What?"

"I saw you," I say, continuing my rant, then lower my voice. "It was you. In my dream. I saw your eyes, Noah. Nobody has eyes like yours."

A slow, predatory smile lifts both corners of Noah's full mouth until he is broadly smiling. "Dreaming of me, Poe? That's— Ow!"

"Shit!" I say in a hiss, almost in unison, shaking my head. I broke it that time. I know I did.

Noah grabs my hand, and when I try to jerk it back he pulls me closer and holds it steady. His dreads slip over my wrist as he bends his head to inspect my hand. He lifts his head. "I don't know what's got you so riled up, girl, but I had nothing to do with your dream." He grins. "Not that . . . whatever you dreamed I wouldn't want to do, because apparently you're wound up about it," he says cockily. "But swear to God." He looks at me. "I'm innocent this time."

Suddenly, other things about the dream come to mind. An unusual accent. An even more unusual language. Hair that was silky enough to drag my fingers through . . .

"Damn," Noah says, studying me. "You're makin' me jealous, darlin'."

Maybe it wasn't Noah after all.

Somehow that disappoints me a little.

Noah smiles broader. "Let's go get this lethal weapon a bag of ice before it swells," he says. He hooks me under my chin with his knuckle, forcing me to look at him. "Next time, ask first. I'll never lie to you, Riley."

I'm looking at the most sincere pair of mercury eyes I've ever seen. I think I must be an idiot. "I'm sorry."

Noah's face softens. "Not as much as I am."

I immediately know he regrets not being in the dream.

So, if not Noah, and not Eli, then who?

When we turn around, the entire WUP team is standing on the steps. Watching.

Victorian's brooding stare feels like a ton of bricks.

"Lover's spat?" Jake asks, grinning. "Do tell."

"Kiss off," I say, passing by. "I wrongly accused Miles of being in my dream. No biggie."

Jake laughs. "Can't trust a vampire, Ms. Poe. Don't you know that by now? Especially one like Miles." All the guys erupt into laughter.

"Ignore them, Riley," Sydney calls out.

I ignore Jake's jab, since I'm sure he's just trying to rile me more so I'll stay angry at Noah. Which I won't.

In the entranceway Noah turns to me once more. "You can trust me, Riley," he says quietly. His eyes hold mine. "I'd never do anything you wouldn't want me to. Ever."

Without waiting for a response or a reaction, he turns and heads into the kitchen.

Speechless, I follow.

"We've got to get you ready for tonight, dar-lin'," Noah says, putting me at ease by changing the subject. "Jake had your and the other girls' gowns ordered. Pretty sweet, if you ask me." He grabs a bag of frozen peas from the freezer, turns, sits me down at the table, and covers my hand with the vegetable bag. He looks at me. "You won't see me there tonight, but you bet your sweet ass I'll be there. Whoever this is you're dreaming of"—he pauses as his gaze lights on mine—"he's dangerous, Ri. He can infiltrate your dreams, just like Valerian and Victorian Arcos. It may be just sexual now, but you don't know what he is or what he'll turn into. Especially if it's one of the Fallen. Which I suspect he is."

"What's he want with me?" I ask. "I'm . . . nothing. I'm not an Archivist. And I damn sure don't have a pure soul."

Noah's gaze weighs heavy on mine for several moments. "You really don't know, do you?"

Slowly and bewilderedly, I shake my head.

Noah smiles and chucks my chin like a little kid. "Then you probably don't need to know," he says. "Wouldn't want your ego getting, well, bigger than it already is."

I punch him in the thigh with my other hand. "Whatever." Still, I'm puzzled by what he means.

The others soon file in, and Darius, the only one

not in the group, comes in from the library. "I think the second relic is below the Marimae House."

We all turn and stare.

"You're joking?" Jake asks.

"Not one bit," Darius says. He holds a tome, and, in the pages he has opened, a map. An old map. Of Edinburgh. He points. "More than one battle between the Celts and Lowlanders occurred in the area, and more than once directly in the place of that house. Below it, some of the old catacomb passageways pass."

"I'm going with Ms. Maspeth," Gabriel says, crossing his arms over his chest. "If this otherbeing beckoning Riley is indeed one of the Fallen, then the relic may truly be there."

Jake nods. "My thoughts exactly." He turns to Lucian. "You'll go as Ginger's escort, as well. You'll all take separate cars. I'll acquire an invitation for the two of you." He looks at me. "I believe you'll have to give only your name at the door."

I nod. "Okay. Sounds good." I glance at the clock on the wall. "Five forty-five. I'm going to get ready." I nod at Noah. "Thanks for the ice."

Luckily there are two bathrooms on each floor. I find one and soak in the tub for at least forty minutes. My hand already feels better and the swelling has gone down. Nice thing about having tendencies, I guess. Fast healer.

I wash my hair, don't have to shave because of that fine investment of laser hair removal, and, finally, before I'm pruney, climb from the water and wrap my hair in a towel and my body in another. I add a little something to my look that I've been aching to bring back—maybe because it's how I looked when I met Eli, and I desperately want to go back to the way things were. I make my way down the corridor and to my room, and, of course, I have company at my door.

"Yes, Victorian, I'm going to be careful. Promise." I smile at him.

He returns a grave one back. "I fear for you this time," he answers solemnly.

"Oh, you haven't before?" I say.

"Well, of course," he answers. "But this . . . with the dreams . . . it's out of my control."

"You used to do the very same thing to me," I accuse. "Only you never quite took it this far."

He stares at me. "My point."

I sigh and give a nod. "Taken." I move to my door. "You and the others will be there," I remind him. "Gabriel and Lucian inside, with us."

"That gives me some comfort."

I smile and head inside my room. "I'll be fine, Vic. Promise. By the way, how's Abbey doing? Jake says you've been checking on her?" That Victorian Arcos has found a soft spot for an almost vampire is . . . slightly astonishing. Curiously so.

"I shall hold you to that. And Abbey is . . . well. Better, anyway." He's silent for a moment. "Something about her strikes me, I suppose." Silence again. "I'll see you soon, Riley."

Closing the door, I shake my head and gather my

makeup—something I've really not had any use for since being in Edinburgh. Tonight, though, is different.

I'm solving a puzzle. And hopefully catching a killer.

Lying on my bed, wrapped in a sleeve of fine plastic, is a formal dark purple gown. Off the shoulder with a snug bodice and tulle skirt, and lined in silk, it's . . . breathtaking. Nothing I would've found myself in had it not been for this particular event. Beside it, a box. I open it and beneath the tissue paper lies a pair of black strappy heels.

Perfect.

Climbing to a different spot on the bed, I sit cross-legged and apply my makeup. I'd give anything right now to have some decent tunes to put me at ease. Maybe a little Emilie Autumn, or Five Finger Death Punch. Maybe a little Paramour thrown in. Definitely some Adam Levine and Maroon Five.

Queen. Eli loved Queen.

Loved. Past tense. How I hate that word. Eli loves Queen. Better.

As I apply my base and powder, accent my brows, and brush on varying shades of smoky plum and black eye shadow, I'm pulled back to the days when I rose each morning to face a crowd of happy, excited customers getting sometimes their very first ink, or those returning for their fifth, sixth, or fifteenth. I miss the hum of the Widow, the tattoo machine, and I miss the artwork. Especially the freehand. Music blasting through Inksomnia's kick-ass stereo system, and Nyx scurrying all over the place, hugging.

Nyx. How I miss my wacky best friend. I hope Eli's brother, Luc, is taking good care of her.

Luc. Phin. Josie. Elise and Gilles. Eli's family. God, they're going to be devastated when they hear of Eli—nope, not even thinking it. Not until I know for sure. Preacher and Estelle. They love him, too. Jesus Christ. I've got to make sure . . .

A sob rises in my throat like a lump, and it hurts to swallow past it. Shame floods me as I recall the dream I'd just had with another. How could I? How could I have so willingly . . . forgotten? Or mistaken? How? How did I think it was Eli? It seemed so damn real. Like it was truly him. Until the eyes . . .

Seth. My brother. Preacher and Estelle. I want to hug them, smell them, hear their voices so badly, I ache for them. I know I haven't been gone that long, but I miss them all.

I take a deep breath before the tears fill my eyes and ruin my makeup.

Pulling off the lid to the eyeliner, I stare into my mini mirror, lean close, and line one eye, ending with a small sweep upward at the corners. I connect the sweeping line to the one side with my inked angel. As I'm applying my second coat of mascara, I notice something out of the corner of my eye. My gaze slides behind me in my mirror. I turn around.

The little girl is there. Dressed in black. Skin luminescent. Eyes and hair as dark as her dress. She's watching me. Kind of reminds me of how Eli's sister, Josie, used to treat me. A lot of staring, no talking.

I don't know what she wants or why she seeks me

out, but she no longer frightens or wigs me out. I just let her be. Maybe she's just curious about what I'm doing to my face. "Makeup," I say out loud. "Most girls wear a lot of it to formal events." I continue sweeping my lashes. "Why are you still here? At your school?"

I wait, but no answer. She's there—I can feel her presence. But she remains silent.

"Well, I'm here if you ever want to talk. I know what they think of you," I continue, trying something else. "Of killing that teacher by scaring him to death." I turn and look dead at her. I smile. "You don't look so scary to me."

Her eyes, black orbs with no pupils, gaze at me long. She doesn't smile, exactly. But her face sort of . . . relaxes. Or maybe I'm just seeing things.

Finished with makeup, I bend at the waist, shake my towel loose and hand-dry my hair. Jake had placed a blow-dryer in the top drawer of the chest, so I find it, plug it into the crazy-looking UK plug in the wall, and dry my hair. Done, I brush it out with a wide-tooth comb. I look at myself in the small mirror atop the chest. I stare at my newly placed hot-pink highlights. Jet-black and straight as a board is okay, but, damn, I missed my highlights. Eli always loved them. And now my hair's grown and hangs nearly to my waist. I've lost the tan that I'd gained over the late summer at Da Island, when I'd gone through vamp-venom detox and my skin was back to lily white. I turn and look at the little ghost girl and grin. "Up or down?" I ask her, and although I get no real answer, I see her eyes shift to the top of my head. "Up it is." Moving back to my bed, I gather a handful of bobby pins I'd stuffed into my bag, return to the chest and mirror, and pile my hair atop my head in a messy modern style. I have several long, straight black and pink wisps hanging about my face. Not too shabby for a made-up do. Grabbing a pair of black silk panties from the top drawer, I keep my back turned and ease them up under the towel. With the girl's eyes steadily on me, I move back to the bed, pull the plastic off the dress, and slide the zipper down the side. With my back turned, I drop the towel, step into the dress, and pull it up, over my shoulders, and ease up the zipper. Smoothing my hand down the snug bodice and waist, I turn around and look at my ghostly audience. She's looking at me, first at the dress, then lifts her gaze to my eyes.

I smile. "You know, I think we look a lot alike, me and you," I say. "Don't you?"

The very slightest of lifts occur at the corner of her mouth, just as she gives an even slighter nod of the head.

Then, she shifts her gaze to the far side of the room. To the trunk. She moves toward it and stands there.

I look at her. "I know you're trying to tell me something." I study her longer. She points to the chest, but says nothing.

I ease toward her slowly and glance down at the chest. I open it. Inside, the scathe Gawan of Conwyk gave me. The box of holy water cartridges lays by its side.

Along with the Pict verse.

Then, Lily looks at me, turns her head, and points to the bed.

Where I'd laid Eli's medallion before taking a shower.

Our gazes hold. "Do you think I can find him?" I ask her.

At first, she just stares at me with those gaping black orbs. Then, she nods and points back down, to the scathe.

"With that?" I ask her.

Again, she nods. Then, she turns and crosses the chamber and stands beside the hearth. She simply stares at me. Somehow, those black orbs beckon me. She points to the hearth.

A loud rap at the door sends her into a blurred vapor. Then gone.

"See ya," I whisper, staring at the place she'd just pointed. I'll talk to her again. Later. Then I turn to the door. "It's open."

Noah walks in, and I hear his intake of breath at the doorway. "Damn, Poe," he says after several seconds. He walks over to me, gives me the twice-over, his gaze lingering as it goes from the hem of my gown up to the bodice. Those mercury eyes finally meet mine. "Damn. The pink is back. Good."

I give him the twice-over, too. He's dressed in a tailored black tux. Sun-bleached dreads are pulled back with a black leather and silver clasp. His face is marked by ridiculous beauty no man should ever possess. He had to have had the shit beat out of him before he became a vampire. Pretty boys always get beat up.

A slow smile transforms his face. I don't know how to describe it. Part arrogant. Part predatory. Part . . . endearing.

Only if you know and love him, I guess.

I remember a time when I wanted to beat him up, too.

I meet his gaze. "Damn," I say in return. "You clean up pretty nice, Miles. But I didn't think you were going to the event. Only lurking outside."

"Jake says to lurk outside, you need to look as if you belong inside," he answers. He stretches one arm out and dusts off imaginary lint with his hand. "Not bad, if I say so myself."

I roll my eyes. "Hold on, let me get my shoes." I turn to the bed, pull the heels out of the box, and slip them on. I walk back to him and look up. "I'm almost as tall as you are now."

Noah's jaw muscles flex as he looks at me. His eyes are smoky gray. "You're beautiful, Riley. In a gown or a sweaty pair of training pants. Either way," he says. "Exquisite."

Heat floods my scalp. "I think you're making me blush," I answer, and pat my cheeks. "Are you wearing your special hoodoo concoction that keeps your sexuality tamped down?"

Noah has a special feature. He's so sexually potent and alluring to females—of all species—that he has to wear a charmed mixture of hoodoo herbs around his neck, or females everywhere will throw and claw their way into his pants. Sounds like something he'd love, I know, but, according to him, after a couple of centuries of it, he grew weary. I can tell you firsthand, though, when he's not wearing the charm, he's . . . a mess. Let's just say that. A freaking mess.

He grins. Wide.

I shake my head. "Oh, wait one more sec." I go to my chest, grab the feather-light sheath and strap and my silver dirk, slide it up under the skirt of my gown and attach it to my thigh. I ease the dirk into the sheath. I eye the scathe's hiding place, in the trunk. I want to take it but Jason had said the best place for it was gripped in my hand. That's a no-go tonight. For now, it stays. My hope soars now with the possibility of finding Eli. Even if it means delving into the Underworld. I sure as Hell will do it. In a heartbeat. "Okay, ready." Noah, whose gaze is kinda stuck to my thigh, shakes his head and sticks out his arm for me to take, and I do. "Let's go," I say, and look at him sideways. "Arrogant, pervy ass."

Noah's laugh fills the corridor.

"Who were you talking to when I first came to your door?" he asks as we head downstairs.

We pass the darkened alcove midway down the corridor, and I see Lily in the recesses of the shadows. As we pass, I smile and give her a little wave. She literally smiles back at me. "Oh, someone who reminds me a lot of me."

Noah's questioning look makes me laugh out loud.

Downstairs, I have to catch my breath. Honest. I gasp. Out loud.

Imagine a room full of vampires, werewolves, and immortal druids, all in black Armani tuxedos and lovely formal gowns. Breathtaking is all I can say. I admit, I'm the . . . oddball, I guess. I'm the one with the dragon tattoos exposed and the wing on my face. Where Ginger and Sydney are stunning in their gowns, Ginger in a champagne blush and Sydney in soft plum, they have jewelry to match. I wear no jewelry. My ink, my art, is my jewelry. I don't even have earrings.

"And it is spectacular," whispers Noah in my ear. I squeeze his arm.

"Riley, simply gorgeous," Jake says in front of everyone, making me want to roll my eyes and punch him for singling me out. "You'll be in a cab alone. Gabriel and Sydney, MacLeod and Ginger, you'll be in separate cabs. Darius, you ride with Arcos. Miles, you're with me. We'll arrive first. Riley," he says, looking at me with admiration and a quick twice-over. "You will arrive last."

I nod. "Got it."

Outside, the night air is heavy, but not so much brine this time. That sweet, cloverlike scent rides the chilly breeze, and Peter hands me a silk wrap as I wait for my cab. "You look lovely, miss," he says. "I would drive you myself, but—"

"Oh, that's okay, Peter," I say hurriedly, remembering the ride from Hell he gave us from the airport. "But thank you for the wrap. And for waiting with me."

He grins. His nose is, as always, red. "You're most welcome, miss."

I watch the sun drop as we wait outside the Crescent, and the sky once more has turned varying shades of purple and gray. Soon, my cab arrives, and Peter opens the door for me. "The Marimae House, please sir," he tells the cab driver. Then hands him twenty pounds. "This should cover it."

"Aye," the cabby answers. "Cheers."

"Cheers," Peter answers, and waves to me.

I wave back and we take off to New Town.

Traffic is heavy, and the cab driver takes several side roads that I'm unfamiliar with—especially once out of Old Town. I can see, though, why even though it's called New Town, the ground itself is still as ancient as Old Town. Which is why a particular battle was fought between the painted warriors of the north and the lowlanders. By the time we arrive, I'm stunned. Marimae House is a large manor home, at least three or four hundred years old, and it has a wide, sweeping circular drive that we pull into and get in a short line of black cabs dropping off guests.

It's precisely seven p.m. when my cab stops at the front entrance. A concierge is there to open my door and assist me out. I don't need assisting, but I allow it anyway. The damn humming has started up in my ears again. I guess I should've seen a doctor by now. I ignore it as best as I can, push it aside. It dulls.

The manor home is of aged stone and five stories high. With an impressive front face, it has two fountains out front with mermen and mermaids spewing water. I can vaguely see a large garden in the back as I start up a two-flight winding staircase

The moment I enter the home, I search for signs of the WUP team. Way across the room, I spy Ginger and Lucian, standing together near an enormous and intricately carved hearth and sipping a drink. They don't see me. I continue to scan the room. No sign of Sydney and Gabriel. No telling where they are. Probably digging up the garden, looking for the relic.

I see no sign of the others. I continue to walk through the manor. In the next room is a huge parquet dance floor, and several couples are twirling around to ancient music. Ballroom music. Never did learn to dance like that. I'm more of a dirty dancer, I guess you'd say.

"Miss, would you care to dance?"

I turn around and face . . . a very old guy. Cute, lots of white hair going every which way, but old. I smile. "Sure."

He leads me out on the dance floor, and that's when I catch a glimpse of Jake. He's watching me from a table of drinks, where three women are all vying for his attention. A slight smile lifts his mouth and he gives me a slighter nod.

Prick.

He then excuses himself and walks hastily from the dance hall.

"You're very good," the old man says to me. I look down at him. "Thank you."

"I like your markings," he says, and grins widely. "And your pink hair."

I try not to laugh. "Well, thank you very much."

We dance a few more minutes, until I notice the guy is actually getting a little winded, and we stop. "Thanks," I say, and he ambles off. Before I can even glance at the crowd, a voice whispers at the back of my neck, close to my ear. "Don't turn around."

My insides seize.

"You're an exquisite dancer," he says, his voice silky smooth and oh, so familiar. "Walk straight ahead into the next room."

I make my way through the crowd of charity-event goers and into the next room, as instructed. Only a few people occupy it. Chairs and settees are situated about, and I feel his hand now at the small of my back. It sends shivers down my spine. I hate that.

"Just at the far end of the room is a doorway. Go through it."

I'm not nervous, like life-in-danger nervous. I'm . . . anxious. I want to see whoever this person is. I walk ahead, find the door, open it, and go through it. It's another dimly lit room, rather a passageway. One small lamp hangs overhead and gives off a soft amber glow. The sound of metal clicking reaches my ear. The door is now locked. The chamber is chilled, empty. We are totally alone.

Strong, callused hands move to my shoulders

and slowly turn me around. My breath lodges in my throat when my eyes meet my company: long, silver-blond hair hangs straight past his broad shoulders, half of it pulled behind his head and secured. Eyes nearly the same color as his hair stare down at me, and they look like liquid metal. Full lips, sensually curved, sit above a square chin and strong jaw. Perfectly shaped brows lift. "Not what you expected?" he asks.

"No— Who are you?" I manage. His beauty is so great, it almost hurts to look at him. Literally.

His sexy lips curve. "My name is Athios." His eyes move to where his hands rest on my shoulders, and his fingers skim down my arm, tracing my dragons. His gaze lifts. "You are the most exquisite woman I've ever seen," he says, amazement lining his unusual accent.

"What do you want with me?" I ask, uncomfortable with how sexual this stranger makes me feel simply by touching my arms. "Why did you want me to come here tonight? Why do you sneak into my dreams? I thought you were . . . someone else."

He smiles. "I . . . don't know. I couldn't help myself." His silvery gaze lingers on mine. "I had to see you again. I have only imagined you. Like this. Inside your head. Inside my head." His gaze drinks me in. "But to see you in life, standing before me, under my touch? I can't believe you're real."

His words even turn me on. That low hum is beginning to get the best of me, and my concentration is slipping. Why is my body reacting to him? I'm angered at myself for even thinking it. I want to leave, yet I don't. "You are one of the Fallen."

His jaw muscles flex. "Not willingly, but yes, I am. And you're one of the hunters."

Slowly I nod. I can't seem to take my eyes off his . . . eyes. They're mesmerizing. His scent, his entire being is intoxicating. I don't understand it, and confusion makes me frown. The ringing . . . it's starting to make me dizzy again. The hum is now a whine, like the low-pitched sound a dog hears. I want to cover my ears.

"What's the matter?" he asks.

I shake my head. "Ringing. In my ears. Hurts." I clasp my hands over my ears.

Athios grazes my temples with his fingertips, and the humming stops. " 'Tis the relics, I fear," he says. "Your acute hearing is attuned with their low frequency."

I blink. I've been hearing the freaking relics the whole time? Now my body heats, and I can't take my eyes off of Athios. Again, I frown.

"What is it?" he asks. His hands skim down my sides, pulling me closer.

"I don't know," I answer honestly. "I . . . know this is wrong, yet I can't help myself," I say. "You are controlling me."

"Why is it wrong?" he asks. "Do you not recall the other night? The one we shared with such passion?" He lifts my chin with his hand and forces me to look at him. "How can that have been anything but right?"

"You don't know me," I say. "I know that the Fallen seek pure souls. Mine is anything but, so don't get any funny ideas about sucking mine out of me."

Athios laughs low, deep. "That's the farthest thing from my mind," he says. "And I do know you, Riley Poe. From the very first encounter, I scanned your entire soul. I know what your very first cognitive thoughts were, all the way up until now." He grazes my jaw with his thumb. "I know your whole life. And I admire the person you are. I envy your fiancé. You're an amazing woman."

"Well, I don't know you at all," I answer, feeling the drug of his touch against my skin. "How do you know my fiancé?"

"You know me better than most," he answers, ignoring my question about Eli. "Please hold still, Riley," he whispers, drawing close. "Just for a moment."

I go deathly still as he leans toward me, head bent, and brushes his lips over mine. His silky hair slips over my shoulder, and the sensation across my skin makes me shudder. His lips are full, pliable, and they move expertly over mine in a possessive caress, tasting me with his tongue, pulling at my bottom lip with his teeth. My hands move to his chest, up the collar of his tux, and around his neck to pull him closer. His hands move over my back, pulling me against his body. I can't seem to get close enough. His lips claim mine seductively, softly, slowly, and I sigh into him. What's wrong with me? Why can't I stop? Instead I urge him on, moaning softly against his mouth.

"Athios," I whisper, kissing him back. "Beautiful." My mind whirls, and deep inside, I grasp onto what little control I have left. My hand moves to my thigh, and slowly, I inch my gown's hem up. My fingers grate my blade, and I release it from the sheath. Gently, I lift it until the blade rests against Athios's throat.

"Get off of me," I say with a growl. Control is barely in my grasp. I press the blade harder, and Athios flinches. "Now."

Athios pulls back just a fraction. "Impressive."

"Turn her the fuck loose before I take your head right here," a voice says vehemently in the corridor.

"Do as he says," another voice demands. "Now."

Two bodies fly toward us, and I'm shoved backward against the wall. My head smacks the hard, sharp stone and immediately I'm dizzy, and I feel drugged. The bulb is hit and is swinging on its long cord, making shadows and light dance all through the passageway. I hear nothing but fists, grunts, and swearing at first, then the sharp clang of steel against steel. I see nothing; it's pitch-black.

And I know that voice, those curses, belong to Jake. The other is Victorian.

The fighting continues, and I try to stumble up to help. *Stop it!* I demand to anyone who will listen. No one does. *Jake! The second relic is here somewhere! He just told me!* Still, the fighting continues as if no one hears me.

In the fast flashes of light as the lamp swings back and forth, I see Victorian and Jake have both

changed; their jaws are dropped, fangs protruding,
eyes ablaze. It does nothing to deter Athios. Then, all
at once, everyone freezes. No one makes a move or
a sound. The air chills even more inside the chamber,
and a fierce wind blows through. Suddenly, two
more have joined. They stand by Athios. Older. Both
wearing tuxedos. One lifts his hand toward Victorian and makes a rising motion, lifting his writhing
body up. Jake lifts his sword and charges the two.
Then, before I realize what's happening, the one
makes a quick flick of his wrist toward Victorian. He
completely . . . vanishes.

I pull every ounce of concentration I have into a
small, condensed ball in the center of my chest. I
focus on the two Fallen. *Leave here. Now!*

Nothing happens. No one moves. I strain harder.
Pain, seize their bodies!

This time, I can barely make out their faces.
They're pinched in pain. One points toward Jake.

Jake! Leave here now!

Jake's face, although filled with rage, charges both
Fallen. I aim and throw my blade at one of the older
Fallen. It lodges in his chest. They go down, and Jake
escapes the way we came through.

Then, everything changes. The room is tilting—at
least it feels that way. I shake my head to clear it, but
that makes it worse. A black shade is being pulled
over my eyes, or a shadow—I can't tell. Just before I
black out my body is lifted, and I feel space and air
flying past me at lightning speed. It's almost nause-

ating. Soon, though, my stomach is at ease, and I'm floating into darkness. . . .

"Victorian!" I bolt up, my eyes scanning my surroundings. My vision is blurry, and it takes a few seconds for it to clear. It's almost dusk, which means yet another full day has passed. Gulls scream overhead. The heavy scent of brine fills the air, and the crashing of waves against rock echoes. It's cold in here, damp, and as I look around I realize I'm in ruins that I don't recognize.

Memories rush back.

Victorian is gone.

The other two in the passageway were the other Black Fallen. And they'd had the power to make Jake Andorra freeze in his tracks. They've sent Vic somewhere. He just . . . disappeared. Or was he dead? Christ, was that it?

Two? I've lost two now?

"I'm sorry."

Throwing the covers off, I find I'm still wearing my gown. I snatch up the hem and feel for my blade. Miraculously, it's still sheathed. I grab for it.

"You've no need for that," Athios says. "I won't hurt you."

"How do I know that?" I ask.

"Because I would have already done so. Besides, I left you your dirk."

"The other two—Black Fallen?" I ask.

"Yes," Athios answers. "My . . . brethren, so to

speak." He says that with disdain, and it's unmistakable.

"They killed Victorian," I say, and an uncontrolled sob rips from my throat. "Fuck!" I say, then scream it louder as it echoes off the decayed stone. "Fuck!" I move to what used to be a grand arched window and look out over the ocean. A fierce, cold wind blows against my face, and I welcome it. It dries my tears.

Victorian and Eli are both gone. I can't even come to grips with it.

"I was warned about the powers of the Black Fallen," I say out loud, facing the sea. "I really didn't believe it until last night." I turn to Athios. "You are unstoppable."

Athios, his jacket removed now, still wears the remainder of his tux. The tie is loosened from his starched white shirt. He moves closer. "I'm not like them."

I study him for a moment. I believe him. "What about Jake?"

"He escaped. Thanks to you."

"How?" I ask, bewildered. "They could've gone after him. Followed him out to the party."

"Because," Athios says, moving closer still. "They preferred instead to come after me."

I'm not sure what that means, but I don't think it's good. "You know we've found the first relic?" I ask.

Athios nods. "Your team has found the second, as well," he answers. "And soon to find the third."

"How do you know that?" I ask. I know he's

moving closer to me, and I allow it. I know he won't hurt me.

"Because it's here." He swipes his arm. "And the inscription on the second relic is quite explicit."

Confusion webs my brain. "How in the hell do you know that?" I ask.

Athios is standing in front of me now, and he lifts a thumb to my eye and wipes the edge. "Smeared mascara," he says. "Because. I am the one who hid them."

"So, you're not the younger of the Fallen," I say. "You're the oldest."

Athios nods. "Just . . . younger in appearances. I was younger when I became an angel. But after so many centuries of life on earth, I can hardly be called young anymore."

I feel myself being drawn to him again. "Athios, please. If you're using your angel/Fallen mind-woogie on me, don't." I look at him. "Please. Let me have my own faculties. For now."

He simply stares at me with those silvery metal eyes. "I find myself wanting to touch you. Always. It's . . . difficult not to."

I don't know how to respond to that, so I don't. Instead I question. "So, if you're not like them, what are you like?"

Athios smiles. "I'm a Death Walker, now," he states.

"What's that mean?" I ask.

"I made an ill-fated mistake as an angel by hiding the relics and, ultimately, the Seiagh. I wanted them not only for myself, but to keep them away from others who wouldn't know how to properly use its magic. It can be a dark, evil book, and I've seen too many souls turn black because of it." He looks out at the sea. "But because I hid it for my own gain, no matter the reasoning, I was banished as a Fallen." He turns to me. "And the only way to rectify myself is to see its destruction." He laughs softly. "Which, ultimately, leads to my own."

I meet his gaze and hold it for sometime, mesmerized once more by the silver beauty. I shake my head and look out over the ocean. "Damn, Athios."

He laughs and slides a little closer to me. "The North Sea is a tumultuous beauty. Is it not?" he asks.

I watch the water for a moment, at the constant white caps that tip the dark water. Seabirds dip and dive into it for fish, and the crashing of it against the rocks foretells its fury. "Yes, it certainly is."

"Much like you," he says. "Riley Poe."

I turn to him, lean my elbow against the derelict wall of the ruin. "Where are we?" I ask.

"Tantallon Castle," he offers. "A grand fortress in its prime. None other like it, save Dunnottar to the northeast."

"How is it no one is around? Tourists, I mean?" I question. In the distance, I see the parking lot. Totally empty. Nothing but green grass and ruins.

"I've charmed it," he admits. "Even from my brethren and yours. But it won't last long."

"How long?" I ask.

He lifts my chin with his knuckle. "Long enough."

"Athios," I look at him. "I don't know you. I don't know what's real and what's not. And I've just lost my fiancé. This . . . isn't right. I would've never done it on my own."

"Well," he says, and takes my hand and places it in his. "Get to know me."

My head spins, the world darkens, and I slip into another life, another time. . . .

Part Ten

❖ ⊱━━◦❖◦━━⊰ ❖

ABSOLUTE RESTITUTION

And then there stole into my fancy, like a rich musical note, the thought of what sweet rest there must be in the grave.

—Edgar Allan Poe, "The Pit and the Pendulum"

All along, I've known how wrong it's been to take advantage of Riley, even knowing she'd just lost her love. I can't help myself. She's everything I've always wanted. Aye, I've used my powers to lure her, and I make myself forget at times that I've done such because her reaction to me, to my touch, is so powerful . . . it's what will help me survive what I'm about to endure.

—*Athios*

Just that fast, I'm back.

I've just witnessed Athios's entire life. And death. And rebirth.

He smiles down at me. "Now you know me."

It somehow comforts me to know Athios is truly not a Black Fallen. He's a victim of circumstance who took the fall. A big fall. His heart is pure. And unlike the other Fallen, he has never stolen a soul. He instead visits the emergency room, where the dying are headed out the door anyway. He uses a little of their life force to maintain his substance here on earth. No one hurt. No foul done.

And he's only doing it until the Seiagh is found and destroyed.

"Why did you wait so long?" I ask. "If you've known all along where the Seiagh is, why wait?"

"It was written that way," he says. "Not until the Archivist arrives could events unfold. Ms. Maspeth only just arrived a year ago. I had no choice but to let things unfold as they would have naturally."

"So, by now my team has found the second relic?" I ask.

"Yes." He glances at the sky. "It won't be long now until the third relic is found." His gaze returns to mine. "I fear there's going to be a war, Riley. My brethren have created an army of Jodís. They'll bring them all. No match for your team. And my priority now is to keep you safe."

Yet another man wanting to ensure my safety. Where were all these guys when I was boozing it up and smoking weed as a teenager?

"No, your main priority, Athios, is to make sure the Seiagh is destroyed."

He gives me a slight nod. "Correct."

"You know I'm going to fight when my team arrives and the Jodís and Fallen get here?"

Athios sighs. "I feared as much. But, yes, I guessed you would." He looks at me. "Please know I never meant any harm to come to your friend," he says. I had no idea my brethren had followed us. I would've taken you . . . elsewhere." He sighs again. "But I wanted to ensure your team found the second relic."

"What about my fiancé? Eli?" I ask. It almost hurts to say his name now. And I'm not sure I want to hear his answer.

"Your fiancé?"

I look at him.

He glances across the ruins, in the opposite direction of the sea. "They're here."

I glance in the direction Athios does, and although I don't see anything, I believe him. I can hear voices in the distance.

"Riley, please," Athios says, and cups my jaw with his hand. "I don't think I'll get to say a proper good-bye once this starts," he goes on. "Can I have one last thing for my soul to keep?"

"What—?" The moment my mouth opens, Athios lowers his head and claims it with his. Long and possessive, his velvety warm tongue gently and slowly explores me, tasting the corners of my mouth, suckling on my bottom lip. His hands move down my back to cup my bottom and pull me tightly against him. Fire shoots through my veins and my hands wrap around his neck and, God help me, I can't stop. I kiss him back.

I kiss him good-bye.

His mouth slows, his lips resting against mine, gently kissing, inhaling. "Thank you," he whispers against me. "Like it or not, you'll always be with me, Riley Poe."

I pull back and look into his mesmerizing eyes, liquid metal shimmering in the fading light. They're almost the color of his hair now, which also has an unusual shade of silver tinting it. I don't understand any of this. Not a bit.

But it's real. That much I know.

Then Athios kisses one cheek and whispers something in my ear in that foreign, painful language of angels. He does the same with the next cheek, the next ear. It sounds . . . familiar. How, I don't know, especially since I just thought it was so foreign. But I've heard it before. He pulls back and looks at me. "You'll be safe now. But still, be careful. Watch your teammates. They'll need it. And when the Seiagh is destroyed, take cover. A gale like you've never experienced will occur."

"Okay," I say. "What about you?" I ask. Somehow, and for some reason, I care.

He smiles. "I'll be fine. And also, know this. You may still have a chance to rescue your mate. And, your friend. Your mentor, Conwyk, gave you a . . . tool. Speak to him. He'll know where you can look for your man. Now." He sweeps down and takes a final kiss from me. "Until, Riley Poe."

"Riley!"

Out of nowhere, a tumultuous force as fierce as the North Sea appears. It's Noah, and his rage is evident in his morphed appearance, the change in his voice. He lunges at Athios like a bolt of lightning. The wind picks up, and before my eyes, Athios disappears.

Gone. Like a vapor.

Noah swears and grabs me by the shoulders and turns me to face him. He doesn't even change back. His face is full-blown vampire, jaw unhinged, fangs dropped, and mercury eyes on fire. He shakes me. "Are you okay?" he all but growls.

"I'm fine!" I yell over the wind. "Victorian," I say. And that's all I can manage.

"I know, honey," he says, and for a second I almost want to laugh. A full-blown vampire calling me honey. It strikes me. "Eli and Vic might still be alive!" I yell. "Athios just told me!"

"We'll search after this"—he sweeps his hand over the air—"is over!"

"Promise?" I holler back.

He nods. "Here!" he yells, and hands me my sword. "Be careful!"

I roll my eyes.

The others hurry into the ruin. "Riley!" Sydney and Ginger yell simultaneously. "Are you okay?"

"Yeah, fine," I holler back. "Let's get this done!"

"Follow me," Darius says, and we all run along the parapet, down a winding flight of derelict steps and across the courtyard to another ruined building. He ducks inside, and we all follow. Everyone is wearing training gear.

I'm still in a formal gown.

With a sword.

Inside, Noah leans close. "You scared the hell out of me, Poe," he says. I look at him, and his familiar mercury eyes, very different from Athios's, now that I've had a good look at both, comfort me. "Don't do it again."

"It's here somewhere!" Darius yells over the steadily raging wind. It's whistling and whining through the cracks and holes of the old kirk we now stand in. "Sydney?"

"There!" she yells, and Darius moves to where she points. To a recessed altar in the stone.

"Ah. I see you've found it for us," a voice calls out. "Perfect."

My words, Riley. Use them. Now. The words whispered across my cheeks. The painful language. I stare at the remaining Black Fallen, and I know I have to act fast. Dredging up the words Athios placed in my head, I will them out, past my lips, onto my tongue. So painful, and nausea stirs in my stomach and my knees weaken. Still, I say them, just as Athios had said them to me. The Fallen stare at me, their silvery gazes fixed, wide, and . . . frightened. They aren't moving. Standing still as death. But their monsters are in full swing.

Shit.

A thunderous sound kicks up, and I realize it's not thunder but voices. Deep, grumbling voices. Lots of them. I glance out over the field and see a small army moving toward us.

Tristan de Barre. Gawan of Conwyk.

And about fifteen big-ass guys dressed in full chain-mail armor.

With swords.

"Sydney! Riley!" Jake calls out, and I turn and catch the first Jodís head of the evening. He'd lunged so fast that I almost missed it.

"Riley, help Sydney!" Noah yells.

"Not until they get up here!" I say, inclining my head toward Tristan and the others.

I fight. Hard. And somehow we push back the two Fallen and the Jodís enough for Sydney and I to ease in behind Darius. Lucian and Ginger transform—and

I mean fast. Like, blur—wolf. I'm not sure if ripping a Jodís' head off is the same as hacking it off with a sword, but it looks like it has the same effect. Lucian, an enormous black wolf, rips the head off a Jodís with his jaws and spits it out, and the white, gross, screaming pile of pus ensues.

That'd be a yes, then.

The roar of warriors almost deafens me, and I see just enough of Tristan, in full steel chain-mail and helm, hacking his sword like it was another of his own appendages, to turn to help Sydney. To my surprise, she's already got the stone covering the Seiagh halfway out. "Almost got it—"

"Riley!"

I turn just as one of the Fallen lunges at me. They must have broken free of the spell Athios gave to me. Why he didn't use his willy-nilly powers on me, I don't know. But I react. In my gown, I leap high and swing with all my might toward his head.

I watch it roll for a few feet before it disintegrates into a pile of ash.

Like the rest of his body.

When I land, Sydney has the Seiagh in her hand. My insides shake as I hear her incite some verse, and the language sounds a lot like the one spoken by Athios.

In the next instant, Sydney retrieves a silver dirk from her waistband and jabs it into the Seiagh's center. With a shout, Sydney drops the old tome. The ancient volume bursts into flames. It is destroyed. Never again to harm humanity.

Or another innocent angel.

The storm has ceased now, and the only thing ringing through the ruins now are the sound of steel against steel, steel against rubbery gross neck, and the thuds of heads hitting the stone floor. When Sydney and I run from the kirk, the scene in the courtyard and in the ruins is like a scene from a medieval movie. I jump in and start swinging until the last Jodís falls.

But there is still one Fallen left, and he's standing in the center of the courtyard surrounded by Jake, Gabriel, Darius, the lupines, Noah, and the warriors. I know what the Fallen are capable of, so I use what control I might have to keep him from attacking. Darius recites a verse in his own language, then lops off the Fallen's head in one swing. It's the end of the battle. Tristan, Gawan, and their men stand, sweating, but all alive. Not one innocent life lost.

Piles of dead Jodís are everywhere.

"Damn me, girl," Tristan says, walking up to me and pulling off his helmet. His long dark hair is plastered to his head, and brilliant blue eyes gaze at me with a twinkle. "You must've had a fine, fine instructor. You're amazing with the blade."

"And in a ball gown, no less," Gawan says, joining him. He, unlike the others, wears no helmet nor any armor. Still sweaty, though, and larger-than-life. "Fine fighting, lass."

Just his ink markings alone would scare off most, I think to myself. "Thanks, guys," I say, and wipe my forehead with my forearm. "I had great teachers."

"I'm surprised no tourists were milling about," Tristan says. "Usually they're all over Tantallon."

I know why, but I'll tell them all later. I doubt they'd even believe me right now that one of the Fallen wasn't quite so Black, and he'd used a charm to keep innocents out.

"One of the Fallen escaped," Jake says. He rests against his sword and eyes me. "Disappeared into thin air."

I guess I'll be explaining that one a little sooner than later.

"Let's go home," Sydney says. "I'm starved."

A roar of grumbling *ayes* fills the ruins. It will take a small army to feed Tristan and his men, for sure.

I smile at the big Dragonhawk knight. "I'm glad you came," I say. "Even gladder you didn't get dead."

He gives me a crooked grin. "Aye, woman, me also." He cocks his head. "You've got to come to Dreadmoor soon. My wife, Andrea, wants to meet you."

I give a nod. "I accept that invite."

Tristan smiles and moves off to speak with Gabriel.

"Riley," Jake says beside me. "I'm . . . sorry. About Arcos. I . . . couldn't—"

"I know, Jake. It wasn't your fault," I answer. "I knew that right away. Besides," I look at him closely, "he may be with Eli."

He nods. "You have a lot to tell me, girl,."

I smile. "I do."

With a sigh, he pushes off his sword. "Let's go home."

As a group, from afar, we must've looked like a big reenactment troupe or something like that. Who would've thought, though, that this gang of warriors, including one in a ball gown, was from other places, other times, once dead, vampires, werewolves, and one human with tendencies?

No one. In their right mind, that is.

"Riley, the scathe?" Gawan asks.

I look at him. "I've been told you might can guide me to a good place to look. I'll need your help."

He grabs me by the shoulder and squeezes. "I pray you'll ready yourself in something other than a gown?"

That's all it took. One little touch from Gawan.

And I'm there. . . .

Gawan stood, frozen to the very last step, and stared at the beauty whose gaze he couldn't tear away from. Their eyes were fastened within the mirror's reflection, and they stayed that way for a score of seconds or minutes. He knew not which.

Suddenly, it hurt to breathe, and every muscle burned as his body tensed. Unable to move, he simply stood. And stared.

Before he knew what was happening, his lips began to move—at first a whisper. A stunned, coarse whisper. The ancient Welsh verse barely reached his own ears.

Not once did his gaze leave hers.

"I mewn hon buchedd a I mewn 'r 'n gyfnesaf—" he began, his voice breaking like a lad of sixteen.

"Adduneda 'm cara atat forever 'n ddarpar . . ." she finished on a whisper.

In this life and into the next, I vow my love to you, forever, Intended . . .

Gawan's throat closed, his heart slammed into his ribs, and a tidal wave of memories crashed over him, yet his feet, thank the saints, began to move, closer to the woman standing barefoot upon his straight-backed chair, staring into his oval mirror. His woman.

His Intended.

It was then he noticed a tear sliding down her cheek, her body trembling. A small black purse she'd been clutching slipped from her fingers and fell to the floor.

When he reached her, he grasped her around the waist and set her on the floor. Slowly, he turned her around.

Her eyes were squinched tightly shut, tears trailing out of them and down her cheeks.

With a ragged breath, Gawan lifted her chin, and fought the crushing urge to pull her into a ferocious embrace she'd not be able to tear free of. Saints, he wasn't even sure he could manage another bloody word, much less a score of them. Christ, he remembered.

"Ellie, open your eyes," he said. "Now."

Her body shook beneath his hands, and he squeezed a bit tighter, just in case she started to slip to the floor. Her breathing, like his own, became labored, as though she'd been running for her very life.

Slowly her lids cracked open, and the most beautiful, tear-soaked, blue-green eyes stared back at him. Her mouth moved, but no words came out.

Gawan bent his head closer.

And then, he quickly realized, no words were needed.

Ellie threw her arms around Gawan's neck and pulled

his head down. Their lips met, settled, and simply melded.

Wrapping his arms tightly about her, he lifted her off the floor and allowed memory after memory to assail him, reveled in the familiar feeling of his Intended's lips against his, the taste of her on his tongue, her soft body, made just for him, pressed against him.

Then her mouth began to move against his, and he pulled back, reluctantly so, just to hear her sweet words.

"You found me," she said, in between a series of wet, sloppy kisses. "Gawan of Conwyk." She bit his lower lip. "Junior warlord." She dragged a slow kiss across his mouth. "Angel extraordinaire." After a long, sensual kiss that nearly made him shout, she whispered against his lips, "My Intended."

A thunderous bellow echoed across the great hall, followed by several more, and as Gawan and Ellie turned around, they found the entire Dreadmoor garrison, along with every ghostie within a hundred kilometers, standing behind them, cheering.

Ellie laughed and buried her face into Gawan's neck. He held her close, and he drew in a long, delicious breath tinged with the scent of her hair, her skin, her. "My Ellie of Aquitaine."

And then he had no choice but to let his Intended down, for there was an entire garrison of knights who wished to hug her—the Dragonhawk himself, included, not to mention one special young knight in particular.

"Jason!" she exclaimed happily, and launched at the lad with more spirit than a fierce Welsh Wode maiden in battle.

To the lad's credit, he apparently had been awaiting her memory to return from the moment she left England. He caught her in full leap, and squeezed her thusly.

"My lady Ellie! I've missed you!" he said, and quickly found he'd have to muse over fond memories at a later date.

Not only were there many a fierce knight about the great hall who stood rather impatiently to welcome Ellie home, but a skittish Nicklesby, who all but hopped about from one foot to the other, anxiously trying to worm his way into the crowd.

She spotted him and made a beeline for the wiry man. "Nicklesby! Oh, Nicklesby! Can you believe it?" she asked as she all but snapped the skinny man's neck in twain with her fierce hug.

Nicklesby hugged her back, unashamed tears welling up in his eyes. "'Tis a wondrous miracle, aye," he said. "I'm powerfully glad to see you home."

"Move there, yon bothersome Grimm steward, and let me 'ave a word with the lass!"

Ellie turned from Nicklesby's embrace and Gawan thought he'd never get used to seeing such a beautiful smile light upon her face. "Sir Godfrey! Ladies!" she said, as the three Grimm spirits floated toward her.

"Lady! What about me?"

Through the crowd burst young Davy. To the dismay of several knights, the lad plowed through to get to Ellie. "I'm here!"

Ellie laughed and bent over at the waist. "Are you ready for another game of knucklebones?"

"Most assuredly, aye!" he said, just as a barking Cotswold shoved through the crowd, Nicklesby chasing after him.

Gawan's heart swelled as he watched his people embrace his woman. They'd fast learned to love her as an In Betwixt spirit.

They loved her more as a very much alive and breathing woman. His woman.

And as Gawan moved through the throng of people, he pushed Jason aside and peeled Ellie from Tristan de Barre's arms. Gawan drew her close, and over the top of her head clashed gazes with three of the most wily beings ever to set foot in his hall.

Elgan, Fergus, and Aizeene gave a short nod, their broad, knowing smiles most satisfying indeed. They'd acquired their own retirement, after all. He couldn't wait to properly introduce them to Ellie. Indeed, that would wait.

Moving his mouth to Ellie's ear, he first kissed the soft shell, felt her shiver, and then whispered, "Forgive me, girl, but this cannot wait." He kissed her lobe, and then whispered again, "Wed me, Ell. I vow, you'll not regret it."

Ellie slowly lifted her head and stared into his eyes.

The entire hall grew deathly silent.

Gawan's heart ceased beating.

Then a wide smile split her face in twain. "Yes!"

As Gawan pressed his mouth against Ellie's, their teeth clacked together as each one smiled. They laughed, but their laughter was quickly drowned out by the raucous cheering of the knights, ex-angels, and ghosts filling Grimm's great hall.

Overcome with happiness and love, Gawan took his

wife-to-be even tighter within his arms and kissed her good, well, and true.

Aye. He'd found her.

He glanced at Elgan, Fergus, Aizeene, now joined by Nicklesby. They stood grinning like fools. He owed them much.

With a bit of help, he'd found his Intended.

And bleeding priests and saints above, he'd not let her go again.

"Wow," I smile at Gawan. "I gotta admit. You medieval warlords make for some seriously romantic guys." I elbow him. "Slick move in the mirror."

Gawan grins. " 'Twasna planned, my lady. 'Twas fate."

I nod. "I believe in that now," I say. "And it's why I need you to walk me through what to do again if I find myself going after . . . an Earthbound, or anyone else who may be being held hostage in that otherworld."

Gawan looks at me and his eyes twinkle. "Very well." He rubs his chin. " 'Tisna here, in Edinburgh, though," he admits. " 'Tis farther north. In the Highlands. St. Bueno's Well. Young Jason mentioned it to you before, aye? With the holy water. I was wondering when you'd get around tae askin' me about it."

I search his brown eyes. "You just point me in the right direction, Grimm. I'll take it from there."

Back at the Crescent, I'm packing my stuff. I pack up Eli's, too, and my eyes sting with tears. I sincerely don't believe he's dead. Not anymore. Vic either. But it's going to be Hell—literally—to save them both. I'll die trying.

Just then, a slight movement out of the corner of my eye catches my attention. Slowly, I turn. It's Lily. She's standing against the wall. Staring at me with those black fathomless orbs.

I smile at her. "I've got the scathe all packed and ready," I say to her. "I'm going to find Eli. And Victorian." I study her little ghostly figure. "Thank you."

The corner of her mouth tips up.

Grabbing my bags, I shoulder them, then reach into one. I withdraw the pouch of hoodoo herbs for protection and set it on the dresser. I smile at Lily. "For you. Just in case you need it."

Lily turns her head and stares at it.

"Ready?"

I turn my head to find Noah at the door. When I look back at Lily, she's gone.

So is the bag of herbs.

How she pulled that off I'll never know. But I'm glad as hell she decided to show herself to me.

I stare out the window as the plane ascends, leaving Edinburgh behind. Beneath. Whatever.

It's more than leaving Edinburgh. I feel as though I'm leaving Eli behind, too. And Vic.

And I guess I am. Sort of. But not really, according to Gawan.

Leaning my forehead against the double-paned glass, I stare into the clouds. What's real anymore? What's really out there? Do any of us know for sure? And how in the holy Hell do I get my head back in the game without Eli?

Strong fingers slip through my hair and squeeze my neck.

"You'll make it through this," Noah says, mercury eyes sincere. His lips tip in a solemn smile. "I make it my solemn vow to see you make it through this."

I give a slight smile. "Thanks, Noah."

"Besides," he says, and pulls me close. "We're in a plane with two werewolves, four immortal druids, and another vampire besides myself. We're heading into a were-war. We need you, Riley." He looks at me hard. "I need you."

I meet his stare and it comforts me. "I know. I'm here, Noah. I'm not going anywhere." I glance out over the jagged cliffs that peer through the misty clouds. We're headed to the Highlands. Inverness, and into wolf country.

Werewolf country.

And, yeah, there's a war raging between the clans, and it ain't purty. Only I won't be joining them. Not right away, that is. I've got a mystical well to visit first. St. Bueno's. I pray it holds the answers I'm looking for, so once we land in Inverness, I'll be taking off. Alone.

Eli would want me to be strong, stay safe.

I'll do my very best.

Just as my eyes drift shut, a voice interrupts my thoughts. It's familiar, achingly so.

Your men may still be alive, but you'll have to go after them. I canna promise they are there. Riley Poe. Be careful . . .

My eyes dart around the plane, and I search all faces. No one else has a voice like that besides Athios.

Who was supposed to die with the Seiagh.

What the?

Where? I ask.

You're headed in the right direction. You'll know it when you see it. Hallowed ground, oldest in Scotia. Tell no one. You've got to do this alone. . . .

ALSO AVAILABLE

FROM

Elle Jasper

EVENTIDE
The Dark Ink Chronicles

Newly-bitten tattoo artist Riley Poe feels herself changing
in unimaginable ways. Eli Dupré, her vampire lover, has
seen the change in her and fears for her humanity. His
rival, Victorian, tells her she must see the patriarch of the
vampire cult that attacked her to save her soul. In the
vampire cult's fortress in Romania, Riley will face her
worst fears—and the dark powers threatening to destroy
her. And she'll have to do the one thing she's been
determined not to do: put her trust in Eli.

**"Sultry, sexy, spooky Savannah—
the perfect setting for hot vampires."
—*New York Times* bestselling author Kerrelyn Sparks**

Available wherever books are sold or at
penguin.com

facebook.com/ProjectParanormalBooks

S0432

ALSO AVAILABLE

FROM

Elle Jasper

EVERDARK
The Dark Ink Chronicles

When Savannah tattoo artist Riley Poe is ambushed by an undead enemy, she inherits some of the traits of her attacker—and a telepathic link with a rampaging vampire. Now, she's experiencing murder after murder through the victims' eyes. And her new powers will not be enough to stop the horror—or the unending slaughter...

"A must-read for all major paranormal fans."
—Romance Readers Connection

Available wherever books are sold or at
penguin.com

facebook.com/ProjectParanormalBooks

S0336